# The Girls of Yesterday

# The Girls of Yesterday

## A NOVEL

## Michael André Fath

iUniverse, Inc.
New York   Bloomington

*The Girls of Yesterday*
A NOVEL

Copyright © 2009 by Michael André Fath

iUniverse books may be ordered through booksellers or by contacting:

*iUniverse*
*1663 Liberty Drive*
*Bloomington, IN 47403*
*www.iuniverse.com*
*1-800-Authors (1-800-288-4677)*

Because of the dynamic nature of the Internet, any Web addresses or links contained in this book may have changed since publication and may no longer be valid. This is a work of fiction. All of the characters, names, incidents, organizations, and dialogue in this novel are either the products of the author's imagination or are used fictitiously.

ISBN: 978-1-4401-8021-7 (pbk)
ISBN: 978-1-4502-5262-1 (cloth)
ISBN: 978-1-4401-8022-4 (ebk)

Printed in the United States of America

iUniverse rev. date: 8/24/2009

*This novel is most lovingly dedicated to my mom, Elizabeth;
and, to her best friend Norma Bornarth (may she continue
to rest in peace with our Lord).*

## Thanks to

Jade and Sierra, not only daughters but soul mates, and their mother Kris; Jennifer Abbott (my Texas love); my manager Christian Scarborough, graphic designer Stilson Greene, my attorney Joe Ritenour, and photographers David Sharpe and Madeleine Harrell; Navy Commander (ret.) Georgia Gill (my cousin love); my brother Vic and his daughters; my brother Eddie (rest in peace) and his daughters; my close friends, who are much too numerous to mention, and surely know who they are; and, to all of the amazing women in my life that have helped me to understand myself (and them!) with their God-given intuitive perspective and insight!

# Chapter One

"I am but a pauper, a princess she,
A sad situation, regretfully,
Yet every day as she plays in the courtyard
She passes a glance unto me."

The Magic King

# I

God, was Mary Jean Lowell heart-stopping gorgeous. I had almost forgotten how stunning her natural beauty was. I say almost. It had been a few years since I had last seen her, high school graduation to be precise. I'd been away at college and had preoccupied myself with chasing skirts of the southern college variety (and formidable opponents they were, I might add!), whilst trying to get a degree, for who knows what reason, as I certainly had no idea of, or set course to, the futures that so many of my compatriots seemed to avariciously follow.

At any rate, I was looking into her eyes, sitting on the couch in her apartment, proposing marriage. And I'm talking about a do or die, no holds-barred, gut-wrenching declaration of endearment and commitment that had in some way taken over my entire inner self, in a manner that was wholly new and surprising to me. It was as if my subconscious mind had figured something out and had dictated this to my body, while leaving "conscious" me on the sidelines to observe.

Why would a soon-to-be senior college boy like myself, looking at finishing school with a bang (or several, or many for chrissakes), want to commit to anything, let alone matrimony? I had, up to that point, been having the time of my life away at school. I was young, full of an overwhelmingly spiritual and physical zest for life. I was probably looking at many unique relationships with all sorts of girls down the road, many, as in the past, that had offered such a passkey into the true wonders of this special part of our world that only God could have dreamed up for us. Yet I'm sitting there, teary-eyed, asking for her hand, and asking for her forgiveness for breaking up with her before our senior year in high school, after having had gone steady for the previous two, which was a lifetime back then you know!

Why had I ended our relationship in the midst of those hallowed and golden years of high school? She was virtuous! That's why. And all my friends were getting laid, so what goddamn choice did I have? I was in love with her, to be sure, but in lust with the possibilities that my 12th grade year had to offer. This superseded any amount of compassion I held for her, and it was to be a hard-ass lesson I would later learn. I can only claim youth and innocence as my excuse. I was also asking her to break up with her fiancé who was going into the Marines. Yes, what a low class thing to pull, when Dan's away at boot camp, but "all's fair," as they say.

Mary Jean was loyal, too fucking loyal, if there was such a thing. She was loyal to a fault, or better yet, loyal to a higher degree of life and its true meanings, something of which I had very little clue at the time. She was committed to me in high school, and even when I was a jerk, she hung in there with me. She would have stayed in love with me for life. Jesus, did I have stellar hindsight and the most fucked-up foresight in history, when it came to girls. I can honestly say, though, that I was always in love with every one of them! I truly mean and believe that. I was the pillar of commitment, even if it was for only a day, a week, a month or a year or two.

Mary Jean was the most beautiful girl in the county, or even, arguably, the state of Virginia, for that matter. While on a break at a dance I was playing with my one of my high school rock and roll bands, I can remember introducing her to James, a high school friend of mine, who was so shocked at her beauty that he was literally speechless. Now James was someone who wasn't shaken very easily. Girls would flock to him, especially the pretty ones. He'd always had that cosmic appeal, that one cannot define very readily, but you know and accept that it exists…some have it, most do not. James was good-looking and very sure of himself, at least as much as one could possibly be during his teenage years. Yet Mary Jean stopped him dead in his tracks, and I was lucky enough to witness one of life's subtle and yet profound amusements, as harmless as it was, of one's inability to function due to an immediate scrambling of one's synapses as a direct result of a vision of a real life goddess. She had that innocent power of overwhelming beauty, coupled with a very gracious personality and a wholesomeness that was absolutely sincere. Deadly, but in a nice way. I had barely a clue as to what a treasure she was.

"Why couldn't you tell me this before?" she says.

She's crying, my heart is aching.

"You left me with a broken heart and shattered dreams, something that I never recovered from."

I respond with the desperate and not so brilliant, "I don't know, I guess I was too young, too confused," (and in my own reality, too trapped).

Geez, no shit! We were all too young, I was just younger. What a woeful display of making my case for the hand of the most magnificent young woman in the world.

My sister, Loretta, always told me that Mary Jean was the one. But then she told me the same thing whenever I fell hard for a girl. That is, if she approved of her. But, Loretta did remind me from time to time, and it was always a remembrance that gave me a dull physical pain in my heart, that Mary Jean was extraordinary, so special in the sense that we probably all lose someone of this type, someone that we truly think of many days of our lives, someone that occupies that one place in our hearts and minds that no one else ever enters.

"I adore you," I said, "I've always loved you," (even when I was following Patricia Barnes into the woods for an encounter of the closest kind, next to the A&P grocery store, or for that matter, any one of several encounters with several girls I was "in love with" at that particular moment).

"I cannot stop thinking about my life with you, and how romantic our future together could be," I said.

Sounds banal, I know, but nothing was closer to the truth.

Loretta whispers into my ear that I'm making a slight (but at least not absolute) fool of myself, and that she understands my pain. I just wish that Mary Jean could talk with her, and then she'd understand and say yes to my declaration of everlasting and undying love.

"I wish that things were different with Dan and me," she says amidst tears and choking on her words. "You know how I worshipped you in high school, but you crushed my heart, and I had to carry that pain all through our senior year!"

Jesus, adolescent love is such an overwhelming force. And it's funny how devastating it is when you're the one on the wrong side of a dream, but how clueless you are when you hurt someone else. I can honestly say that I did eventually learn this lesson, and liked to think that I actually "preserved" someone's heart later in life. I can thank Loretta for this. She knew me better than anyone in the world, and being female, she could always make, for me, the connection between the real and spiritual worlds that we boys and girls reside.

5

"I'm so sorry," she said, as she consoles and holds me, "I wish this had never happened, but it's too late."

At least she didn't toss the "I hope that we can be friends" thunderbolt into my stomach and up my ass. She did know me well enough to realize that that would have been an insult to my entire psychological make-up, especially my quixotic notions of our imaginary "Camelot," something that I desperately longed for.

This is something that I will never understand. How does one ever, and I mean ever, settle for second best? I knew that she loved me in a far different manner than Dan. But I also knew, and was resigned to the fact, that with her, it did not matter. Remember, she was the mistress of compassion and loyalty. I guess maybe I thought too highly of myself back then. Sure, like unrealistic confidence was never an affliction of the young-adult masses!

I left that day in total desolation and a bewildered state of mind. In my car, Loretta put her arm around me, held my head and let me cry into her chest. The smell of her hair and skin could calm me under almost any circumstance, and the strength that she exuded, both physically and mentally, was a measure of security that I always longed for, and a comfort zone that I required. She was famous for rescuing me from my broken hearts and depressions. She was the coolest sister anyone could ever hope to have. She was the most understanding and faithful friend I had ever known. I firmly suggest that maybe she was one of the very best to walk the face of this earth. This is not just a declaration of emotion, but rather a statement of experience and fact.

\*　　　\*　　　\*

You see, cancer had taken Loretta less than a year ago, and I'll never forget the utter magnificence and dignity in her dying. I remember playing my acoustic guitar for her as she lay in bed, allowing the morphine to give her a brief respite from the excruciating and goddamn unfair pain. She adored my music and faithfully supported me in all of my various melodic endeavors. She was also there for me when I almost broke my neck in a high school football game; she was there for me when I broke my hand sliding into home plate during a Babe Ruth League game. When I cracked my ribs, she sat with me in the hospital for a week, and when I battled Billy Barnes at a Saturday night dance, she congratulated me after the fight, which everyone said was even (and weren't almost all adolescent fights in the overall scheme of things, really draws), but because Billy was the toughest bastard this side of the ninth grade, it was a victory for me…one of the highest order.

So, I was returning the favor. My sister Loretta, my hero, whom I loved more than life itself, was lying there, fighting the good fight, and I was doing my damnedest to comfort her, and trying to keep her from any absorption by osmosis of my own inner suffering.

I also remember her refusing to succumb to pissing and shitting herself, as she became weaker and weaker. She was class personified. I was very lucky to be there with her, to shave her legs in the bath, to brush her hair, to massage the sickness out of her body. I was there to whisper into her ear, as she lay in a coma,

"It's okay to leave now, it's okay to give in, please let go, I'll take care of everyone, I'll be with you soon, I promise."

She's with me each and every single day, much more than anyone can hope to realize, with me in a way that is so real that I talk with her, walk with her, and generally carry on as if she's almost always physically by my side.

God, I missed my sister, and my very best friend, and just maybe my real reason for existence. Loretta, Loretta, oh Loretta!

# Chapter Two

"Today she is the wind and the sun,
She is the light in the sky,
She is really both of us child,
She is the rain that falls on her grave."

Just You and Me Child Today

# II

I grew up in the South, not the deep and mysterious South of which the horrors of the civil rights movement were indelibly etched upon our collective souls, not the South that many northerners loathe and detest and fear for some odd reason, but the South nonetheless. The rights of passage for a southern boy are wholly unique and, unless you grew up there, inexplicable to most who lived their formidable years in the North or elsewhere. True, growing up is growing up, but coming of age in the South has its own charm, its own beauty and grace, its own vanity, and its own disgrace.

I grew up with greasers, preppies, country boys and rednecks (there is a huge difference of the latter two, by the way). Though some of us were of a different ilk and thought of ourselves as somehow unique and unencumbered by the societal boundaries thrust upon us by an ignorant environment, we found that being nonconformist had its downside, and many times this was a very scary thing to experience.

In the tenth grade, I remember fighting two brothers, both of them older, at the same goddamn time. Fat fucking chance I had, me with my "mod" attire, replete with Beatle boots and fur vest. I got the shit kicked out of me, but I hung tough because I knew that I surprised them. I did not look threatening in the least; in fact I was always on the small side and did not get into weight lifting, formal boxing and the martial arts until later in life. I have always had that essential survival ability, though, of the ability to "see red" when attacked. It is a mysterious phenomenon in that these two sides or personalities of me are quite removed from each other. At any rate, I survived another of the many altercations that we all experience growing up with idiots, and to this day I remember almost all of them vividly. I do not like to fight in the "street" (the gym is another matter), because I feel that it is <u>always</u> a life or death situation and react accordingly, but I do owe those two boys a surprise and maybe the hands of fate will someday grant me that opportunity. I've always despised mean people and firmly believe that they will fail miserably at some point in their lives.

Anyhow, my greaser and total outcast friend, Johnny Martin (who could very easily have passed for a young James Dean), was so proud of me that I thought he was gonna kiss me, which was so far beyond taboo that it would not have even registered on the "I'm gonna kick your ass" scale that a lot of southern boys daily weighed themselves, and his affection went very far to take the sting out of my face and body.

What was strange about this beating, though, was that I was not just some rock and roll freak juxtaposed upon my cracker brethren. Keep in mind I was also a jock. In the ninth grade, I was a defensive back on the junior varsity football team, and every summer since I was eight years of age, an all-star baseball player, and by the end of my senior year would have all-conference honors as a defensive back and be headed to college to play basketball. It's just that by the tenth grade I had become so enamored by The Beatles, The Yardbirds with Jeff

Beck, Jimi Hendrix and Led Zeppelin, that I found myself extremely compelled to emulate these new heroes of mine, rather than those professional athletes that so previously dominated all of our southern bedroom walls. It seems as if I would always balance these two idioms, though, never really favoring one over the other until I was much older. I gather that these two older brothers just couldn't tolerate the fact that they were just confused and dumbfounded by my desire to push my own boundaries.

These same two also wanted to beat up another new guy in the neighborhood just because he shaved his legs, and I assure you that he was no wimp! In fact, Jake was quite tough, tough enough to survive in that environment of the ubiquitous redneck asshole, especially during those warm months of t-shirts and cutoffs where he was oh-so-exposed. Personally, I felt that if he wanted to shave his legs, so what. He had great looking legs and why should just the girls get to have all of the fun. My sister Loretta was a huge fan of Jake's, not just because he was a good-looking guy, but because she was so tickled by the fact that a boy in our "country" midst could be so odd and courageous.

Jake also played bass in a very cool and popular soul band at the time, with some of the members hailing from a rival high school. This, in and of itself, was a dichotomy in the general make-up of our collective male schoolboy personalities. I mean, fraternizing with the enemy? This goes to show that the music really did matter, that it could overpower many built-in social mores, even with a bunch of country boys. I would also see this firsthand, as I was cultivating, even then, my own "guitaristic" approach to communication and acceptance. Maybe there's a connection with some of this violence directed at those in the rock and roll limelight versus those on the "athletic stage". I say "maybe" at this point because later in life, I found this out to be very true!

Loretta wanted Jake and me to retaliate with these two bullies.

"Jessie, why don't you and Jake just surprise them one night and beat the ever-lovin' shit out of them?" she rhetorically and emphatically stated. "They're such fucking trash anyhow, you guys could take them, Jake's a lot tougher than everyone realizes, and besides, I'd help you."

"Jesus, Loretta, they're seniors for chrissakes, I was lucky not to get killed," as I plead my case to my own sister's prosecution, and knowing truthfully that, for adolescent boys, two years difference in high school is a huge gap in the "kick-ass" world. Also, I was not of the make-up to just go and attack somebody. Remember, I was of the "survivor" mentality; my strength was in self-preservation, not in aggression. I was later to learn, though, that this would change as I would one day go after someone, on Loretta's behalf, with premeditation and heartfelt intentions of maiming and destruction.

I knew that my sister's purpose of justice was only so serious, especially after she had cooled down a bit. In reality, she was more magnanimous that I could ever be. We were, though, so very close in spirit that she felt what I felt, and this was a connection that both of us would cultivate to a much higher degree later in life. And besides, even though she was privy to the occasional slap by our angry father, most girls (thankfully) do not have to experience the wonder of a solid punch in the mouth, delivered from an energy source bent on cruel destruction! At any rate, I left those "sleeping dogs" to "lie in state" for an as yet to be determined length of time.

I never, ever heard my parents utter the word "nigger," or any other racial epitaph for that matter, and believe me that where I grew up, this was generally unique. My dad was a professional artist and semi-professional soccer player, and being Hungarian and French, had that cosmopolitan approach to life that was so wonderful to experience. It just might also have been that due to the fact he was fighting the

Japanese in The Philippines during World War II at age 16, he had learned firsthand, very quickly and early in his life, of the value of people and life, no matter their race or religion.

It's funny but strange how the prejudices of the south have even their own prejudices. I mean Blacks and Jews and Northerners were "niggers" and "fucking Jews" and "fucking Yankees". But Italians were Italians, Germans were Germans, and the west coast guys were just strange. We were ourselves a strange lot, those of us growing up in the South. I use the collective "we" loosely because, yes, I am a Southerner, but no, I did not hate any particular group of people, save for those nasty fools who continuously harassed those they must have despised and secretly feared, whether they were white or black.

For the life of me, I cannot fathom the desire of my parents to live in a county that integrated only when it had to. My neighborhood was I guess what you'd call a "country suburb". Most of my parents' friends were, for the most part, educated, and this truly carried its weight upon us kids growing up. Those friends of theirs that did not have the benefit of a formal education were intelligent and very good people, nonetheless, and I can unequivocally say that my parents never, ever discriminated. My dad never even got the chance to experience the college scene as the war had a tendency to distract him from his pedagogical pursuits, and believe it or not, war gave him an opportunity to escape some of the nasty existence of a childhood in and out of orphanages and juvenile homes. My mom had a college degree in chemistry, though, and was a public school teacher and guidance counselor, after her initial stint as a chemist with a national health organization. So between the two of them, I had a better than decent chance of successfully growing up with some good sense and compassion.

At any rate, they were good people. Oh, I had the occasional severe beating from my dad, when I mouthed off or got into something nefarious, but for many of us in the South, showing up at school with a black eye during the middle of the week was business as usual. Dad had his violent side, but for some reason my sister and I always forgave him. He did smack Loretta a few times, probably to show mom and us that he was indeed a contemporary man and did not discriminate between the sexes, but not in the same way that he would hit me. Sometimes it did take more than a few days to come to some absolution for him, but inevitably we did, very possibly due to the fact that we always remembered from where my father came.

As I said, our schools integrated when they were required to. That meant that all of the Blacks that lived on "Nigger Mountain" were going to school with us. No big deal for me, my nanny (up 'til the time I was nine, when I was old enough to take care of Loretta and myself as both my parents worked) was a robust and vivacious black lady named Nellie, whom I dearly loved. She never "smelled awful" to me, I adored her personality, her skin was a gorgeous reddish brown, and I even liked her curly hair ("kinky" was a term that I would later learn from some racist jerk). She loved Loretta and me as if we were her own, and this affected us greatly. Loretta was compassion personified and, under the guise of Nellie and my mom, benefited to such a powerful degree that her own general make-up was so much more ethereal and spiritual than anyone I've ever known.

With regards to race relations, Dad had his own benevolent effect on us as well. He and mom would give these dinner parties out in our yard for his various soccer teams. Back then, soccer was not a very popular sport in America, and the "international element" of these professional teams was obvious, to say the least. We had no soccer team in any school I had ever attended, and certainly no country-ass white boy would be caught dead with those knee high sports hose, except for maybe Jake when he did not feel like shaving his legs for some reason!

Anyhow, there would be Nigerians, Sudanese, Italians, English, Germans and Dutch, eating pasta, drinking wine, and generally having a superior time on our front lawn. Loretta and I would always have the time of our own young lives at these parties. We thought that it was just superb to witness and experience all of these people in such festive conditions.

My dad was hilarious in that the drunker he got, the more European or African his own accent would become, depending on whom he was talking with at any particular time, and Loretta and I would always remember how we would laugh and laugh and laugh. Of course, I'm sure that possibly the wine we snuck had a bit to contribute to this as well.

So integration was no trauma of mine. It was such a non-event to me that I cannot recall the actual time-frame of that happening, only that it pissed off the general population of knuckleheads, but at least nothing too dramatic was imprinted upon our young and absorbing minds.

Yes, there were specific episodes that imprinted their way upon my evolution. I remember Squeaky Jackson, my cornerback mate on our varsity football team in 11th grade, coming back to the defensive huddle and telling me that some white boy receiver had just called him a "nigger that couldn't cover his own momma," and me telling him to tell that fucking redneck that Squeaky's own mom was too fast to cover, but that Squeaky had been "covering" that white boy's own mom for the past couple of months! Needless to say, we all were swinging at each other before the next play even got started, and anyone that has ever played high school football knows what a glorious thing an on-the-field brawl could be.

It's funny how Loretta, watching the previous events from up in the stands, could know exactly what was transpiring. It was as if she was always a section of my brain, installed there to be of use whenever her survival skills were absolutely needed. After that particular game, she looked at me as if I was some sort of hero, nothing to do, mind you, with the fact that we won, but that I had once again participated in something more than just a good deed, something beyond my own current and conscious scope, something of which only she was all too aware.

*     *     *

I remember the true joy that lying in the sun and feeling the warmth on her face gave Loretta when she was sick. She would get so tired that I would carry her outside Mom and Dad's house and place her in a lounge chair, positioning her so that the rays of the afternoon sun would bathe her body just so.

We would reminisce about our childhood, of course, but she was always more concerned for my future well-being. She was knowingly preparing me for life after her death, and how to survive the perils of being involved with, and counted upon, the many close friends and family I had and was to gain. Loretta knew that there would be many days that someone would truly rely on my countenance, and many days that my strength and energy would be all but depleted.

Now I know that she knew then that she was going to be able to "stay in touch" with me. Maybe this was one of the reasons she wasn't so scared. Mom and dad were understandably frightened and devastated, and I was out of my fucking mind with a different kind of grief, one of abject loneliness. Loretta and I knew of her special abilities, even when we were very young, but only she could have possibly realized the true extent of her spiritual abilities to help guide her own brother throughout his life, to truly have her own after-death purpose for someone still living.

To this day, one of the most splendid and courageous things I have ever witnessed happened during one of these very afternoons in the sun. She had been lying there, listening to a recent classical composition of mine on the guitar, just as peaceful as she could be. The morphine she was taking was then only in small doses, and her coherence was fairly sharp.

All of a sudden she had this stricken look on her face and pleaded,

"Jessie, please help me, quickly, I've got to get to the bathroom, my stomach hurts really badly," she was grimacing so intently and my tears were starting to flow because of her obviously severe pain.

I tried to comfort her there on the spot, not knowing what was going on, and thinking that another spoonful of the blue painkiller would help. But Loretta got very angry with me and shouted,

"Goddamnit, Jessie, now!"

I was totally confused and thought that she was dying at that very moment.

"Please, God, not now, please give her another day."

Her grip was like iron and she was actually hurting me, but it did not even matter, and as I got her into the bathroom, she screamed at me to close the fucking door.

She then released her bowels and started crying uncontrollably. I was standing outside the door, finally realizing the total nobility of her strength. No way was the deathly ugliness of cancer going to fuck with her dignity, no way was my sister going to mess herself as long as she drew a breath. No way was the god-awful and debilitating menace that raged throughout her body going to lessen one fucking degree the grace and magnificence of my hero and soul mate! No fucking way!

# Chapter Three

"Your first kiss, an innocence so tender
Touching my face I'll fondly remember,
You take my breath, so suddenly,
As swift as the tide and as completely,
You I wanted and I knew, it could not be..."

Looking Through Tear Filled Eyes

# III

Indian Summer in the mountains of Virginia is unlike anything else on earth. *God's Country* is a description used for many of the lovely land and seascapes that He created with a most divine sense of artistic and intuitive ability, and the celestial nobility of these mountains found in Miss Virginia's domain are a tapestry that is as compelling as anything on this planet.

The crystalline smell of the air can invigorate, beyond expectation, the most lifeless of us, and yet the pungent aromas of these alpine leaves, that are still green with summer but ripening with fall in their veins, can so intoxicate one as to rival the most prodigious cocaine/ heroin popper found in any drug connoisseur's private reserve.

My own personal feelings aside, as I'm one of those whose lifeblood is synonymous with the sea, there is definitely an atmospheric "pressure" found in those hills that permeates the soul, charges the psyche, and flourishes as an unyielding specter, affecting everything that it touches.

Mountain people, plainly and simply, are unlike any others. The sheer isolation, that is the environmental prerequisite of many of these folks, imparts a certain philosophy of life that separates these people from everyone else, and some of this is good, and some of this is bad. In these hills, one can certainly feel that freedom in everyday life apart from the "normal" constraints that bind those of us not included in this "hillbilly" society. Unfortunately, there is also an obvious lack of cultural integration that has a tendency to diminish or even close a lot of healthy minds that are educated in some of these mountainous areas.

I had this experience firsthand, as I went to college in the heart of the Allegheny Mountains of the mid-South. Reading the local paper during my first days there, I remember two very distinctive headlines (at least they were to me): one, a big governmental agency bust of a huge moonshining ring that was operating in some godforsaken back-hills part of Tennessee; and the other, a feature on the dangers of rattlesnake-handling during some cracker fundamentalist revival meeting. I say "dangers" because two people had died from being bitten (while clearly being stupid). Maybe the two go hand-in-hand. At any rate, this was my journalistic welcome to this nether region of the country that had enticed me to pursue my higher education.

Snake-handling, really, I mean give me a break. I told you there was a huge difference between country boys and redneck crackers. One's pursuit of spiritual healing and cleansing is fine, I went to church and everything, but snakes? Jesus Christ! This was the shit that you heard about as a kid that scared the hell out of you. I mean, in a sense, is this really that far removed from the ugliness and utter insanity of cult Satanic worship, which, for all intents and purposes, is a diametrically-opposed discipline? I guess this is where derangement stretches in all directions and shows no prejudice: "all lunatics are welcome!"

I respect different religions, in the sense that if you live your life taking care of your family, loved ones and friends, treating *all* people with respect and basically obeying moral and most legal laws, you will achieve divine absolution in the end, regardless if you're Islamic, Buddhist, Hindu, Christian, Jewish, or whatever. I have known many wonderful examples of each of the aforementioned, and am firmly convinced that we will all be welcomed into the arms of our Lord come judgment day, regardless of the bullshit that those headline-grabbing psychotic fringe idiots of each doctrine proscribe to.

Most of these fundamentalist assholes feel that their way is the only way. To me, this is in direct conflict with what God is all about. I've heard many of these people express the belief that many of us are going straight to hell, those of us who are sane enough to have a difference of opinion with this kind of ignorance and abject stupidity. Thank Christ these revivalists are a distinct minority, especially the reptilian sects whose diminished brain capacities overwhelm their abilities to actually do much harm to the "outside" world.

Snake-handling, give me an ever-loving' fucking break! What a bunch of obtuse assholes.

I'll never forget meeting Jess Butkus for the very first time. Jess was to become my very best friend in the world, almost instantaneously. He was an extremely good-looking black guy who grew up in these mountains and, miraculously, by the tender age of eighteen, had already developed a very cool and intuitive outlook on life and its real meanings, especially growing up where he did. I mean, I saw my fair share of racial prejudices and such, but where Jess grew up, this was a different scene altogether.

Black "lawn jockeys," "Alabama porch monkeys," and just plain ol' "nigger statues" were a dime a dozen as ornamental household fixtures where Jess lived. I had seen a few growing up where I did, but this was a very uncommon chattel. In short, Blacks were still second-class citizens where Jess lived, and to his supreme credit, he transcended the incomprehension of his environment.

Don't get me wrong and think that I feel that the South was all reactionary. On the contrary, I'm very, very protective of my birthright, and am a fervent lover and guardian of the South's history and way of life. And I know many like myself who, when the middle finger is pointed in our austral direction, will jealously stand up for our Southerly existence. Just ask any ill-prepared, ignorant Yankee motherfucker who has done so.

Jess was going to college on a full ride as a result of his being an all-state high school linebacker. And its God's all too familiar sense of humor and irony that Jess' last name was also the same as his childhood hero, the Chicago Bears' hall of fame linebacker Dick Butkus.

Jess was also an unbelievable operatic tenor. I mean, he had a voice that could kill. This was also a dichotomy in his background, which surely shows how one can truly rise above the constraints thrown upon all of us, at one time or another, from our restrictive surroundings.

I was in the gym working on my jump shot. Even though I also had an athletic scholarship, I did not have the high school accolades, at least in basketball, that Jess had, and I was not even guaranteed a place on the team. So, I was putting as much time in as I could, especially knowing that the coach was all too aware of who was working out… and who wasn't.

I could shoot like no one else on campus, though, and as a matter of fact, one of the star baseball players, J.P. Finney, asked me to help him with his own jump shot and he absolutely tore up the intramural leagues later that winter. He would make a basket and just look up at me in the stands and wink and smile. In my own games, I would do the same, as we had that shared jump-shot-athletic-bond that only we could relate to.

Yes, I could "shoot the lights out," as they say, and this was a very good thing, as I was the smallest player on the team and needed each and every advantage and skill I could muster.

"You know, for a short motherfucker, you've got a nice touch," a voice (that later would be instantly associated with the legendary Jess Butkus to anyone on campus) boomed behind me.

I turned, partly pissed-off but mostly bewildered, as to who in their right mind would say such a thing to an utterly complete stranger, and saw a ridiculously handsome black guy, grinning from ear to ear, waiting for my reaction.

"I think that you probably meant to say 'massa, when I's dun fru pickin' dis here cotton, cain I gets you to show me how you shoot dat round ball, 'cause I ain't never seen even no black motherfucker ever shoot like dat' ," I answered, surprising myself to no end at my improvised eloquence.

Of course I smiled greatly, as to the fact that this guy was an instantly recognizable force. I mean, one can tell these things, if one's been in enough battles. And a genuine and very profound accord was immediately formed between us, the beginning of what we would eventually discover to be a marvelous friendship.

"Hi, I'm Jess Butkus, you gotta a dream shot for a white boy. Where'd you play ball?"

"At White Oak High School, it's in the northern part of Virginia, sort of near Washington, D.C. I'm Jesse Mouchebeau," I replied, introducing myself to this inimitable spirit that was rapidly becoming supremely infectious.

We didn't even comment on the irony of having literally the same first names (though mine was pronounced Jessie), it was almost like this event was intended to happen, something beyond our immediate capacities to grasp.

Jess told me where he had gone to school, and commented upon the redneck population that inhabited his township:

"There were more fuckin' crackers around there than I care to remember, but hey, it's home and they learned not to fuck with me."

I somehow knew that this all-state linebacking terror wasn't going to take any shit from anybody, at any age, at any place; he was just that powerful. And what was equally amazing to me at this time was the fact that we were talking like we'd grown up together. It was the same manner and fashion of dialogue that we would undertake for years to come.

"It seems to me that this part of the state could be the white trash capital of the world. I mean, I grew up around rednecks and all, but I keep feeling like I've stepped back in time in this ignorant ass place," agreeing with him.

Even in college, the local manner of life had a way of slipping into our psyches, whether we desired it or not.

Which is very amusing coming from one such as myself, whose main high school cheer (unofficially, of course) was, and this is no lie:

*"Alakazzip, kazzip, kazzam, son-of-a-bitch, goddamn,*
*Horse's ass, bull's balls, Valley High (or whomever), fuck you all!"*

I still smile today over that one. Yes, it was totally stupid, but hey, we were kids, and it did shock the ever-lovin' holy hell out of opposing players, teachers, parents and administrators the first time they heard it. I can even remember seeing Mr. Cross, my English teacher, screaming his guts out and throwing up his middle fingers during that cheer, of course in his time-honed and perfected manner of stealth. I guess it served as some sort of necessary catharsis for him, and maybe he was just getting back at those idiotic students of the past, however many years that he had put up with, who had not a clue as to the importance of grammar, the wonders of language and the miracles of literary masterpieces.

"What the hell kind of name is 'Mouchebeau', French or something?" he asked, taking the ball from my hands and knocking down a shot from the top of the key. "You know, if I decided to play basketball, you'd never make the team," he chided as an afterthought.

"As a matter of fact, it is," I replied. "You see, though, my ball handling skills are my best asset," dribbling around and through my legs ala Pete Maravich, one of my own personal sports heroes.

And as I do this, Jess steals the ball and drives to the hoop, making me feel like he could probably take my position on the team if he so desired. As I said, he was a superb natural athlete.

I had to work hard at basketball, and only God knows why I chose not to pursue my own natural abilities found on the baseball diamond. As a Babe Ruth League shortstop, I was always a first team all-star. My fielding skills were legendary and I would consistently hit for a .400 plus average. I even was approached several times by major league scouts and considered the minor leagues, but having known several ballplayers to go that route and fail, I was convinced to pursue my higher education, and besides, I loved hoops even moreso!

Alas though, most of us (save for the Jess Butkuses of the world) suffer these dilemmas of adolescent confusion. And it does take an inordinate amount of trial and error to sort out our collective paths of excelling eventually in those gifts that God bestows on most of us. When we do, however, it is a wondrous thing. It's just that it would be so nice to experience these later-in-life accolades earlier, while we're in the throes of post-high school insecurity and unbridled passions. Not after we've missed out on all of the eighteen year olds that could have been our own goddesses and whom we would have worshipped for time eternal.

Jess and Jesse. We immediately fell into a very profound relationship. One that was spiritual and even bordered on the supernatural at times. It was a connection between a black boy and a white boy, plain and simple.

And I am one of those who believes very few people who say that they do not "see the color of our skins," that they just see the "person inside," those politically correct social soapbox saviors that are just a tad bit too touchy-feely. I think that it is our nature to observe and make distinctions of all types. It is a very splendid thing to marvel at the magnificent beauty and variety of skin tones found in God's personal palette.

I knew Jess was black, and would, in jest, call him a black country ass motherfucker, not just a motherfucker, because he was a black (not red, not blue) motherfucker, plain and simple. I was a white-ass "frog" (the designated colloquial French slur) motherfucker and I laughed every time I was so designated. Eventually, Jess and I would call each other nigger (which was strictly taboo), and at first this messed with my head, but I later figured it out, and was amused by the complete and utter silliness that these slurs really are. We knew what the deal was. We knew, in our hearts and souls, of the "real life" meanings of these little oral manifestations, which truly meant absolutely nothing.

Jess Butkus and I, Jesse Mouchebeau, were in our own naïve way, conducting our own college courses in race relations and proper human behavior, and unbeknownst to us, would affect a decent amount of the student body and even some of the general local population, both black and white, without consciously trying. We were just having fun living life as it's supposed to be, maybe partly even as divinely proscribed, well, maybe not quite that righteously, after all, we were growing young men. What a concept!

*     *     *

Loretta called me later that night, as was our customary routine and promise to each other. She was a senior and very much looking forward to her last year of high school, but was not feeling as spirited as she had in the past. I could tell that something was really bothering her, although if her previous several years' behavior was any kind of barometer, she would deal with her own demons in her own way. Loretta was never one to sulk or burden anyone with her woes, even if they were very serious. Of course, from time to time, she would admit me into her own private sanctuaries, but lately it seemed as if she was protecting me from something. I sensed this greatly, but not enough to really figure anything out, at least not then.

We both were experiencing major separation anxiety, and if it were not for my new environment providing me with a fair amount of distraction, I would have been very depressed. I did travel home as much as I could, but it was a ten-hour trip and time seemed to be in short supply, what with me stressing over making the team and delivering a reasonable attempt to get decent grades. Never mind the all-out pursuit of my dream girl, or girls as the case would many times prove to be. I have often proved to the world that one of my most compelling attributes was my total dedication to the research and solving of the mysteries of the opposite sex!

I was also spending a serious amount of time with Jess, when he wasn't crushing skulls on the gridiron. This was, I realized later, my subliminal attempt at a surrogate sibling, as well as the obvious sensation of a newfound life-friend.

"Jesse, honey, are you feeling like you'll make the team," she asks in her soothing, but nonetheless breathy and sexy voice, and with her patent sincerity.

Almost all of my high school friends, male and female, had commented, from time to time, on the beauty of Loretta's speech and her command of the English language, as well as the aural elegance of her voice. And it just seemed right that her sheer physical beauty was so matched.

"I just know you'll do fine, you shoot better than anyone in the state, and besides, you know that I can tell what's going to happen, even though I'm far away."

And from several past experiences dealing with similar situations, I knew she was absolutely correct.

"I'm okay, you know how insecure I can be sometimes, but Jess has been great and he really does think that I can cut it."

Loretta and Jess had talked with each other only by phone at that point, but had hit it off as to be expected.

"I miss you Loretta," I continued, "I feel like something's wrong, but it's weird, I can't figure it out, and it's not school or anything. Are you feeling alright?"

"I'm okay, Jesse, although I have lost a little weight and I don't know why. My appetite is gone and you know how I love to eat. I think that I just miss you terribly and I love you more than I ever realized."

If this seemed like strange talk for a brother and sister, maybe it was, although to us it was perfectly natural. We did fight once in a while, but never seriously, and these events always seemed to have a purifying effect on the both of us. Needless to say, this delighted our parents to no end. I unequivocally know now that my sister's and my relationship was the single most gratifying aspect of our childhood for our mom and dad.

Loretta always had boyfriends, but I truly believe that they were not a life necessity for her. She was an authentic pioneer spirit, and could survive just fine without romance being a daily requirement, unlike me of course. Don't get me wrong, she appreciated the opposite sex, but in a manner that was very detached and amusing. I think that really intellectual people have this personality trait in general, and Loretta was indeed so very special. Little was I to realize the profound impact of this conversation at this time next year.

"How're Mom and Dad, are they getting along better now?" I ask, referring to a recent trend in their mutual behavior. "Are they driving you nuts or what"?

"They seem to be much better, but I think it's because they are worried about you and me," she replies. "Mom is constantly feeling my forehead, like that's going to solve anything."

Mom's holistic approach to medicine was a constant source of amusement for us, including my dad.

"I just can't wait to see you during fall break, when we can spend time in our rooms talking all night like we used to," she added, "and please give my love to Jess, and tell him to look out for you or I'll smack his black hiney! Bye, my adoring brother."

Loretta's anxiety later turned out to be very perceptive. I know now that she understood what was to happen in the extremely short period of the next two years. She was all too aware of her own body signs, and these signals, to her, were an obvious read. As I've said, she was intuitively so far beyond the rest of us that most of these incidents of enlightenment had no release, other than possibly with God.

Why didn't she tell me at first? Well, of course, she was protecting her older brother, something that had started taking place during my high school years. I cannot remember exactly when, but it surely was amusing to finally realize that Loretta's insight was the answer to many of my enigmas, and not the other way around, as in previous years of my protecting her.

How could I ever exist without this lovely creature? Maybe God does place these noble people in our midst for a brief glimpse into his celestial psyche. Maybe this is also why he takes them back, far too soon, and nearly destroying us in the process. I would eventually learn one of the hardest lessons of survival in existence.

# Chapter Four

"Damn you old man, really open your eyes,
We hand you two mirrors to 'see',
Your subtleties knife us with searing pain,
We have nothing to lose, only gain."

The Insurrection

# IV

In college, dinner was a sight to behold and a very special event to witness. The infamous ghetto game, "The Dozens," would be played out in such grandiose fashion and style by those of us so inclined to make this treacherous pilgrimage and, dare I say it, sacrifice, that even the most steadfast and hardened of observers would often cringe at the cutting and deadly dialogue that attacked those most sacred aspects of each of our personal lives.

This was the very nature of the game, a game much akin to the art of fencing, a game that tested one's resolve and IQ, and forced one into instantaneous mental reactions and timing. One had to be quick-witted (and loud) enough to parry the ceaseless and caustic personal attacks on, say: one's mother, one's dick size, one's acne, one's haircut, one's girlfriend (or boyfriend, God forbid if some poor gay soul was so careless), one's clothes, one's ethnicity (niggers, spics, Jews, honkies, q-tips, slant-eyes, etc., were equal in the game's "constitution"), one's intelligence (of course the dull-witted were butchered and cast aside in a matter of seconds), one's sexual prowess (and God forbid, once again, if the word got out on any such kind of inadequacy), one's hometown, one's health, one's financial status, one's parents' occupation, one's siblings' shortcomings, and the same with one's aunts and uncles (again, Lord help us if any of them did jail time or drank or drugged excessively in public), etc., etc., etc. I do hope that I am making myself clear on this particular aspect of our cultural playtime. Nothing; not one single aspect of anyone's life was not fair game.

This may seem like a cruel and heartless (and ridiculous) way to spend time, but very often it was absolutely the funniest affair I ever had the privilege of attending and participating.

Jess was an absolute master of "The Dozens". His booming tenor voice would cascade over all of us and reverberate within the dining hall as no other's voice could! Volume had its advantages, and this was leveraged to the hilt by the incomparable Jess Butkus. But he was smart and quick as well. He could assimilate a thought and "gouge" the nearest bystander within seconds, leaving him (or her in very rare instances) disemboweled and "standing dead in his tracks".

I, on the other hand, did not have the "vocal" acumen of Jess. I was also at a disadvantage as I was the only non-black to regularly attend and challenge. There was always "open season" on this white boy, as well there should have been. I mean, wasn't I totally responsible for all of my black brothers' ancestors' pain and suffering? Did I not personally captain several slave ships from Africa to our American shores? I was also probably personally responsible for J.P. Finney looking like a fucking Mexican bandit (he really was a carbon copy of Pancho Villa), as I'm sure that one of my Mexican grandfathers most likely raped one of J.P.'s black grandmothers and pillaged his hometown of Knoxville,

Tennessee! Plus I'm sure he stole all of J.P.'s family's money and land. I mean, my white ancestors were the dregs of the earth, weren't they?

I did have the intelligence, however, which in this case was much more of the "street" variety, versus say "classroom" intellect, and the reaction skills necessary to survive.

And most importantly, I had something that was to become the most powerful weapon of all in this perilous game of mental attrition. Something that would enable me to not only compete with this veritable array of skilled verbal and sometimes physical warriors (occasionally a fight would occur, as even we could let things get out of hand), but something that could bring Jess Butkus, the undisputed champion of "The Dozens," to his knees; something that would compel each and every participant of these oral tournaments to challenge me, knowing full well that I could always beat the best of the best. And anyone who has ever competed in anything serious knows how debilitating this can be.

I had the delirious pleasure of invincibility. I had firsthand knowledge of what was a mortal sin, in the eyes of my African brethren. I had the most profound and intimate knowledge of my best friend Jess Butkus' intoxicating penchant for oral sex with his female partners (him "delivering"), which in the eyes of my black compatriots was as taboo and gross an act as just about anything.

Remember that this was many years ago, in a time when our sexual mores were a little more defined and presumed; a time when interracial relationships occurred but were even less acceptable than today, and a time of just plain stupidity and close-mindedness with most of my soul-brothers.

J.P. Finney was as "like-minded" as Jess, but had the good sense to never divulge his predilection for this customary "French art". I did some research, though, on all of my opponents, and gathered some invaluable information in a variety of categories, on each and every one of them. And whenever necessary, "pulled out all of the stops" in battle, much as a Commonwealth attorney pursuant to his or her dreams of higher political office!

Jess was not so fortunate with me from the "get-go," however. In a weak moment of confidence and loving friendship, he told me of some of his passions, this being one of them, and gave me enough information to initiate a little detective work and ultimately corroborate his accounts. The all-powerful Jess Butkus did indeed have his Achilles Heel! And I, "Jesse the Archer," had an entire quiver of arrows poised and ready at a moment's notice.

Of course, Jess could deny anything that I "brought to the table," and told me so, after realizing his fatal error. But our black brothers were very, very sharp, and he and I were all too aware of this fact. He knew in his heart that his eyes and body language would betray him at a crucial time, and he knew that I knew this as well.

So, the invincible and incomparable Jess Butkus, after several excruciating minutes of panic followed by one or two seconds of lucid thought, made me a deal.

"Jesse, you absolutely cannot tell those other motherfuckers about this," Jess commanded, or at least tried to, realizing that I had his black ass "dead-to-rights".

"My reputation is at stake and those country-ass niggers will crucify me," as his command quickly dissolved into an appeal. "I'll cover your ass anytime you ever need me to, I'll back you up, any place, anytime, if you keep this to yourself!"

I knew that Jess would do all of the aforementioned anyhow, so he really did not have a "leg to stand on".

I'm sitting there taking all of this in and, much to my amusement, am realizing that I now have got a "get out of jail free pass" that's going to be good for an infinite number of transgressions. I mean, I've got Carte Blanche with the one and only Jess Butkus. Yes, he's my very best friend, but I'm no fool; I mean I have enough insight to realize that, coupled with my own skills as a "dozens" debater, and with help from the very best at that game, I will be able to whip ass on my black opponents at will. I was a happy sonofabitch at that moment, needless to say, and could not wait for lunchtime the next day, as the cafeteria was the battleground for most of these encounters.

"I will honor your request, oh wise and mocha-skinned fuck-up, and will expect only the utmost proficiency in your offer, whenever the need shall arise," I answered with a proper British accent, to make my point crystal clear, "and sincerely hope that you never, ever fail to provide the very best of your skills, or the consequences will be such as you have not occasioned and suffered."

I succeeded in making my point, because Jess was speechless for a moment, but then broke out laughing, and I joined him. We came to a truce that night, and this held steadfast throughout our college years, something, as I stated earlier, that completely "blew the minds" of all our friends.

The very next day I sat down at one of our designated tables in the cafeteria with much anticipation but some anxiety. Today I would know if I could truly reign as the "white massa" amidst my black "slaves," or if I would fall to the "African rebellion" that my compatriots would viciously impart upon my esteemed self. I mean, this was "their" game and heritage; how dare a white motherfucker like me even think to ascend to the highest ranks of order in this particular universe. It was one thing being a well-respected opponent, but quite another being the best. You see, I could "hang" with any one of them, at any time, but it was Jess that constantly kicked everyone's ass, including my own, and it was Jess that I had to defeat in order to gain everyone's proper respect and, dare I say it, fear. Yes, we did take this seriously, as it was a "mini right of passage," of sorts.

Immediately J.P. Finney started in on Dennis Hall (an outstanding freshman running back, and was even featured in *Sports Illustrated* during his stellar senior year of high school):

"You sure looked like shit when that linebacker caught your slow monkey ass on that sweep play, you non-runnin' motherfucker, shit, might of cost us the game if Bobby *(Dennis' big brother who was an all-American defensive back and punt returner)* hadn't of run that kick back. Fuck, Dennis, you runnin' like a corn-fed white boy or something."

"Just listen to this Mexican-lookin' nigger talk like he's an athlete or something," Dennis whispers in his soft-spoken but deadly intense delivery, "Shit, what the fuck do Mexicans know about running, other than when they're stealing hubcaps?"

As I said, J.P. was a carbon copy of Mexico's most famous outlaw, and never did any of us let him forget this fact!

"At least I got some speed, nigger, thirty-three stolen bases last spring," J.P. counters, proud of the fact that he led the conference in this category, while his team suffered a losing season.

"Yeah, thirty-three steals with everyone whippin' y'all's asses all over Tennessee, shit I could'a got forty on those sorry ass pitchers you faced. Christ, most of 'em were in shock to see a real live beaner on the base paths," Dennis counters back.

Now Jess jumps in with his customary conquering mode:

"J.P., your mamma musta really liked those swingin' Mexican peters to bring your sorry ass into this world, you short fuckin' jalapeno pepper-eatin' motherfucker," delivered with Jess' rapier efficiency, wit and heartless style.

It was now getting "deep," and sometimes the smart thing to do was to wait, and jump in only when there was a sure "kill," never minding the fact that Jess always did with profound efficiency. A war of attrition has its strategy, and very often it was fatal to be premature.

We all saw that that last "cut" really got to J.P., as we really suspected that he did indeed have Latin blood somewhere in his family line, but was so very proud of his black heritage that this was never really acknowledged by him. These black friends of mine were very noble, even at this naïve stage of our young lives.

At any rate, Dennis was laughing and laughing hard, so hard in fact that the rest of us were joining in and J.P. was really fuming.

Dennis added, "If you can't take the heat, might as well take your base-stealin' ass back to Mexico, 'cept it's hot there too-maybe go on to Alaska or something, you do look like a black-ass Eskimo anyhow. Maybe your mama was humpin' up there while on summer break from all of the wet-backs she was seein'."

But Dennis was sitting next to J.P. (most of the time it was wise to have some geography between you and your opponent, especially if he was crazy enough to pull some wild ass stunt or worse, could kick your ass) and this would prove to be "fatal".

While Dennis was chuckling, J.P. grabbed (as lunch menu fate would have it) his baked potato, wrapped in tin foil and still very hot, and jammed it onto Dennis' hand, held it there, and yelled, "Now, motherfucker, here's some heat for your ass, you slow fuckin' non-touchdown gettin' country ass motherfucker!"

He burned the shit outta Dennis' hand, or at least Dennis' scream led us to believe that!

Now we all were laughing so hard that many of us were in tears, I was laughing maybe a little too much because J.P. started in on me.

"And you, you skinny ass white wanna-be-black roundballer who's got no game," (at least my height was left out because poor J.P. was a good three to four inches under my 5'10," and he also could not "rank" on my shooting skills, because even then, they were becoming legendary, and I did teach him to improve upon his own shooting skills), "got no chance at beating out those quick black brothers *(the guards ahead of me on the team's depth chart).*"

Before I had a chance to defend myself, Jess, as was so customary, as he held no reverence for anyone at anytime, "jumped" in on me as well; and he obviously had suffered a total mental lapse as to our previous "pact".

"Yeah, Mouchebeau, what the fuck do the 'frogs' know about roundball, anyhow. Seems to me that all your non-warrin' German ass-kissin' (I told you that this shit got deep) ancestors want to do is lick each others' pussies and peters and cuss all us Americans… fuckin' French faggots."

Uh-oh, a most fatal flaw in Jess Butkus' attack on me: the brief, but albeit tell-tale mention of the licking of body parts!

As all eyes were fixated upon my white countenance, waiting for me to crash and burn, I calmly looked at Jess, the master of all masters in this domain of verbal warfare, and indelibly etched upon every single combatant's mind the response: "If your fat mama's ass didn't stink so much, your shoe-shinin' daddy might not have to go out and be eatin' on all those white trash whores in your town, motherfucker!"

Boy did I cut right to the chase, I mean ranking on one's mom's ass is the lowest (and most dangerous) cut found in the "dozens" rules of etiquette, and the mere mention of "shining shoes," forget it! I did know that Jess's dad was a very well-respected man in his community and was a member of the police force for well over twenty years, but no one else did.

I then looked hard at Jess and said, with not too little emphasis:

"And anyhow, what's wrong with lickin' a little hiney now and then, Jess? Some of you black fuckers ought to try it sometime!"

As I said, mentioning one's mom, or even dad, in such a manner, was taboo, and sometimes ended in a serious ass whipping if the offended party was in the right mood! And here I offended the baddest motherfucker in the school.

All souls were immediately silent, anticipating at least an all-out verbal assault, by king Jess, on my masculinity, my whiteness, my athletic inadequacies, and my family.

Jess was frozen by the implication I delivered and could not respond, knowing that I could deliver his black ass to "hell in a hand-basket," if I so desired.

"Yeah, well fuck you too," he replied, with a most definite air of resignation and deflation.

His response was not even close to the resplendent intellect that Jess Butkus was associated with. In fact, it was very far from being acceptable by all there, and as a result, suffered an unmerciful attack by J.P., Dennis, and Blakely, a standout basketball player from North Carolina.

I will give it to Jess, though; even when slammed hard, he could "outfight" anyone, and proved himself once again by destroying all comers. The once invincible Jess Butkus had been taken down, maybe just one notch, but that was enough to sway public opinion.

It's just that by leaving me alone, he crowned me the new king, and everyone knew it. Even though I was fair game at anytime, Jess could always overpower the others by the sheer volume of his tenor vocality. The others knew that I had something "deep" on the mighty Jess, and to them, that was worth its weight in gold!

This held steadfast throughout our college years, much to the utter and complete annoyance of my entire black kinsman. Oh, I parried and thrusted with everyone, and I suffered some minor skirmish losses, but I remained unscathed. Yes, we had many, many battles, but I ultimately "won the war". The WHITE KING still reigned!

\*　　\*　　\*

Loretta and I were very calm "under fire". Many childhood incidents gave the both of us a certain coolness and detachment when calamity struck.

But I really feel, though, that we were given this character trait by God. He, in His infinite capacity, set us on our collective ways to assimilate those various events of growing up that so shape our souls and psyches.

This would, of course, come in very handy when I was fighting in the bars, or Loretta was defending her honor and fighting her own personal demons. It is always helpful, moreover, when one is attempting to shield a less fortunate soul.

Yes, we are all influenced by certain occurrences, some very apparent, some not so cognitive, of evolving from birth and on, within this world of ours.

One event, though, would shape my life in a way that very few others would ever come close to.

It was a very brisk autumn evening, a perfect high school football night, charged with rosy-faced cheerleaders, helmets cracking on the gridiron, and many hardcore fans in the stands. You could smell the fall air, the trees, the grass field, the sweat, the vibrant passion of so many being basically caught up in the same wavelength!

Boys and girls in love held hands and kissed, wearing each other's Peters jackets, sucking on each other's fingers, and generally being oblivious to the surrounding energy that only a schoolboy game could give.

I was working in the concession stand, as was customary for the varsity football players at a junior varsity game. Things were very lively as the Jayvee team was beating an archrival and we, the varsity, were expected to do the same the very next night.

Mr. Karbone ordered a chili dog from me and commented, "You boys gonna whip those asses from Central tomorrow night?"

"Yes sir, we're ready to take it to them," I answered respectfully, as Mr. Karbone was always considered to be a "little off in the head," but had several wonderful kids that went to school with me, one of which was playing in that very game, and another on my team.

"Well, Jesse," he continued, "I'd like to see these guys get one more win," which was an odd thing to say in that both the jayvee and varsity had several games left on the schedule and were very good teams.

Mr. Karbone was acting strangely, and I knew that something was up, but hadn't quite yet learned to fully "read" my own intuitive signals, something that would be "born-again" that very evening, in such a manner as to save my own ass many times in the future!

"Why sure, Mr. Karbone, we're both going all the way this year," I replied, and added, "Jamie *(his son)* is really havin' a good game tonight."

"Yeah, he is at that," he mused. "I'll miss him and the others".

Now I realize that hindsight is easy (Jamie was an athlete of such grandeur, even in the 10th grade, and his older brothers and sisters either were blessed with the same athletic prowess or as exceptional scholars), but I figured Mr. Karbone's statement to be one of an ordinary parent lamenting the inevitability of his various offspring moving onto their respective futures, via graduation, marriage and whatever.

I was starting to get uneasy, though, and I have never forgotten "his eyes". The eyes are a dead giveaway in battle; those of you that have experienced any time "in the ring," any street fight, or worse, know exactly of what I speak!

He said, "See ya around, kid."

Alarms were starting to go off in my head, my muscles started feeling like rubber, and my blood pressure was rising very rapidly. These bodily reactions I later learned how to control, much to my own self's improving sense of preservation, but I was "jelly" that instant.

Loretta was standing just outside the booth and I went out and grabbed her (and to this day, felt like God was propelling me).

"Jesse, what's wrong, you're white as a ghost!" she cried.

I yelled, "Get down, something's going to happen," and ran after Mr. Karbone.

I was less than fifteen feet away, and closing fast, but not fast enough.

Mr. Karbone yells, "Everyone get back, get the hell away".

I witnessed, in excruciatingly slow motion, Mr. Karbone pulling out a .22 caliber pistol. He then grabs Mrs. Karbone, puts five shots into her face, looks up into the heavens one last time, and uses the last shot to blow his brains out.

Now a .22 pistol sounds like a firecracker, so this horrific event was still seconds away from sinking into the collective minds of the general public in attendance, but I knew well of what I had witnessed.

Loretta grabbed me and in her unbelievable aspect of calmness under fire told me that I was going to be all right. I'll never forget her looking into my eyes with a fervent stare and understanding. Never mind the pandemonium that was beginning, she was protecting, and maybe even saving to some extent, her big brother's psyche at "that moment of truth".

She sensed that the real danger was over and focused on the healing that was going to be necessary, even at such an incredibly short time span from the actual shooting.

People were going crazy. Some were crying uncontrollably, and many were in shock. The stands were emptying at such a rate that both Loretta and I feared for some getting trampled, but that did not happen. Thankfully others were rising to the occasion and helping to maintain control.

Poor Jamie Karbone, realizing what had happened, ran off the field and was not found until the next day, crouched in a fetal position in the attic of our high school, and Lord knows how he got there.

The utter magnificence of his brothers and sisters all rallying together was as inspirational an event that I have yet to witness.

They buried their parents, lived and supported one another throughout their school years, and moved on with their lives, never accepting charity from anyone.

Loretta and I knew that they were special, and that they were blessed. God obviously had His plan for the Karbone family, and as nightmarish as it was, delivered them from any future evils.

Loretta and I talked all night about what had happened. Our parents were obviously concerned, but eventually left us alone, as they probably were equally as shocked and confused as we were, and really didn't know what to say. I think that they did their own praying that night, to a God that preserved their children from harm.

Loretta was very calm as she sat next to me, talking about things other than "the event". She was mentally massaging my mind, as only she could and as skillfully as a veteran psychologist. She was protecting her older brother and best friend, and was spiritually enriching us both.

Loretta knew, she always knew. This is why God touched her; this is why God took her back.

I mean, I can take witnessing a murder and suicide up "close and personal," and as fate would have it, this would not be the only time. I can survive the most wicked of bar and street fights, those events that many times can lead to serious endangerment and even death. I can "keep my head" in a disastrous accident, not panicking when an overturned car is leaking gas and there are four kids that need to be cleared out. But I will never, ever get over the utter debilitating feeling of inadequacy, of not being able to save my own sister from that most evil of enemies, her own cancer.

She was there for me and taught me how to be there for her. Loretta and I were indelibly etched with a collective imprinting upon our souls of dealing with disaster, but in much different ways.

These ways would manifest themselves in the coming years, and as I think back upon our time together, I realize that God does indeed work in many strange ways.

And as I get older and wiser, I realize that most everything that we are involved with is a divine test, a right of passage onto something very glorious.

# Chapter Five

"Try and explain our laughter again,
You cannot truthfully say,
That we didn't feel so incredibly real,
All those times that we walked in the rain"

In The Rain

# V

A brother and sister's relationship can be many, many things. Loretta and I would probably qualify as the distinct minority in terms of what we meant to each other, and more importantly, how we treated one another.

I mean that I do not believe that we represented the "norm". Yes, there are many sibling relationships that are strong and respectful, but ours went beyond anything that most had ever seen, and anything that our close friends and family had been privy to as well.

For starters, when we were toddlers, we were always helping each other; at least this is what mom and dad would constantly remind us throughout our lives. Even though I was a year older than Loretta, she was walking before my slow ass could. I think that I was 20 months of age, doing my level best at holding on to whatever furniture that was available, when Loretta, at her tender age of 8 months and maybe a few days, glided across the floor like some little, cute, curly-haired version of Baryshnikov, waltzing by me in a toddler's version of Ginger Rogers and a stoned-drunk Fred Astaire.

In a few days, she was grabbing me and actually helping me to balance myself and inevitably walk right beside her. I mean that she was my teacher and terra firma before I was two years of age!

There was this sparkle in her eyes as she watched me take my first couple of steps. It's almost as if she was on her mission before she could talk; which brings up another of Loretta's super-baby qualities: her ability to communicate without even speaking. Never mind the fact that she was forming entire sentences by the time that she was 15 months, and of course guiding my linguistic excursions as well!

I know that mom was cognizant of Loretta's abilities to a point, just as dad was all too aware of my deficiencies, not as compared to other very young boys my age, but as balanced along side our little super girl. But this never seemed to matter as Loretta was so far ahead of "the curve" that I was always given some deference, just based on common sense alone.

My motor and verbal skills gradually caught up with my sister's, and by the time that I was four (she being three), we were playing, talking and even reading on more or less an equal level. Of course, there are many, many different plateaus of achievement in childhood development and just when I would think that I was holding my own, or dare I say it, even starting to surpass my younger rival, Loretta would completely mystify all of us with yet another accomplishment; like the day that she learned how to swim, or rather the day that we knew she could swim.

Mom had enrolled me in a swimming class when I was five. She was absolutely adamant about us learning this potentially life-saving skill, as we lived next to a very large lake, and my grandfather's place, where we spent many blissful summers, had 230 feet of waterfront on the Chesapeake Bay. Most of all, though, mom still had a very vivid memory of being carried out to sea one summer, while lifeguarding at the beach, by a very mean and nasty riptide, and only her excellent aquatic skills, which included the essential mental ability of not panicking, saved her!

At any rate, here I am in class one summer morning, all of us freezing our little asses off (why are swimming classes always at 8am?) and wondering where our little pee-pees were hiding, trying to master the sacred art of the breaststroke. Most of us were at the same level of incompetency, so at least that particular trauma wasn't the foremost thought in our collective minds. Rather, we were simply terrified of sinking into the many, many fathoms that lurked below us, never mind that anyone could clearly see the bottom of the local pool.

Usually the moms would start to show up 10 to 15 minutes before we were finished, to socialize and check on our progress. Well, mom always brought Loretta, who of course wanted to take the class but was one year shy of the minimum age requirement, and needless to say, this bothered her to no end. Yes, of course she "knew" that she could out swim all of us, but bided her time with a patience and manner that was well beyond her youthful four years. Little did we all know that she was secretly plotting her strategy and waiting for the perfect moment to pull her own little "Amelia Earhart" stunt, something that would be a major part of the neighborhood talk for weeks.

So here were mom and Loretta watching all of us flounder around like a pack of physically-challenged dolphins, when my little sister, having, oh so slyly, removed her tennis shoes and jacket, takes off with a swan dive right into the deepest part of the pool. She then starts into the American Crawl, much as she had observed Buster Crabbe, when he played "Tarzan" in the movies.

You see, this was so typical of Loretta's and my perceptive qualities. I am watching Tarzan and am wondering how he could be so super-human (and of course secretly wishing that I was with Jane in some treetop locked in a most passionate embrace, as even then I was completely enamored by the female body, plus I actually had a girlfriend named Jane at the time).

But my sister, well, she was analyzing the mechanics of one of our Olympian swimmers, mentally taking notes, physically practicing somewhere secretly as a sort of dance routine, or "Kata". Loretta was the most observant and perceptive person that I have ever known, period!

There is my little sister, swimming for all she is worth, heading straight for the other side of the pool. By the time that the instructors could react and go get her, she was out and running back over to my mom.

Of course everyone was in a daze at having witnessed so bold a move by a four- year-old female munchkin. Mom was extremely angry at first and rightfully so as she was scared, but when we all started cheering, as the alternative being a feeling of serious emasculation at such a tender age, smiles broke out on everyone's faces, including the lifeguards.

This was Loretta's way; something that I would grow very, very accustomed to over the years. Loretta's way was also to inspire, and guess what? Every last one of us learned how to swim that summer. I know that God always surprises us, and it is not always pleasant, but here he showed us "the light" by offering up the miracle of my little sister, duty bound to guide us through our apprehensions of keeping afloat in the water that ubiquitously appears in our neighborhood swimming pools, ponds, lakes, rivers, bays and oceans.

I mean, how were we not going to learn how to swim after seeing such a display, by someone so much smaller? Even my friends and I could figure out then that, if we failed in this endeavor, we would be the lamest group of five-year-olds to inhabit the earth. I knew that my sister had just helped to catapult ourselves onto yet another plateau in the mountain range of life, and I will always have transfixed upon my mind, the pure, natural beauty and grace of her little image flying through the air and water, like some mythical creature in a fantasy world. My little sister, God's little gift!

*     *     *

I lived in a small house that was just off campus, but considered "on-campus," and we adhered to all of the laws and decorum that my college rendered unto its student population and faculty.

Upstairs lived Monty Price, a seemingly harmless little guy with no obvious skills or direction, and a very wacked-out sense of humor. Yet, somehow he managed to charm the rest of us to the point that we would include him in almost all of our adventures and parties. Monty will always be remembered for his ridiculous but nevertheless indelible statement: "spring has sprung, fall has fell, and winter has went!"

In the room next to him lived Tim Bates, a renegade wild-ass from the streets back home that was equally comfortable drag racing at the local track or running various scams with his acquaintances. Obviously, he and I became very good friends, as I had this knack and passion for outlaws.

In the suite downstairs with me lived two other guys that were also on the basketball team: Burton Rocks and Joseph Smith. In fact, that is precisely why we lived in this house. Since our college was small, the best that the administration could do to keep their athletes "in line" was to have small groups of us rooming together in different places. None of us on the basketball team save for one or two of the local rednecks, wanted even a part of the jock dorm. It was mostly a football haven for the aforementioned provincial players, and the "jock" fraternity, with whom I'd have my later share of battles!

Burton hailed from a very historically rich and cultured, but small southern Virginia city. He was a decent high school player, but like me, he improved his game by leaps and bounds during his senior year, and his workout with the head coach during the summer after his graduation from high school netted him an even greater scholarship than was originally awarded. It also helped, in light of the fact, that Burton was a good 6'7" and still growing, and he was white.

I strongly suspect that there was an unwritten quota for our Caucasian brethren on the basketball team. I say this because of several incidents pulled by our coaches and administration. But this was something that I could never prove. My college did have a propensity for hiring cracker coaches, though, and this always bothered me to no end.

Burton's improvement during his four years at college was nothing short of remarkable, as he took his game very seriously. He and I would also date roommates at a nearby all-girl small college later during our junior year. Burton adored music, most styles, and this suited us just fine as our stereos were constantly blasting the latest Led Zeppelin, Stevie Winwood (Traffic and Blind Faith), Marvin Gaye, Sly and The Family Stone, Deep Purple, Jeff Beck, Jimi Hendrix, The Temptations, Smokey Robinson and The Miracles, etc.

I kept my classical and jazz records to myself for those quiet times that I would need to escape the madness of freshman and sophomore existence.

Joseph Smith was a black version of Rudolph Valentino. I mean his drop-dead movie star good looks rivaled even Jess', and he commanded a game on the court that was just as remarkable. He was a senior and only 6'3," but possessed jumping skills that allowed him to play small forward. Joe's "game" was way ahead of its time. Looking back, I could definitely see hints of Julius Irving ("Dr. J"), the future professional hall of famer, in his approach to the game. He and Blakely Younger, another guy on the team, both came from a small and rural coastal North Carolina city high school, that was well regarded for its basketball team and players that went on to make names for themselves in the many various divisions of college and university programs. In fact, and it got to be a running joke of sorts, we were always running into their former teammates on rival squads throughout West Virginia, Kentucky, Virginia, Tennessee, and North and South Carolina.

Interestingly enough, though, Joe never participated in our "Dozen's" battles, and this was due to precisely two facts. One, his dedication to the opposite sex was even, dare I say it, more centralized than even Jess' and mine and occupied literally all of his spare time, and two, Joe had a dark side that even he was afraid of. He was not above threatening someone with a gun or knife, and any of us that ever "got into it" with him, were always wary. But above all, he was a good guy and we had many notable shared experiences. The most legendary, albeit rumored as it was an "unofficial event," and they still talk about it today, was the party we threw that fall.

It was homecoming weekend and we were (as young college boys are inevitably prone to do) preparing for a most commemorative party. Even though our house was small, we had enough space with our downstairs living room, bedroom suite, kitchen, den and foyer to host a coterie of 30 to 40.

Our plan was to invite all of the players on the basketball team and their dates, plus some other friends, Tim Bates' guests, who thankfully numbered just a few, and Monty's contingent, which numbered none, save for all of us there at the house. The football players were on curfew, as the big game was the next day, and even my buddy Jess couldn't slide out of his dorm. In fact, I had tried to get him to move in with us, but the administration was, by now, well aware of our profound relationship and thought it best to "let sleeping dogs lie". Besides, Jess being a football player, had already been assigned to a dorm way back in August during summer football practice.

With the other athletes, including J.P. Finney, and various friends, we figured on 50 or so, and actually were "right on the money" with our prognosis.

Now, alcoholic beverages were forbidden in the dorms and campus housing. Also, women had to be out of the rooms by midnight on Friday nights, and in their own quarters by 1 a.m. It was always a totally amusing adventure to witness and experience, that of the one-hour "twilight zone" that lay between the aforementioned curfew times, and, of course, we were inevitably and always "pushing the envelope," so to speak.

The chances that I took were legendary by the beginning of my sophomore year. One had to possess the stealth like qualities of our finest elite armed forces commandoes to evade campus security, and most of the time it was a supreme challenge, whilst being drunk on your ass, with a date that was equally plastered and wining about her dorm mom's predilection to restrict anyone caught after hours. Plus, there was one factor that always preyed upon our minds and souls and that was the Dean of Women's well-documented penchant for chopping our collective male balls into oblivion. Her infamous tirades on matters such as "the evils of men," "the casualty of the penis," "the deterioration of society as a result of boys waving their penises," etc., etc., had everyone realizing which "team" she represented. To us, the "Dean of Women" initials on her desk (DOW) always stood for "DICKS OFF WOMEN"!

So alcohol was forbidden? Right! Our house was famous for its "buffalo piss" recipe. This was an always-improvised beverage as the ingredients were based upon who donated what. It was required for every participant to contribute a pint of "whatever your distilled fancy happens to be". I mean that everything was fair game, and you'd be quite surprised how, when added to a decent fruit-based punch, vodka, gin, Southern Comfort, and even scotch made for a very nice concoction. Beer and wines were off limits, as even we had some sort of class and dignity, and maybe a little common sense. Plus, the barfing factor was kept under epidemic boundaries and proportions. This is not to say that some inevitably suffered at the hands of fate of the porcelain gods, but these lapses were actually few and far between!

Our parties were always under control, and I have to believe the reason for this was that most of us were good kids that never really wanted to physically do irreparable harm to our own bodies. Yes, I heaved a few times, as others, but was keenly aware of alternate ways to have fun. Plus, my personal tolerance for booze was very little. I always had a very high metabolic rate, and knew that alcohol would literally race through my system.

Our homecoming affair was smoothly taking its course. In fact, so smoothly, that no one noticed how the night was slipping away. I mean, with the right music, dancing, drinking, small doses of smoking reefer, et al, time can take on a surreal effect, and it was, for many of us, our first homecoming We had dwindled to maybe 15 or so, including my housemates Burton, Joe, Monty and Tim. The rest of the basketball team had gone on to their respective dorms, as we had our own restrictions. I looked at my watch and it startled me for an instant. It was well after 2 a.m.

Well, we weren't making any real noise, and our house was off the main campus, so I wasn't too bothered.

"Hey Burt, Joe, you guys want a hit off this joint?" I offered to my basketball compatriots.

"Sure 'nuff, Jesse, the look on your face says it all," Joe replied. "This Traffic tune is the shit!"

My date declined as she was well "in the bag," but still maintaining a lot of control, especially since we were past curfew. We had it worked out anyway, as to how we were sneaking her back into her dorm.

So here I was, sitting on our couch with Suzanne, joint in one hand, bottle of wine in the other, and basically minding my own business, when I happened to glance in the direction of our kitchen, which was just off the side-door entrance. Well, in walks the Dean of Men, with two campus security guards, heading straight for our living room, and looking me dead in my eyes.

We were busted, plain and simple. I mean, my own personal transgressions were instantly threefold and of the utmost serious nature, save cheating on an exam. I mean I was obviously, and somewhat energetically, breaking the 2nd, 3rd and 4th commandments of the college's doctrine of proper behavior.

I could see the "writing on the wall": "College basketball player expelled from school for infractions ranging from alcohol and drug abuse, to curfew violations with an underage co-ed"; never mind the fact that Suzanne was 18 years of age, and this was our very first time for missing curfew, that I drank only socially, and I got stoned very rarely.

The wheels in my head were turning and I was envisioning a serious ass-whipping from my dad, based partly upon the idea that he was still in charge of and responsible for me as I was still a minor, and mostly upon the idea that he still could!

Mom would be mortified. She always had a vision of me as the son who would invariably use good judgment in any given situation. I later realized that I did indeed fit that description in her eyes as in the big scheme of life; these sins were indeed minor, especially when stacked up against the potential horrors of adult "real-life".

Burton, Joe and I were all put in the campus patrol car and taken to the Dean's office. Our girlfriends were similarly escorted to their respective dorms with the promise of a later meeting with their own Dean and, for some godforsaken and unknown reason, Monty and Tim were left alone, as were those few other friends of ours that were also there at the end.

Well, wouldn't you know that I was in for lesson number one regarding "the justice system," that of the time-honored tradition of light sentencing for "those that matter". You see if it wasn't for the fact that Burton and especially Joe were so valuable to the basketball team, my ass would've been shipped out of there like I was some sort of Yankee malignancy, spreading doom and destruction throughout the South.

Instead, both of my roommates each copped a plea of nolo contendere, and equally and magnanimously accepted blame. But most importantly they made the point of letting the dean know that they were as guilty as me, with respect to all of the charges. So, if the Dean was expelling me, he'd have to expel them, and we sort of suspected that that was not going to happen.

I looked at the clock on Dean Jarid's wall and noticed, by then, that it was 4 a.m.

"What do you guys think?" I whispered to them, "Seems like we're either supremely fucked or they will just brush this under the carpet."

"They're not messin' with my scholarship," Joe answers, with the conviction of a young man that is going places in this world. "I will blow the whistle on some shit that I know that goes on in here, and they'll be sorry as hell!" Joe came from an impoverished family, and there was a real sense of urgency in his statements, as this was most likely one of his only opportunities for a "free ride" at this stage of the game, given the serious nature of the charges.

"Christ," Burton answers, "you'd think that we stole some exams or something, or robbed the student union."

"My dad is gonna beat my ass," was all that I countered. I figured when I survived that, I'd have to join the Navy, anyhow. "Good-morning, Vietnam!"

The Dean went and made a couple of phone calls, and then told us that we would hear from him within the week.

"You young men are really, really in serious trouble, and I hope that you realize that you may well have ruined a great chance to make something of yourselves," Dean Jarid said, in a most somber tone of voice.

I figured that we had a fifty-fifty chance of good or bad news. What I was counting on, though, was the fact that the three of us represented one-quarter of the basketball team, and that Joe was seriously invaluable, Burton was somewhat invaluable, and I was "chopped-liver," but still considered to be the best pure shooter on the team. My instincts told me that we would not be expelled, simply because of Joe's "net" worth, and from what he had previously uttered about indiscretions on the part of our college.

We then went home, utterly exhausted, and for some strange reason, were also famished. So we did the natural thing that so many of us getting the munchies would do at this ungodly hour: we went to the truck stop, just off the Interstate, four exits south, and feasted on biscuits and gravy, sausage and eggs. What a meal for the three "stooges/felons". What a way to kick off homecoming weekend. What a way to fuck up our lives!

One week later, my suspicions were validated. We were let go, "scot-free," so they say. Our only punishment was that we were on "special-circumstance probation," whatever the hell that meant. I suspect that that was a brand new term for really fucking up, but having the where-with-all in having some clout and also having something on the administration that could ultimately cause irreparable harm.

As it turned out, Joe was prescient beyond reproach. He later told us that when he was being recruited, he was offered different kinds of "under-the-table" monies; all of it highly illegal, at least as far as the NCAA was concerned. And he reminded the administration of that fact. What balls!

And he had absolute proof of another even more startling fact: that certain well-known former members of one of our championship football teams were not only betting on college games, but had close relatives and friends that belonged to the local chapter of the KKK, a practice that continues to this day. Something to this effect was often rumored in our midst, but never proven.

This was a dichotomy that often plagued my thoughts. How could blacks and whites fight for a common cause on the gridiron, and then want to harm each other when not playing ball?

Joe knew the details, and as I later found out, all of the black athletes knew. Each and everyone one of them, most likely due to some instinctive and obvious survival mentality, would share this information with each incoming class of black freshman, even the non-athletes. What a genius method of self-preservation, and I was duly impressed. I had not a clue until Jess filled me in and made me swear on my sister's virginity that I would never utter a single word, as this was serious business. In my black brothers' eyes, no one of their kind was going to get fucked buy the white man, at least in this particular environment.

Pure hardball, of a most noble variety; this was real life, plain and simple!

*     *     *

"I hear you pulled a big one down there," Loretta said to me, during our first phone conversation since I got the news that I wasn't getting thrown out of school. "You really cut it close this time Jesse."

I wondered for just a second or two as to how she was so informed of my current affairs, and then realized that she and Jess had been quite the phone companions themselves. As I have said, over and over, she was my guardian angel.

"Yeah sis, this was way too close, although it's easy now to be relaxed and laugh about it, considering the shit we got away with." I continued, "Everyone down here is talking about it, although Coach Melling is totally pissed at me, never mind that Burton and Joe were equally involved. It's my ass that he's taking it out on. He's never given a shit about me anyhow. God he's such a country-ass!"

Of course I would never say this to his face as Coach was a former All-American small college forward, and was as tough as they come. Plus, I think that he bailed hay his whole life and had that upper body development that many farmers have that is deceptively deadly.

"Jesse, promise me that you'll cool out for a while. You know that mom and dad would have a fit if you lost your scholarship."

We were not poor, by any stretch, but my family never had money to throw around. Also, I had friends that were much less fortunate, and having been through Appalachia many times traveling to and from regional colleges that were on our schedule, I was starting to get some real-life perspective on the "class system" in our country.

"Loretta, I swear that I'll behave, or at least not do anything foolish." As I could give up anything other than girls, I would have to be smarter, that's all.

"Jesse, I think that something's wrong with my stomach," Loretta stated in a much more somber tone, while abruptly changing the subject. "Mom thinks that maybe it's an ulcer."

This caught me off guard, as usually Loretta's pattern was to spare her big brother any details that would unnecessarily worry me, and immediately I sensed something amiss. I was not too alarmed, but something felt wrong, even though her statement was nothing out of the ordinary. Years later, I would play this conversation over and over and over in my head, something of which I could never rid myself.

"Jesus, sis, are you okay?" I tried to be as positive as I possibly could. "You're too young and healthy to get an ulcer. Are you worried about anything?"

"Not really, honey, it's only every-so-often, and it goes away after an hour or so."

Loretta would call me "honey," "darling," and even "sweetheart" when she was concerned about me. This was her style, never mind that she was in pain. It was always me, her brother and protector Jesse that she invariably championed.

"My appointment with Dr. Samuel is tomorrow and I'll let you know," she continued. "I'm sure that it's something simple."

"Babe, please call me everyday," I answered. "Please don't leave me in the dark if anything is wrong."

"Babe" was one of the affectionate names I used for my sister when I felt equal-said regard for her.

"I promise you, Jesse, that I will share everything, even if it's bad news, although I know that I'm fine."

Well, later she would concede to me that she always knew something was wrong with her, and I was not in the least surprised as I felt that my sister knew just about everything.

"By the way, Reece asked me out again," she added. "I think that we're going to a party at his house."

Reece Davis was attending a community college near home, and I really did not know him well, as I only met him once and did not care for him. He had taken Loretta to her senior homecoming dance a few weeks earlier. Loretta was always attracted to the "fringe element," just as I was, and I chalked this one up to her quixotic nature.

"I love you, sis, more than you can imagine," as I started to end our conversation with a few tears streaking my face. "You are the best thing in my life!"

"Jesse, my sensitive artist, athlete and brother of my dreams, I thank God everyday for being your sister, and for giving me my real-life hero. I love you, too."

We hung up and my tears were flowing - "Please God, give her a chance!"

# Chapter Six

"In the morning, as I rise,
Only the dreamers have my eyes,
Only the dreamers are tryin',
And the schemers are lyin,
And they keep on denying me,
Can't you see...?"

Only the Dreamers

# VI

Loretta was getting dressed for her date with Reece later that night. She always looked absolutely stunning in dresses, especially cotton summer ones and, with this being an exceptionally warm fall evening, decided to wear her favorite blue dress with the pastel flowers. This never failed to take my, her own brother's, breath away...needless to say of the effect on her various boyfriends!

I have always melted at the sight of a pretty girl in a sundress. I absolutely believe that it is the singular most complimentary article of clothing a woman can wear.

Negligees, fishnet stockings, pant suits, daisy-duke shorts with halter tops, Danskin leotards, tight jeans with 5" pumps, and even athletic gear, are all wonders of the world when adorned by beautiful girls.

But I tell you, and I have maintained this since I was a child, that the vision of a radiant woman in the aforementioned trousseau touches my inner soul, and I am forever grateful to God for allowing me to be constantly overwhelmed by the simplistic beauty that this projects.

Now Reece Davis was a hardass when he was in high school. Not really an outlaw, but "fringe element" just the same. He was a former jock that had a real mean streak, not the kind that is necessary when in "battle" on the field, but the kind that bullied the innocent and the weak from time to time; again, not really evil, but dangerous just the same.

He was a very good-looking guy with loads of potential, but something about him raised my hackles. This has always been a gift of mine, to spot trouble before it explodes. I got along with him okay, considering the fact that I had only met him once. My sister was one of the finest looking girls in the county, though, and this did wonders for my own particular status; still, I always sensed a looming battle with him on the horizon.

Loretta had her "perimeter" attractions as well. She had the hots for Reece, and this bothered me to no end, as I could not imagine my beautiful YOUNGER sister having sex. I liked to imagine her as a virgin, but sincerely had my doubts, especially since she and Jake (he of the aforementioned bass player and shaved legs ilk) had dated for close to six months before realizing that they were better suited as best friends. To his profound good taste, Jake never mentioned their sex history to a living soul, and my respect for him grew and grew. Otherwise I would have heard, I mean this was high school for chrissakes!

I shared almost everything with my sister, but some things were sacred, even between us.

She and Reece were going to a party being held at the house that was rented by Reece and three of his community college buddies. They often had Saturday night bashes, and you'd think that people would learn to stay away, especially since the local cops were constantly being summoned to the scene for out-of-control obnoxious drunken preppies acting like they owned the fuckin' world.

At any rate, Reece came and picked Loretta up in his glass-packed and overblown GTO, which was another reason I did not care for the son-of-a-bitch. I mean what a fuckin' redneck car. I told you that I grew up in a county that was forever notorious for the ubiquitous provincial and inane behavior of many of its inhabitants!

His car is roaring in my parents' driveway and instead of getting out to meet Loretta at her door (never mind the social grace of parental acknowledgement), he toots his fucking horn! What an ever-lovin' asshole!

I have a serious problem with rude behavior, and while it is very true that many of us who were reared in our bucolic surroundings did not really have the chance to be so refined, some of us, however, took the time to learn to be respectful (plus a sharp jab or right cross from my dad did wonders to remind me of proper etiquette).

I am also constantly amazed by my girlfriends of their surprise of my graciousness with respect to their well being, and wonder just who the hell they have been hanging out with their entire lives. I mean what's the big deal about holding the door for: your mom, sister, grandmother, children, aunts and uncles, neighbors, the people you run into at the post office, movie theater and grocery store, etc.? Isn't this just "normal" behavior? Well, apparently not for a lot of folks.

Standing up from the table when your lady needs to be excused is a delicacy that is slowly becoming extinct. Maybe this is my southern upbringing and culture coming into play, but I do love the decorum.

It's like dancing, and as much as I love rock and roll, I do not care for the gyrations of the "Gene Kelly inept" whilst agitating to the sounds of the aforementioned.

The tango, however, can be one of the most sexually compelling and yet sublimely graceful events one can witness or, even better yet, become a participant.

The waltz: what an absolutely lovely maneuver to experience, and the sheer tradition of such can be overwhelming.

I also have seen women Flamenco dancers in their sixties look as vibrant and seductive as any 30-year-old movie starlet.

At any rate, here we have Reece gunning his engine, honking his horn and waiting for my lovely and graceful sister to be subjugated to his crass behavior. Little did she know that he had already been drinking (and quite a bit at that, I might add), and that his true reason for not getting out of his car was due to his state of inebriation.

Little did she know that the events to follow would change the course of her, and my, life forever.

Little did we know that our love for each other would become so much greater and that our spirits and souls would evolve to such a level as to literally frighten us into thinking that if we were ever separated that we would not survive!

Loretta hopped in with Reece and off they sped towards a destiny that redefined her life and that redefined her spirit, which led me to "step across a most sacred line".

Things were already in fast gear at the Davis house. Lights were flashing, rock and roll was blaring, and the booze was flowing as if there was going to be a prohibition law introduced to our county the very next day.

One thing about Steppenwolf, Iron Butterfly, Zeppelin and Hendrix: when coupled with the right liquor and designer drug, they will get one fired up to the point of no real return to normalcy at any time soon.

Loretta starts dancing in a way that only she was capable of, a sort of tribal theater that she alone was privy to and that only she understood. Usually this would raise the eyebrows of even the most tolerant and sensitive, but with my Loretta, anything was possible, and even better, acceptable!  She just had that sparkle, as if her guardian angel had just atomized her with the loveliest pixie dust this side of Tinkerbelle.

Reece's roommate, Butchie, was groping his slut of a girlfriend to the point of ridiculousness.  He was another loser in the "charm school system" and had about as much tact as a hungry great white shark, roaming through an ocean of plump, juicy sea lions wallowing about with their "come hither and rip my guts out" behavior.

Because of Butchie's behavior, Reece started to follow suit, with his "boys will be boys" pattern, and made Loretta an especially potent bacchanal.

Compelled by the spirit of the moment, and genuinely having a great time, Loretta flushed down the deceptive drink, with the speed of a cheetah and the grace of a gazelle, and it was her own special quality of delicacy that enabled my sister to look magnificent whilst chugging God knows what in the midst of a most raucous celebration.

Everyone was dancing and yelling and drinking and drugging.  Reece's other two roommates, both named Billy, were just as intoxicated as Reece, apparently having started the festivities together earlier that afternoon.

Couples then started into their sexual phases of the evening – some pairing off into their respective automobiles, others grabbing blankets off of the front porch for the fields behind the house, and still others making headlong forays into the semi-finished basement.

As I alluded to earlier, I have never condoned the preppie existence: everyone with their button-down shirts, jeans and loafers with no socks, expensive cars (red-necked or not), and enough money to really not have to work; but life is what it is, and I do not begrudge anyone for their affluence.  It's just that when proper and gracious behavior is replaced by condescension and snobbery, I start to get irritated, and when provoked to the degree of overheating, I have been known to rage, as you shall see.

Reece was dancing with Loretta and, lo and behold, another drink materialized and was placed in her hands. Loretta blasts this one down as well, and started to feel a bit lightheaded, in fact "heavy-headed".

"Reece, darling, I need to sit down, I'm feeling too dizzy. What's in this drink, anyhow?"

"Just a little surprise I've developed over the years, nothing to get worried about."

"Yes, but what the hell am I drinking? It tastes like fruit punch, but with a kick that hits both my head and stomach at the same time!"

"Loretta, you'll be alright, I promise you, and you've probably had enough anyhow."

Enough was the under-fucking-statement of the year! Reece had used grain alcohol (which was 180 proof) to spike his perilous punch, and Loretta had had the equivalent of eight mixed drinks – too much to handle, too much to physically bear.

"How about coming to my room and lying down, until you feel better?" Reece proposed with his not-so-noble intentions.

"Yes, I really need to take it easy, just to lie still for a few minutes," Loretta countered.

Reece led Loretta back to his room, which was located in the rear of the house – a master suite isolated from seemingly all.

Loretta literally fell onto his bed, while Reece deceptively locked his door and switched on yet another of his stereos.

Where does an 19-year-old going to community college get the money for two stereos, and I am not talking about those little compact record players, but component systems? Did I miss something while growing up? Was I absent that day when the "gliding through life on a non-resistant coaster" lecture was given?

I guess so!!

At any rate, Loretta was lying there on his bed, her gorgeous legs and thighs exposed to the wrong guy. Her underwear was provocative, to say the least, and in this case only served to promote the heinous act that was to follow.

Reece started to fondle and kiss Loretta, and at first she was obliging. After all, she did have some of her faculties intact, and she was most definitely attracted to Reece.

"I've waited for this for such a long time," Reece cooed.

"Oh, Reece, me too," she replied.

I guess this is where Reece felt that he had his "green light," because, instead of a lovely interlude of kissing, even with Loretta's intoxication pre-eminent, he pulled up her dress and pulled down her underwear in a flash, Loretta's shoes having been lost eons ago.

"Reece, please don't, I'm sick and so dizzy!"

"Come on, sweetheart, we've always wanted to do this, you know you want to."

"No, I don't, Reece. I'm going to be sick and this is not the time!" Loretta's words becoming more slurred and obscure by the minute.

Reece then thrust his fingers inside her vagina and she shrieked and started to fight back, her legs kicking and her stomach lurching.

Now Reece was a powerful guy, and on a sober day Loretta might have fought with some clarity and success, but on this given night she was much too overwhelmed by the loss of her natural instincts and faculties.

Without even removing his jeans, he thrust himself into her, while pinning her arms above her head and raped her for several minutes, as he too was intoxicated.

Loretta had briefly passed out and, at this point, was just a lifeless figure, abused and ruined by this animal of a human being.

Reece then momentarily passed out while Loretta came to.

Realizing what had happened, she started to sob, thus awakening the "sleeping giant".

Without another thought, and reacting to the most sickening, humiliating and de-humanizing act that many, many women have had the utter misfortune to experience, Loretta then punched Reece in the middle of his face, actually breaking his nose in the process.

"You goddamn bitch," Reece yelled, and punched Loretta back, cutting her eyelid severely.

She started to bleed profusely, and this enraged Reece to yet another degree.

Loretta countered by clawing at his eyes and screaming her guts out.

"You fucking animal! You son of a bitch!" Loretta cried, while seemingly fighting for her life.

Reece then grabbed her by the throat and started to choke the life out of her.

Most likely the only thing that saved Loretta was the fact that she then violently threw up, and I am talking about the type of vomiting that can be associated with a severe case of food poisoning. The kind of expelling that is usually associated with an experience akin to dying.

She fell to the floor in a heap, an abused and wasted wretch of a human being, so trampled and lifeless, sobbing and puking, crying and dying.

Finally the knocking on the door, which was apparently going on for a couple of minutes, was answered.

"Jesus, Reece, what the fuck?" Billy #1 asked.

"Jesus Christ, what the fuck?" Billy #2 echoed.

Butchie came in, and was thusly sobered by what he saw.

"God, Reece, look at her."

Loretta was shaking intensely, and trying to pull herself together, blinded somewhat by the profusion of blood pouring down her face.

"We've got to get her out of here," Butchie's slut girlfriend proposed. "She needs a doctor!" she added, maybe with a touch of grace and humanity.

"Bullshit," Reece growled, "I am not going to take the hit for this. She fucking attacked me because she was drunk and out of her mind. She wanted sex, and then started to fucking go crazy on me!"

Everyone suspected what had happened, but were too allied with Reece to counter anything that he said.

Loretta then, as was her God given ability to do, miraculously sobered up enough to gather her things and, without saying a word, left the room and walked through the house, paying attention to nothing. She calmly strolled out the front door, using her underwear to bandage her head, and proceeded to walk all the way to the nearest 7-Eleven store, where she called a cab.

She then let herself into the high school gymnasium (my sister was the most resourceful person I have ever known) with a key that she obviously had confiscated and took the most important shower (and the longest) of her young life.

Donning an outfit that she so instinctively had in her locker, she then gathered her ruined clothes together, placing them in a paper bag. Loretta calmly walked down the deserted hallways until she reached the boiler room and threw the bag into the furnace, watching the flames engulf her totemistic nightmare.

She did not cry, she did not lament, and she did not curse.

My sweet and darling sister prayed to God. Not for forgiveness for the offensive, for even she had her revenge in mind, but for God not to blame her for what had happened.

My most magnificent sister was concerned for her image unto God, and this is what made her the most unique person I've ever known and loved.

My own sister was the light and love of my life, and events of retaliation were going to unfold in a supremely vicious manner.

Loretta was going to leave revenge up to me, Jessie, her own brother, who she knew would have to deliver, because of our undying and prodigious passion and tenderness for each other.

Equally important, though, was the bond that she had developed with my best friend Jess, who Loretta intuitively knew had the potential to kill, and of which I had not a clue.

Guess what? I had that potential as well, and my dear sister was prescient beyond belief.

I was about to evolve into someone that I had never known or suspected. Jess and Jessie were on a course headlong into a fury of which we had no control, and that would change each of us forever.

I loved my sister to the point of not caring about life or death, and that was to be the most grave and severe lesson of my life to date.

Loretta took another cab home, and most stealthily climbed through her bedroom window. She fell asleep while praying for me and the impact that this night's horrific events would have upon me.

She prayed for my sanity and soul.

I shall never be so blessed!

# Chapter Seven

"And I get lonely,
When I see the children play,
If I could only,
Have one more yesterday..."

Young Again

# VII

Revenge!!! A dish best served cold—the time-honored axiom that has been indelibly etched upon the accumulated psyches belonging to the "fraternity of justice".

Revenge!! Once you cross the line, and I mean the "real" line, your innocence, if still intact, is forever blasted into some monstrous black hole that seemingly devours our youthful compassions and ideals and most likely churns them into fodder, hopefully for future generations to absorb, and then give away when life treats them to their own malevolent circuses.

Revenge! We all think about it. We all have imagined it, quite possibly in some Quixotic fairy tale, quite possibly in a dream following a particularly retaliatory movie or event; most likely, though, when we knew someone tragically affected enough to carry out their own particular vendetta, and concurred wholeheartedly.

Thinking about it, planning it, achieving it, though, is entirely another story. Losing yourself in some sort of psychotic and vindictive time warp will, and I can attest to this fact, change you forever. You will no longer look at life as you once did. Ask those vets that have seen and participated in the horrors of war. Ask those parents who have lost their children to those child-molesting cowards that prey upon our youth. Ask those police officers that have answered those domestic disturbance calls once too often, and found that battered young woman, utterly destroyed in spirit.

Loretta called me on that Monday morning following.

"Jesse, how are you doing my love?"

Something was not right with her voice, as it sounded almost too subdued and relaxed for even my sister's notoriously sexy cadence.

"I'm fine, sis, but we got crushed in our first game; I got to play for a couple of minutes. I hit a jumper from the top of the key, and got two assists, and then Melling yanked my ass right out".

Sometimes I wondered if I was just too "city" for Coach's philosophy, not just in hoops, but also in general life itself. He was a good man, though, and as much as I goofed on his methods and lack of insight into the modern game, he was a "stand-up" guy, and I learned to later really respect him, as I most probably simply matured!

"Are you and that gorgeous Jess coming home for Thanksgiving?" she asked, again with the aforementioned weird intonation.

Now I knew that something was up, as she did not even comment on my basketball game. I began to develop a serious feeling of anxiety and dread.

"Loretta, what's wrong with you, something isn't right!" I nervously asked my sister, feeling the life go out of my legs and the ubiquitous knot exponentially develop in my stomach.

"Oh Jesse, something awful happened, but I'm okay! - You hear me? I am okay!"

Tears started cascading down my face, the salt stinging my eyes as I, most suddenly, was penetrated by my sister's prescience, and knew something grave had happened.

"What is it, babe? What happened?" feeling nauseated and dizzy.

"Are you sitting down? Please sit down while I explain something to you!"

Now I am getting pissed-off, because I am scared, and Loretta's calm demeanor is really getting to me, as I know I am about to hear something that will completely fuck me up!

"Goddammit Loretta," I shouted a bit too harshly, "What the fuck is going on?"

She then told me everything that had happened, in more detail than I probably needed, but that was my sister's profound belief in me as her brother, best friend and now spiritual partner, as she knew full well of my ever-evolving assimilation of her divine intuition. It's like she knew that God, himself, was "passing the torch," for my survival in the days to come.

I was out of my mind with grief!

Never before has something so sickened me to the point of utter helplessness, as I always found ways to respond to my various battle calls in the past. Never have I felt so weak and small and afraid.

I cried and cried, and all the while Loretta kept soothing me back into the reality of the moment and, more importantly, back into a functioning grasp of returning to some sort of "normal" state.

She finally succeeded by actually shocking me with her stark and explicit words:

"Jesse, I want to hurt that motherfucker, I mean really hurt him!"

This hit home with me in a way that had never before manifested itself with my sister's relationship with me. Loretta routinely confided in me, and always shared many of her innermost reflections, but never had I experienced this almost surreal hatred of hers. On the surface, it was very uncharacteristic, but in the moment, it was a revelation.

I was beginning to feel the stirrings of utter hatred and contempt; I was on the fast track to the new and learned experience of willingly inflicting pain and suffering upon someone evil. I was ready to enter into the netherworld of what I have always despised, quite possibly sowing the seeds of what professional assassins may feel when they try to explain to themselves and God the justification of their sins!

Ah, PREMEDITATION! What a concept most evil. What a concept most tortuous. What a concept most divine!

After several minutes of letting our tears languish and just catching our collective breath, I very softly cooed to my treasure of a sister: "sweetheart, as long as you're okay for now, I need to go talk with Jess."

"I know, babe," she replied, "tell Jess that I love him, too, and to take care of my brother."

"I'll be fine, sis, I adore you more than anything!"

"Me too."

"One more thing," I added, "if anything changes with you physically, please let Doc Samuel and me know."

Doctor Morris Samuel was our most trusted friend and confidant, and very few adults ever put us more at ease than he. From tonsils to broken ribs, fractured hands to busted chins, routine physicals to Loretta's very first menstrual cycle, he nursed both my sister and me back to our healthy realities.

Doc Samuel was the first person that Loretta had called when all of this happened, and very likely had "saved" Loretta from God knows what insanity that invades one's mind when something this traumatic happens to anyone.

"I promise you I will," she replied, "and I'll call you tomorrow.

Even though Loretta and I talked frequently, this was the beginning of even more rigorous phone communications, as we began talking at least twice daily, sometimes three and four times, and, to offset our parents' modest incomes, later when basketball was over, I took a part time job in the school cafeteria to help out.

I needed to be with Loretta, now more so than ever!

*    *    *

Thank God that Jess was in his room that morning, having bailed on his Western Civilization class once again. I'm glad, because I would have gone and yanked him out of class anyhow, and this way I could keep my obvious and utter despair more of our secret, than embarrassingly sharing it with anyone else on campus.

I noticed that his roommate was gone, and immediately broke down.

Any other time, I would have not been so weak with this display of emotion, and Jess would have not been so kind with his response, as it was in our make-up to continue the previously detailed practice of "the dozens".

To his credit, he immediately felt the gravity of the situation, as our own psychic bond was once again forged into something even more profound, and beyond our youthful scope.

Jess actually held me in his arms, not withholding any of his love and strength for his best friend. Even the indomitable Jess began to exude apprehension and fear and sensing this I quickly composed myself.

"Jess, this is fucking awful!"

"Tell me brother, I'm here for you."

I recounted the entire story as Loretta had told me, leaving nothing to doubt, nothing for comment.

Jess sat there with tears in his eyes, and for someone as seemingly powerful as he was, I was impacted beyond anything that I had previously experienced; not that Jess wasn't capable of crying, it's just that he was such a bad-ass.

I saw a look in his eyes that I had yet not witnessed. He then calmly walked to the window of his dorm room and, with one ridiculously fast punch, completely obliterated all of the glass within reach.

He then sat on his bed and buried his face in his hands and wept for my sister and me. As I had previously said, Jess was also developing something very serious with Loretta in his own right, something that I had mixed feelings over, knowing his "Valentino" reputation, but also whimsically wishing for us to actually be related.

I stood over him and embraced his head and hands for several minutes, and soon we were both immersed in his blood, from his bleeding hand.

"Hey Jess, we need to get cleaned up, we got blood all over the place."

"Alright. Jesse, you okay?"

"Yeah bro, I'm okay, "I replied, "are you?"

"No, I want to kill that motherfucker!" he answered.

"I will, count on it!" Maybe the most chilling thing I have ever stated, simply because it was the absolute truth.

We both decided to go to a nearby liquor store, Jess never got carded-I always did, and get some spirits to lift ours, and then get some food and go back to my room.

That entire afternoon we drank and plotted a course that would change our lives, and one that would fast forward me into my future as an adult that has "seen too much"!

*    *    *

Jess came home with me for the Thanksgiving break, and was completely and warmly accepted by my mom and dad.

Loretta and I had never hugged so fiercely, and the look that she and Jess gave each other was priceless. Everyone was smiling beyond "facial acceptance".

Mom stated "why Jess, you're better-looking than even our Loretta had warned us about," grinning and reddening my sister's countenance to no end.

"Jesus, mom," Loretta countered, "cannot a girl have her fantasies kept off the 'front page of the tabloids'?"

"Okay ladies," dad chimes in, "you'd think that the rest of us men were invisible, here".

"I think that we all could use a drink," I said, not even realizing that I had started to take for granted, the occasional habit developed by many of us truly experiencing the wondrous freedom from parental restraint for the first times in our lives, being away at school, and something that was, nevertheless, still illegal for Jess, Loretta and myself, and immediately my skin matched the former hue of my dear sister's.

A moment of awkward silence followed, then my dad and mom started to laugh, and Jess and Loretta followed suit. I, on the other hand, took a few seconds to regain my composure, which should not have mattered as both my parents were very wise, and compassionate, and it really was not so long ago that they were themselves pulling the same stunts as adolescents and young adults. Plus, we were raised in the European tradition of wine at every meal, but let's face it, we all knew I was talking about a good stiff shot of something.

I immediately 'zoned in" on the reality of Loretta's and Jess' bond, apparently even more had developed with their many phone conversations than I had previously thought. Yes, something was going on here, and it was much more than casual.

Dinner was magnificent, both my mom and dad could really cook, but there was more to this event than meets the naked eye, and under the watchful surveillance of our most gracious God, a sublime spiritual energy was being manifested that was connecting all of us.

Loretta, Jess and I later talked into the wee hours of the night, revisiting some stark and terrifying events, but all serving as a great therapeutic benefit to my darling sister. She was actually smiling, deeply, from her heart and soul, and made that obvious to us.

I, however, was concurrently experiencing the strangest combination of feelings I'd ever known. On one side of my "mental divide," resided the "I am going to take the high road" benevolent Christian doctrine, and on the other, the malevolent Christian dogma of "burn every last one of the heathen motherfuckers all to hell"!

Both tenets would serve me well, and at this very Thanksgiving gathering, and with Loretta's, Jess' and my "evening conversation post script-pact-spiritual reckoning," this entire maelstrom of thought came to a ridiculously concise closure. I was going to fuck this guy up real bad! I was beyond fear, apprehension, remorse, and most of all, reprisal from my God. Succinctly, I just did not give a rat's ass, and was starting to salivate, much like the infamous Russian scientist Pavlov's dog, and my "dinner bell" was Reece Davis' indelibly imprinted voice etched upon my conscience. The seeds were sown for equity!

\*       \*       \*

Jess and Loretta fell in love that Thanksgiving, but not the physical "throwing sweaters, bumping-happy" sexual explosion that is so wondrous at the beginning of any passionate affair. Rather, a newfound soul mate sort of thing that transcends even our most basic physical desires. The look they shared as we left that weekend to go back to school was priceless, and instead of feeling that I had lost a small part of my sister to this enigma of a young man, I was elated to the fact that Jess and I had crossed yet another sacred barrier, on the path to our life-long intimacy. Plus, I would really need him for the perils that lie in wait.

Loretta now had two guardian angels, and by God we were going to wreak havoc amongst the low-class white trash that had damaged her nearly beyond recovery.

We just had to wait for the right moment!

# Chapter Eight

"Every night I look above,
Hoping to see your light,
Wishing I was flying with you,
Knowing full well that I might,
Someday when my time is right..."

The Nightrider

# VIII

Southern West Virginia University was not our most hated rival. As a matter of fact, my beloved East Tennessee Valley College had in-conference opponents that seemingly forever resided at the top of our antagonist barometer, and we duly prepared.

SWVU was nearly always nationally ranked, and, even though this was NCAA Division Two, occasionally sent a player to the professional ranks. To add insult to injury, they also featured three players from the very same high school power-house that our own Joe Smith and Blakely Younger had previously attended, that state championship hot-bed of basketball talent in eastern North Carolina that would forever plague us with this and a couple of other institutions.

My theory to Rocky Gap High School's indomitable prosperity was three-fold: one, their coach was a paradox, in that he was "old-school" in his values, morals, etc., but most modern in his methods-constantly updating techniques, teaching and philosophies of the modern game; two, he was a very benevolent and wise man, and forever were Blakely and Joe misty-eyed when they even talked about their revered sage, as to how he would counsel his young black and white men about life, without appearing to be too judgmental, how he bridged the gap between generations of young men, sending them out into the world to conquer fairly; and three, this academy was geographically blessed, they were near the sacred ocean, for Christ's sake!!!

When you breathe sea air, something magical happens to many of us, and I, for one, truly know of its most hallowed potency. Blakely and Joe grew up with sand between their toes, seagulls yapping in the skies, and with salt permeating the atmosphere of their childhood years. I mean, how simply marvelous could life be? Roundball courts within earshot of the surf crashing into the rocks and beach; it's no wonder why these two went home as much as possible.

Since the alma maters South West Virginia and East Tennessee Valley were just four hours apart from one another, being much too close to fly, and not far enough to travel on a commercial coach (and one that actually had a bathroom), we all were once again riding that dinosaur of a bus were reverently called "Miss Mabel" in front of coach and other administration types, but in reality her sobriquet being "Miss Maybe".

As in, "Maybe" we will all die this time when "Miss Maybe's" tires fall off their rims and we collide with an on-coming tractor-trailer, "Maybe" we all will suffocate when "Miss Maybe" assassinates us in our sleep with her most prodigious exhaust, or quite possibly "Miss"Maybe" will want to give-up her own ghost, right along with ours, in a suicidal-sacrificial rite of passage when She breaks that front axel and we all plunge off of some Godforsaken mountainside.

Truth be told, we always arrived safely, but our trainer, Phil Betters, who drove Miss Mabel, could always scare us with his uniquely stealth manner of backing off of the accelerator, in just the right fashion, under just the right over-pass, to cause Miss Mabel to fart like a bull elephant that had just consumed far too many bean burritos at his annual "company picnic"!

College athletics, what a misconception by the masses in that we were "superstars," quite possibly the big Division One schools held this to be true for their own celebrity athletes, but for us the reality being that we were just a clique of young men playing a game we loved, and taking the chances that go along with representing your school, against other warriors doing the same for theirs.

This trip would be a sobering experience for me, as I had never experienced what "Appalachia" truly was. I mean, I had read about the utter despair and poverty of these mountain people, but until you see this with your very own eyes, it's simply not the same.

Our drive took us through a particularly clear version of said despondency, that netherworld existing in the southwestern part of the wonderful state of Virginia, tucked away in the glorious Appalachian Mountain range. These "hills" were so stunning in their physical beauty, especially if the sun's cascading rays happen to absorb your attention. I would never get over this most precious gift from our Almighty, yet would question the paradox of the hopelessness that I would see, and yet worse, imagine.

I'm sitting next to T.J. Cooper, a junior guard, who was raised not far from this particular region, and he would educate me, in many fashions and beyond the obvious.

Even though T.J.'s hometown was fairly good-sized, many of his own high school basketball away games took him through here, and it always made him appreciate his own prosperity and family's status.

"Look, over there, Jesse," he said, and I turned my head.

We had slowed down, to a near crawl, as these roads were getting very treacherous with their curves, and Phil was taking no chances driving through here.

"That bridge crossing the stream is made of chicken wire and wooden crates these people most likely stole from the railroad yard," he added, "notice the rock piles at each end, to keep the rail ties in place, fucking perfect sanctuary for eastern diamond-backs"!

I am appalled, as this trestle looks as if it couldn't even withstand a thunderstorm.

"Jesus, T.J.," I exhaled, "that thing is a death-trap, and you could break your leg falling through".

"Maybe some do, but you'd be surprised at the strength, and that particular version has been in place for a couple of years," he told me.

"I don't see any power lines, these people have no electricity?" I ask, incredulously.

"Are you kidding?" he replied, "no electricity, no hot and cold running water, no nearby stores, and besides, they literally have no steady jobs or money!"

I am speechless as I view this deformity etched into the landscape.

"What do they do for money, for food?" I inquire.

"Some of them hire out to the local tobacco and grain farmers during harvesting season, I imagine a few work part time at the railroad yard, they raise some of their own crops, government food stamps and aid, even church 'socials', you know".

T.J. was very "matter-of-fact" with his replies, as obviously he'd been through this scenario before.

I, on the other hand, was captured in a surreal sense of hypnosis, seeing small shacks built literally of cardboard, outhouses I had only seen in movies, pathways that were rags and even more cardboard, etc.

Also, and to add to this horrific sight, were the feral dogs and cats roaming the countryside. I could only imagine the rabies cases contributing to this existing misery.

"Jesus," I said again.

"Jesus, is right," T.J. concurred.

"Christian Reconstructionism," T.J. further elaborated, as we drive away from this valley of despair, "you ever hear of that Jesse?"

I answer with the astute "huh?"

"Down here, these people have their own churches that would make your skin crawl".

I am harkening back to my first days at East Valley and the "snake-handling" episode I had read about in the local paper.

"White supremacy is one thing they truly preach, and it goes way beyond that at times," T.J. continued.

"They hate Catholics, Jewish folks, any kind of 'foreigner', and if you're a tad bit liberal, watch your ass!" he told me. "All in the name of Jesus, what a crock of shit! Worse of all, black people to many of them are literally nothing but animals from Africa."

I am stunned as I listen to this young man of nearly these very same boundaries, having obviously transcended his own environmental ignorance, much as my Jess had.

"Christ, T.J." I finally said, "These people don't look like they even have the time to hate anyone, they're so fucking poor!"

"Many are fine, Jesse, most don't really care for anything other than keeping their families alive. Still, when you get into some of the fundamentalist churches around here, it will scare the shit out of you!"

T.J. paused for a moment and then continued, "Very few of these kids go to any kind of public school, being 'taught' from within their own ranks. So, they just perpetuate this life-style, and some never even get away from these hills, many not even traveling beyond the next mountain or valley".

"There was even one minister and his wife that had several teenage boys and girls basically held in captivity, under the guise of 'adoption', and had psychologically tortured and repeatedly raped them for years, until a local detective, acting like a social worker, cracked the case!"

T.J. was my "older brother" on this team, as his junior status gave him two meaningful years advantage of experiencing college life. Having transferred from a well-regarded junior college, he was new here, but wise just the same, and he was married to his high school girlfriend, which, of course, gave him even more insight into this game of life in general.

He was a schoolboy legend in these parts, and being white, was highly recruited at some of the regional colleges. He attended Franklin Junior College, actually close to our destination of SWVU, because their coach was one of his former high school mentors, and this would ensure that he would start at guard for his freshman and sophomore years there. Why he transferred to East Tennessee Valley, and why I remained here, we both would question until we matriculated, but nevertheless we were here to stay, at least for the time being.

Miss Mabel continued up this mountainside, and down the next, following the same gorgeous "mini-river" that formerly had meandered under the earlier ramshackle bridge we were talking about.

My mind was racing with thoughts of in-bred nastiness, and people with their very own laws, and wondering if anyone ever broke down in this region, never to be heard from again.

I was actually to learn later, and as T.J. had intimated, that most of these people were not evil, on the contrary, some quite engaging; and by my junior year would experience visiting some of these places, getting to know these people on a personal basis, as a part of my psychology/sociology major studies!

I noticed the entire team napping; save for T.J. and myself, and minutes later we both, too, fell fast asleep, with the seemingly endless drone of Miss Mabel's groaning and purring in our ears, and the atmospheric pressure of these ranges grasping our subconscious.

A couple of hours later I hear Blakely and Joe re-living some of their glory years at Rocky Gap High School, which was always their ritual as we neared any institution where said compatriot ballplayers played and carried on with each of their own particular basketball legends.

It's funny how many of us, even in making some of these life-long bonds playing together in our colleges and universities, most revered our high school teammates and games; how that particular school-boy game held our hearts in captivity for a good portion of our lives, and this was duly borne out in numerous conversations I would participate in, or overhear with my college teammates.

I would further guess that the simplicity of our earlier years, versus the complexity of our now rapidly changing lives and ideals, contributed to this nostalgia, and our wanting to go back and re-live our respective childhoods.

We rolled into the stunning campus of Southern West Virginia University, and on this fine fall day, when our good Lord particularly took the extra time to paint His landscape in a most serene and impressionistic fashion, I felt even more alive and special, to be a part of this upcoming and soon to be magnificent battle royal.

"Be prepared to have your asses waxed!" read one painted sheet hanging off a dorm room window, "East Tennessee-Valley of the Pussies" read another, and this one was hanging out a GIRL'S dorm window-verified by Blakely and Joe, having hung out here with their high school mates on a few occasions. "SWVU-NATIONALLY RANKED, ETVC-JUST RANK," cried yet another.

This game had all the feelings of an epic battle, and I know that they were at least cognizant of our potential, and not so much of our history and this year's record, as it still was very early in the season. Just the fact that Blakely and Joe were on our team was enough to give us respect with their own three Rocky Gap players, who obviously had the credentials to lead their stunning ball club.

I loved the feeling of putting on my uniform, but the warm-ups were even more special, as the pants were a very flared cotton/fleece, and our jackets short-sleeved, sort of puffy, and they actually fit very nicely. So much so, that they reminded me of my kick-boxing gear, and sometimes I would find myself, in the middle of our warm-up routine, shadow-boxing and occasionally throwing a roundhouse kick to some imaginary and death dealing opponent, never failing to irk the ever-lovin' shit out of coach Melling, and always cracking T.J. and some of my other teammates up to no end.

We are running drills, getting psyched-up, and basically trying to convince ourselves that we can actually "hang" with this rival when the school announcer screams over the public address system: "and now, your very own Southern West Virginia University Wildcats".

The entire hall erupts into a frenzy, and as I said, these ballplayers were revered, having earned every right to be.

"Wildcats". Now that has a nice ring, and a feeling of invincibility.

We are the East Tennessee Valley "Hornets". Fucking bees, for Christ's sake!

I'll never forget watching these guys warm-up for my very first time, and thinking, "Christ, they're awesome".

Their entire team gets into one line, tallest to the smallest, respectively, and each player, one by one, starts at the free-throw line, and then proceeds to dunk the ever-lovin' shit out of the ball.

Well, I am thinking, "that's nice, but your last guy is my size, hell, even smaller!"

I was officially listed in our program at 5'11," but in reality was 5'10," and that was on my greatest "length" day; in hoops, EVERYONE rounded up when it came to their respective height listings! "Chick" Washington, Southern's standout sophomore point guard, was listed at 5'9"; he too very likely being a good inch, or more, shorter than said documentation.

I notice Blakely and Joe grinning and joshing each other, and, as if the Big Man Himself slid His finger underneath this little guard, found myself to be utterly blown-away when "Chick" grabs the ball and takes two steps, lifts into the atmosphere, and dunks the holy hell out of the ball. Their entire gym explodes and I notice even our own guys "high-fiving" each other.

Yes, Chick was a former teammate of our own Blakely and Joe's, and he used to do this in high school, as well, so our own Rocky Gap High contingent was obviously well informed.

Now, we had "leapers" on our team as well, several, in fact, but the most I could do was to get the tips of my fingers over the rim, having actually dunked a tennis ball, but this was an entirely different league of "sky-ing" ability, and I was dumbfounded.

"Jesus, I hope that I can shoot his ass-off," I am thinking to myself, also musing over the fact that I often dreamed about dunking.

I knew that I would play, at least a little, as by now haven proven myself as the very best shooter on our team, but vastly inexperienced, being a freshman, and fifth on the depth chart, out of five guards, so this little terror of SWVU was going to be either Kelly Woods',

Mark Powers', Blakely's or even T.J.'s concern, before I had to deal with him.

Shit, quick little fucking point guards were the hardest thing in the sports world to deal with, unless your next kick-boxing opponent happened to be 18 and 0; and, a guard that could leap. Damn, I'd much rather cover someone that was "six-four"!

I, too, was very quick, and maybe I instilled in my opponents the same fear, but somehow really doubted that I was on Chick Washington's level.

Later in the game I did discover that I was a better shooter, but that was the extent of it. He was simply stunning, and I learned quite a lot watching this little wunderkind handle the ball, and quarterback his team.

Tip-off was in ten minutes, and we headed back to our locker room for last minute: peeing (most of us), barfing (David Strong was a marvelous forward, who could also shoot "lights out," but let this shit get to him more often than not), "hanging-ass" (my euphemism for going "#2," and who in their right mind has to do that, at a time like this?), and last minute instructions from Coach Melling, which ALWAYS went through one ear and out the other; I mean, if we're not ready by now, it won't matter.

Tonight was a night that made me particularly proud to play on this team. We played brilliantly, so did they, and we were only down by six at halftime. I had not played, but knew that I would as their defense was stifling and David was not shooting at his best.

The second half was even more intense as SWVU knew that their national ranking would be in jeopardy, if they lost to our lowly and un-ranked rear-ends.

Blakely, Joe, Kelly and Mark all were playing "out of their minds," and our power forward, Burton, was really coming into his own as a young, but effective player.

Our center, Steve Hutchings, was also having what was to be his best game of the year, and this kept us in the game.

T.J.'s shooting added yet another dimension, also coupled with the fact that he could actually guard Chick Washington fairly effectively.

Late in the second half, being down by eight, and not seeming to be able to close the gap, Coach called for me to sit next to him.

"Jesse, I want you to go in there and put it up, we need some points right away, and hold onto the damn ball, no turn-overs!" Melling is screaming in my ear, as the arena noise was deafening.

Christ, like I needed Coach to tell me not to lose the fucking ball.

"Yes sir" I replied, "count on it!"

I get in the game, having sat on my ass, mind you, for the entire duration. I'm bringing the ball up the court and Chick, who is guarding me like there's no tomorrow, proceeds to steal the ball and drive in for a lay-up.

Jesus, I hear Melling screaming at me on the sidelines, but do not even look his way, as that usually was a fatal error in that he would yank your ass in a heartbeat, and I knew what I would have to do in order to protect the ball.

I bring it up the court a second time, pass into David, and he immediately gives it back, as they collapsed on him due to his sharp-shooting skills, and I proceed to nail an 18' jump shot.

Melling is screaming again, and I still act like I cannot hear him.

Five minutes to go, we're down by three, and it's getting very tense. Blakely brings the ball up court and passes into Steve, who gives it back to me on the wing and I hit yet another shot. We're down by one!

Chick brings the ball up court, and commits his only turnover of the game when he looks away to try to pass into Red Bryant (yes, another Rocky Gap alumni) and I steal the ball; I then raced up the court and score with a lay-up.

Up by one with three minutes to play, the gym is a madhouse, and we are playing out of our minds.

Coach calls time-out. Why? Jesus, how the hell can one logically figure this move, as we had all of the momentum?

He basically tells us to slow down and protect our lead.

Our lead? It's ONE FUCKING POINT!

I also find myself sitting next to him, as he informs me to "be ready".

No shit, coach. Actually I thought that I'd mull over my literature class' current study of Dante's Inferno, or even better yet, my Western Civilization's look at Napoleon's most fatal error.

"Be ready." Jesus, Mary and Joseph!

Southern scores, and is up by one.

We return the favor, and find us up by one with less than a minute.

They score, and we have the final shot with 20 seconds to go, down by one.

Mark gets fouled on his shot attempt, and goes to the free throw line with just under two seconds left in the game.

He hits the first shot and ties the game, and we are all jumping up and down, knowing if he makes the next one, we will have knocked off the legendary and nationally ranked Southern Wildcats, in their own backyard!

Mark is a stellar free throw shooter, and we all gasp as he takes his shot. It looks good, and seemingly goes through, but as we all know, those of us that have witnessed the impossibility of our "perfect" shots going "in and out," see that this was indeed the case, his wonderful shot looping around and back out.

The SWVU fans scream, knowing that this game is not finished. Overtime!

I am extremely proud as I watch our squad trade blows with our nemesis, and go into yet a second overtime.

Here is where we get our collective asses kicked by a better club, and in this period we fall behind by as much as ten, close the gap to four, and lose by six, with yours truly sitting next to Coach, in all of his infinite wisdom.

Red Bryant, Chick Washington, Freddie Bryant (Red's cousin and also a Rocky Gap standout) and the rest of their team grab some of our guys and hug, many with tears in their eyes.

This is what competition is all about, and Southern West Virginia University's entire student body gave us a standing ovation, knowing that they had truly witnessed something extraordinary.

Chick comes up to me and winks. "You are a fine player Jesse Mouchebeau" pronouncing my name perfectly, and hugs me as well.

"We'll meet again" he continues, "and I hope you and I are on each other, you really deserve to play."

Blakely and Joe had previously extolled my skills to their high school teammate, and Chick was apparently more than interested in this young and inexperienced white boy from "up North".

I reply "Chick, I learned more tonight watching you, than in all my years of playing. Many thanks!"

He winks again, and says "later, my friend."

Hell, yet another young black athlete that touches my heart and soul, and teaches me about competitive life, one who had just led his awesome team in an extraordinary battle of nerves, wits and skill, still having the compassion, and maybe insight, to praise a lowly back-up point guard.

Son of a bitch, I was smiling from ear to ear, as if I had dropped thirty on these guys!

In my heart I believe that an athlete, truly knowing that he or she having played their respective asses off, is at peace with themselves, and the win or loss is secondary.

No competitor likes to lose, but I am one that "lives to fight another day," and if I kept from playing an average game, or worse yet sub-par, then that was a good thing. Apparently all of us felt like we had raised each and every one of our own personal levels in this most recent engagement, and inwardly smiled at the supreme wonder of a battle well fought.

Hell, even Mark, missing that one free throw, knew that he had elevated his own personal game into another realm. He was indeed content with this newfound sensation.

We also knew that we had evolved into a better team this night, and really, this is what it's all about!

East Valley had one more away game, before Christmas break, at Lee University in Virginia next week, and this was a conference foe that, while very good, was extremely disliked, and was going down in defeat. We ALL felt invincible.

Every one of us slept like babies the entire trip back to our school.

*        *        *

Loretta and mom were up in the attic that Saturday night going through their yearly routine of packing away their summer clothes, this late in the year due to an implausibly long stretch of "Indian Summer".

This just may have been one of God's attempts at His healing process for my sweet Loretta, giving her the warmth of the fall sun for an extra six weeks or so, and keeping in her aural senses the gorgeous patter of squirrels gathering their walnuts and acorns amidst the many fallen and very crisp autumn leaves.

"Honey, look what I found" mom whispered, breaking the temporary trance that seemingly had Loretta in another world. "It's my wedding dress, good Lord, that was so long ago," she continued.

She unfolded the garment and held it up to her, pressing the sides against her hips, and turning slowly, as if to relive a particularly serene, yet important moment in her life.

Mom still had her figure, and most likely could wear this sacred garment again, with little or no alterations.

"My, your father was so handsome that day, and so nervous, he actually had to have one of his favorite 'Johnny Walker Red on the rocks' just to calm down" she continued.

Mom continued to muse for another few minutes, completely transfixed in her own brief excursion into nostalgia, so much so that she was totally unaware of the tears starting to cascade down Loretta's face.

"Loretta, what do you think? I bet this would look so lovely on you, maybe when the right…" mom's voice trailed off immediately once she realized the despair and grief so apparent on her daughter's face.

"What's the matter, dear?" mom said, her voice taking on a slight bit of alarm, as she was maybe even more prescient than her gifted daughter.

"Talk to me, honey" as mom laid down her dress and came over to where Loretta was kneeling.

Loretta then started to sob uncontrollably, shaking in my mother's arms for several minutes, before calming and then whimpering into a fade.

"My sweet girl, talk to me, tell mommy what's going on."

"Jesus" Loretta began, starting to get control of herself, "I needed to tell you this before, but was much too afraid for you and daddy".

Now mom's alarms are starting to go off inside her head, but remained very restrained, knowing that this would benefit her poor daughter's hopefully momentary trip into what was so terrifying. She was also starting to rapidly "put together" Loretta's recent behavior patterns that seemed a bit odd, even for her special daughter.

"Remember that night Reece came by…" and immediately mom gasped, all at once gathering her senses, knowing that Reece was a son of a bitch, knowing that this bastard had something to do with her beautiful daughter's "loss of innocence".

She held her baby girl in her arms, stroking her hair, and caressing her soul.

And so began Loretta's reliving of that horror of a night, which would be forever etched into her psyche, leaving a few details out, and graphically sparing mom of any unnecessary pain.

She told mom of Dr. Samuel's counseling and medical attention, and mom, once again, gave her own thanks for this extraordinary country doctor, who had figured so importantly into literally all of our lives at one time or another.

They both sat there for a good ten minutes, comfortable in each other's arms, and body heat.

"Honey, I am going to share something with you, for many reasons, and you are not to tell your brother, and especially your father" mom whispered.

"This is something that I never wanted to relive" she continued, "but God is telling me to do so, and do so, I will."

"I lost my virginity while I was working at a summer camp, between my freshman and sophomore year at Bay College, by a boy that I thought was my friend, someone that I really trusted."

Date rape was not even a part of anyone's vocabulary back then, and many girls of said attacks, were considered "cheap" and deserved such assaults.

"My girlfriend, Sarah, helped me through that, and forever I blamed myself for drinking those beers, and letting him kiss me in his car" mom said, with her tone taking on an edge previously unheard of with her daughter.

"And" mom continued, "until your father and I met, was terrified of dating anyone."

Thank God for my dad coming into my mother's life when he did, which was only a couple of years after this event, and dad, non-withstanding his "hard-ass" side, could be extremely sensitive, when it was most needed.

Yes, I was truly blessed with my parents, and would grow to appreciate them more and more, as life moved on.

Mom did not go into details, other than to simply and repeatedly assure Loretta that life was going to be okay.

Loretta was not pregnant; Dr. Samuel having verified that to her, and Loretta was not physically in any more pain, just the scars branded upon her soul.

Mom had noticed Loretta's gradual discomfort after eating recently, and those minor alarms that were beginning to take their toll upon her own gut instincts were temporarily banished, due to this more "obvious" reason for her daughter's well-being.

Silence permeated the attic, and these two magnificent women held onto each other, with the hope that life would deal better cards for the future, and that they would be able to protect their husband and brother from any more tragedy than these two had seen.

Mom knew that I knew, but felt safe in knowing that I would be distracted while I was away, on campus, secure in my basketball season, and going to my various classes. She was well aware of my reputation for fighting in high school, but also knew that never once did I ever start any said transgression.

She was wrong this time, however, and could not possibly have envisioned the brutality her son would be capable of, coupled with the mighty Jess Butkus, and would read about retribution in the local paper in the very near future, with her own son, the headline "star".

*   *   *

A few years later, mom would start the very first rape crisis and counseling center in our county; to honor my dear departed sister's memory indeed, but to fulfill an even more important mission in life, one that she was chosen for, and one that would help this wonderful woman restore her own faith in God.

Many young women, teenage girls, and even those few unfortunate elderly occurrences would benefit from my own mother's expertise, compassion and intelligence; and, be able to go on with their respective lives with courage and confidence, truly knowing that they were not "damaged goods" but rather "experienced players" in life's sometimes tragic dealing of the cards.

Each, in turn, would be able to give support to someone in need; and importantly, educate the unknowing, with the most essential focus being prevention!

# Chapter Nine

"You cry 'militant, anarchist,
Where is your right,
To destroy what we have made?'
Our violence they say,
Is morally wrong,
We reply, 'it is the only way!'"

The Insurrection

# IX

Donna Warington was a very enticing soul! Her raven-flowing hair, creamy skin, and just enough Mediterranean features to make you crazy, combined with her infectious personality, gave her an extremely spirited vibe, something to which I was definitely attracted.

I am stroking said tresses, lying next to her on the 4$^{th}$ green of our campus nine hole golf course, looking at the stars, and about half lit from the bottle of cheap red wine we were sharing. Magical indeed, as, once again, this was a particularly warm night for this time of year, although we were still both fully clothed, and the camping blanket we were sprawled upon was formidable in its own right.

Our college was truly gorgeous, and, even on this night, one could see the thousands of trees, cascading along the golf course, and in and around the many buildings that made up our campus proper. The duck pond was lit up by a few well-placed and hidden lamps, creating an atmosphere of dreamy peacefulness, as our two regal swans flowing along the banks pushed this vision to that of "storybook" quality.

"We play Lee tomorrow night, you know" I said to this ravishing beauty, "I hope coach lets me play some. He's always on my case for playing too much 'city ball', and is constantly yelling at me as to why I pass the ball between my legs, or why I throw it behind my back, when he says that a perfectly timed boring fucking bounce pass would get the job done."

She listens patiently; maybe too much so, as the joint we were smoking was taking its toll, as well as our libation of the evening.

"You know" I continued, "I almost always get the ball to where I want it to go, and am shooting nearly 60% from the field".

Of course, this was slightly an aberration of statistics as I had only scored a grand total of 15 points so far, in the few games I was lucky enough to play. Still, shooting percentages were all calculated the same, and I had the highest one, plus the highest scoring average for time spent on the court, on the entire team!

Donna sighs "Jesse, kiss me, this stuff is boring, and besides I think that you are fortunate to be a part of a college basketball team, everyone thinks that you are special, anyhow."

Jesus, here we go again with the "I should be thankful just to play, and appreciate my good-fortune" speech, that apparently many of my friends thought, but I let it go, realizing that if I contest this with her, it would most likely ruin the mood, and besides that, Donna was highly intelligent, and could kick my ass in a philosophical debate, even one that featured my beloved basketball as the centerpiece.

I leaned over and whispered to her "you're right, and I am very grateful" feeling my nose starting to take on the Pinocchio growth spurt of said fairly-tale, as my little white lie evaporated into thin air.

I actually was never satisfied with my place and role with this Division Two basketball team, and was ALWAYS pushing myself to succeed beyond anyone's expectations, particularly my own.

I kissed her, and she kissed me, passionately, intensely, and lovingly.

We were two young adults exploring our youth, and finding out what made us click when we were together, in any capacity.

As I said, Donna was special, and her serene nature made her irresistible. I suspected that I was falling in love, not entirely sure, but still thanking God, just the same, for this newfound addition to my already complicated (or at least I thought so) life.

We finished our wine, and continued, touching each other just enough to get aroused but keeping everything in check, as she was not yet ready for sex, and I respected this to no end, as was always my personal philosophy, even without the horrible events of my sister Loretta's too recent past. How could one go through with something as magical as making love, if their partner wasn't equally, if not more so, enthusiastic?

I somehow knew that if I ever had children, they would be girls, and felt a compelling message from God that I was "designed" to someday be a father of daughters; and I accepted this fate and destiny most whole-heartedly.

She turned over and nuzzled her backside against me, and even through her jeans and mine; I could feel an intense warmth, and peacefulness.

Slightly intoxicated, we fell asleep out there on that magnificent night, only for an hour or so, but it was an event I would always cherish, even after we went on with our other relationships.

Donna certainly was an enigma to me, and I to her. I wondered if we were indeed "going anywhere," and it really did not matter at this point in time.

A couple of years later, she recounted to me almost exactly the same romantic impression that it had made upon her, and that made me feel so very fine!

*　　*　　*

Our beloved and feared deity of transportation "Miss Mabel" was in the garage, getting her transmission overhauled, so the mighty Hornets of East Tennessee Valley College was relegated to using the volleyball/basketball girls team's twin passenger vans for this last game before Christmas break, with our conference foe Lee University, up in the southern hills of Virginia's Blue Ridge Mountain Range.

This was just a three hour drive, so traveling in "our sisters" vehicles wasn't too much to bear as again the view was stunning; and as long as you were not in close quarters with Coach Melling in his van, one could discuss: sex, drugs, music, etc., with no panic of repercussion with our God-fearing skipper.

Coach was an enigma to many of us, especially me, as I had never encountered anyone like him in my previous athletic life. We called him "Bullet," behind his back, as his Marine crew cut, coupled with the shape of his dome, truly resembled .45-calibre ammunition! We equally feared and respected him, and as I had already stated, Melling was a storied small-college all-American forward in the recent past.

Coach was maybe 6'3," 210 pounds, so in terms of sheer physical size, he wasn't that overwhelming, but one could sense his inner strength, just by watching him scrimmage with us. I mean this guy could out-rebound Burton, Steve, and even wiley Joe Smith, so not only was Coach powerful, he was extremely quick. Plus, you just knew that he grew up on some backwoods farm, hoisting bales of hay onto the family truck, and when needed, could probably pick the front end up of said vehicle, whilst his brother changed a flat tire.

Bullet was tough, no doubt about it. In practice, when we invariably would get into fights amongst ourselves, he'd actually let it go on, for a few more seconds than what was usual for other coaches to allow, then step in, pull apart the two combatants with his bare hands, all the while smiling with a gleam in his eye.

We ALL respected coach's grit, and, even though I was his polar opposite in basketball philosophy, I admired the guy.

"Now if only he was an outlaw," I would muse to myself!

I felt, usually more than not, that Coach Melling just tolerated me, and my on-court antics and approach to this game he equally dearly loved, just enough to keep me on the team. I was always the first one in the gym in the early mornings; constantly perfecting my jump shot and ball-handling skills, and he knew this. Still, I was also forever looking for new passing methods, most unorthodox, and this drove him fucking crazy sometimes, mainly 'cause he simply would not accept this "playground" approach that I found exciting.

One time at practice Joe Smith laughed out loud when I bounced a ball off of Dave Strong's head, who was guarding him, and then took the rebound that came directly back to me, which I then flicked to Joe breaking to the basket for an easy lay-up. Dave gave me, at first, a very pissed-off look, and then chuckled to himself!

Coach was beyond furious, "that's why you'll never start on this team Jesse; you think this is all a big joke!"

Most of the players are dead quiet, but Joe is still grinning, because I always reminded him of his one-time high-school mate, and our recent nemesis, Chick Washington. In fact, Joe was always quizzing me about my shooting as well, and sometimes before practice, we would drill for a good half-hour, rebounding for each other, and most of the time he could stand under the basket and expect me not to miss, marveling at my shooting prowess.

This is why the great Joe Smith was allied to me in practice, Bullet's wrath or not, purely out of respect for my skill.

"Run 'suicides' (an infamous basketball conditioning exercise) 'til I tell you to stop," Coach screams at me.

I do, for twenty goddamn minutes, all the time telling myself to transfer out of this ridiculous redneck athletic environment. Such was the occurrence for me, several times, in our East Valley College scrimmages.

Mark and Blakely, by now best friends, would just shake their heads with the "when is Jesse ever going to fucking learn" look, but Joe, and a few others, always "got it".

Still, I had to contend with Bullet, so I would always make it a point to sincerely apologize to him after practice. He then would give me his two-minute lecture on how great a player I could be, once I put the team ahead of my own personal achievements.

Jesus was I in for a long four years playing here!

We pulled onto the campus of Lee University, and again, what a magnificent school. While most of the leaves had departed from their respective branches, enough remained to create the gorgeous brown and gray landscape, interjected with the ubiquitous stunning forest pines of this region, that was late fall, God's final portrait before His cleansing winter-white!

I was even more excited than usual, as I was to have my own personal audience this evening. As a last minute surprise, mom and Loretta were making the drive down from Northern Virginia to see me play for their very first time in a college basketball game. Of course, I made it a point to let Coach know, as just possibly he would play me more than usual.

Also, Jerry Buhl and Roger Leeds, friends from high school that were two classes ahead of me and formidable athletes in there own right, attended Lee. They had already notified several of their classmates to witness their "younger counterpart's" roundball adroitness, "live, and in person"!

To add even more drama, T.J. Cooper's hometown was literally in the next county to Lee University, and this being his first trip back, as a member of the mighty East Tennessee Valley Hornets, was guaranteed to bring many of the faithful followers of high school basketball that witnessed his said legendary school-boy days in the gymnasiums of these parts. Plus, Coach Melling had given him permission to go home with his family after the game, as this was our last battle before the Christmas holidays, so T.J. was feeling particularly "sky-high" on this day.

We ran onto the "Jackson-Lee Arena" court for our warm-ups, being aptly named for two of Virginia's historic Civil War generals, and I immediately spotted Loretta and mom in the stands.

Being first in line for our pre-game drills, as I was the smallest player on our squad, I had the distinct advantage of checking out exactly where the opposing cheerleaders were standing, and then always running our team as close as we could possibly get to them, no matter where their location, smiling at the loveliest girls, and asking for phone numbers literally as we waltzed by. My teammates were forever happy with this pre-game ritual, and I never failed to execute. Coach was usually still in the locker room for these antics, so I was spared his wrath that would most definitely follow suit, had he witnessed said behavior on a continuous basis.

As luck would have, being in the throes of my budding romance with Donna, I met Sharon, or rather nearly ran her over leading my troops. She was one of the most stunning blonde-haired, blue-eyed cheerleaders of which so many of our young adult male dreams were made, that I had ever envisioned: petite, obviously very athletic (a trait I always adored) and short hair with those "melt-your-heart" bangs of said locks that framed her face! Still, it was her eyes that completely overwhelmed me; icy and clear, with almost a sea-green tint depending on which angle you were looking.

"Christ," I thought, "here I fucking go again," thinking aloud to myself, as if I could clearly and presciently detail my impending doom with another romance.

Loretta, of course, witnessed all of this, and let me know as I scooted over to her and mom, kissing both immediately, never even minding what my team's first drill was.

"God Jesse," Loretta says, "You will never change!"

She is so happy to see me, and I, her. I am slightly discomforted, though, as she had lost even more weight, which I fully blamed on her recent bout with terror.

"Jess would be here, you know, if the choir wasn't on tour," I answered.

Jess' wonderful tenor voice would someday turn him into a world-class opera star.

"I know, love," she whispered, "I am so glad to see you, and I cannot wait to see you play".

Of course she knew Jess' whereabouts, as their romance was moving forward, even more so than I imagined, and they had already talked this morning.

Mom looked slightly "worse for wear" as well, and this was, unknowingly to me, due to her and Loretta's new-found, yet tragic similarity of their shared "coming-of-age" experiences with the despicable men that so infected their young adult lives.

Apparently both were counseling each other on a daily basis, and this was their own particular necessity. No one, not dad, not Jess, not even me, was allowed in this most sacred and hallowed sanctuary, and, they were healing by themselves, which mattered most of all!

T.J.'s contingent was very vocal, and it made me feel extremely happy to see so many come out to support him.

I grabbed his arm and whispered, "look at her, T.J.," motioning to my newfound goddess.

"Yeah, that's Sharon McGee, I went to high school with her," he answers, looking dead into my love-struck eyes, all the while knowing that he had previously called her to tell her about me, and had accurately predicted my reaction, almost "to the letter," on what was to be this most interesting evening.

God, could the drama get any greater? Could life be any sweeter? Could I be any lower as a romantic human being, with respect to my dear Donna, back at campus?

Sometimes, though, the "thunderbolt" hits us and, depending on with whom we are currently involved, we can simply do nothing to fend off this attack from Cupid's exact and deadly arrow!

I kept thinking of Donna, and looking at Sharon. Jesus, did I absolutely suck as a person. Why could not Donna be here tonight, to meet my sister and mother, and to help this feeble excuse for a young man come to grips with his behavior?

Why? Because this is what the Big Guy does for us! He leads us into temptation, and let's us figure out the "deliverance from evil" part. That's why!!

"Oh well," I thought to myself, "maybe Sharon will be the Lee's football team's middle linebacker's date for the evening, and upon seeing this "killer," my passions will drastically subside".

Besides, I had a game to play!

Yeah, I was quickly "back on track" with my team, and what we needed to do to win this conference game.

The buzzer sounded, and our starting five: Blakely, Mark, Joe, Kelly and Steve were on the court, ready to seriously kick some ass as we, the mighty East Tennessee Valley College Hornets, were indeed the team to take the fabled/nationally ranked Wildcats of Southern West Virginia University into double-overtime, on their own turf!

We were a new force, at least in our own minds, with a newfound confidence and demeanor, and we would not be denied!

Well at least we would not be denied defeat!

Lee University wiped the floor with our collective asses, that evening, winning by 15 points. We could not have played any more terribly, and to make matters worse, Coach Melling put me in the last FIVE SECONDS of this fucking game, and Jesus was I pissed.

I mean, all of a sudden he had this "oh dang, I gotta put Jesse in, his family drove all the way down here" look on his face, and in I went. I almost wanted to avoid his glance and save myself the son-of-a-bitching embarrassment, but I jumped off the bench and checked in at the scorer's table.

Life is often funny though, and I took the in-bounds pass from Blakely, drove past two defenders, who were actually trying to stop me (having witnessed my obnoxious flirting with their very own cheerleader Sharon), even with their insurmountable lead, and calmly drained a twenty-five foot shot, that was "all net".

And you know, it was one of the most memorable baskets I'd ever make, simply for the fact that Loretta, mom, T.J., and even Sharon McGee all screamed as it made its way into the annals of my life story, and the box score. Hell, Burton jumped off the bench, and whooped as if I had won the damn game, knowing my mom and sister were there, and being equally pissed at Bullet for not playing me.

At least T.J. had a few good moments in tonight's contest, but not many, as Melling played him sparingly, as well.

He was samely irritated, but knew that his fans "knew," and thusly was all right. Besides, he was going home to party with his friends, and we were riding back to campus with our defeat.

Jerry Buhl and Roger Leeds came up to me after the game to comment on my great shot, with Jerry stating: "Jesse, I figured if you scored at the average of one basket for every five seconds of play, you'd average 960 points a game!"

We laughed like crazy. God, what laughter can do for the soul! I even forgot the fact that I'd barely played. It seemed not to matter, as my beloved sister, my magnificent mom, my compatriots from high school, and my teammates all meant the world to me; and "hello" now, Sharon McGee!

My mother squeezed my hand before we left to go get our post-game diatribe from Bullet in our locker room and said "Jesse, it's wonderful to see you in your East Valley uniform, and you know, we will see you play many times, so do not stay angry for only playing a little while, life is much too precious for wasted energy," as mom was all too aware of my building dislike for Coach's methods.

I was growing up fast, but confused none-the-less; and, I was sensing something very dramatic developing between my sister and my mom, that left me "out of the loop', so to speak. I always knew that Loretta was prescient far beyond the norm, and was just now realizing from where she gained this incredible gift!

My sister chimed in "sweetheart, you have the most beautiful touch of any player I've seen, and it makes me truly happy just to be here with you."

I gazed lovingly into her eyes, knowing she honestly meant every word she said.

"You know, tonight was more than a game, Jesse," she continued, "and it sure looks like you might have a new friend," glancing over at Sharon and the rest of the Lee cheerleading squad.

"Honey, we'll call you tomorrow morning, and see you in a few days for Christmas break" mom said as they left.

"Please give my love to Jess," Loretta added, "I'm looking forward to seeing him soon," as Jess had been invited up for the holidays, as well.

Enough said, and I was over my resentment with Melling, just like that.

My sister could always pull me out of whatever psychological depths I happened to be residing at the time, and lift my spirits into her world of sunshine.

God, I truly loved her so, and briefly flashed back to the devastating recent events she experienced, but quickly made myself focus on matters at hand, and kissed her and my mom, and said goodbye, as they had a few hours to travel, as well; plus, I needed to make a quick pass by Sharon, in hopes of just hearing her voice.

"Jesse Mouchebeau, it's a real pleasure," said goddess whispered to me in her soothing Southern drawl that instantaneously grabbed my heart and guts.

Yet another that pronounced my surname correctly, and I was indeed impressed.

"Sharon McGee, it's my honor to make your acquaintance," bowing graciously and trying to immediately take on the "Southern Gentleman" demeanor of which I just knew would impress her, or at least make her laugh; and, she did so, with such throaty and soulful timbre as to inoculate me with affection and grace.

Jesus was I so quickly and aptly smitten. Yes, still a lame-ass, with regards to Donna, as well!

She gave me a folded slip of paper, and my heart was racing.

"See you soon" she winked, and it was immediate love.

She knew it, I knew it, and very likely most of the Lee University ballplayers still hanging out on the court knew it, as they fully realized that their very own Sharon was about to get involved with one of "the enemy," and while not strictly taboo, still stung a bit.

I must have "floated" into our locker room, because I do not remember walking there.

Bullet was starting in on us, with that cracker cadence of his, and tonight, of all nights, we just wanted to be left alone. We knew we had just gotten our asses handed to us, and really did not need a reminder. All of us were rolling our eyes, with maximum discretion though, as we were no dummies. Yes, we took a beating, and a very effective one at that, and would just have to get them the next time we met, which would be on our own home turf!

T.J. is sitting next to me, and very quietly murmurs that his friends bought a case of beer for us, or rather those of us lucky enough to secure seats in the van being driven by our trainer Phil, as Melling was captaining the other.

"I had Phil keep the back door unlocked so it's under the very back seat," T.J. said, "it's Rolling Rock," which was our favorite.

Now only to get to the van first, and secure our seats, as no one really wanted to cruise back with Bullet.

"Thanks, partner," I whispered, I owe you one".

"Shit Jesse, I figure you guys will catch enough grief when you hit campus," he countered, knowing that coach Melling was sometimes prone to having his teams practice free-throws for hours on end, in street clothes and socks, after a particularly bad game.

I had yet to experience this, and wondered if tonight this would indeed happen as we did suck from the "charity stripe" against Lee.

Joe, Blakely, Mark, Burton, and I nearly trounced half of our teammates as we vied for our "reserved seats" on the "express bus to intoxication".

We all got situated in our seats when we all nearly had a "group-heart attack" as Coach got on to drive, and since I had already popped open a can from the very back of the van, one could just slightly smell the wondrous aroma of our beloved beverage.

"Christ Jesse," Joe exclaimed in shocked horror, "what the fuck is Bullet doing on this one?"

I am speechless as I can just envision Melling's wrath after discovering our treasure, and wondering how to toss out the can of beer in my hand, before we leave.

All of a sudden, Bullet scratches his crew-cut pate, with a confused look on his face, and gets out to drive the other vehicle. We all exhale with military precision, at our sudden reprieve from the "gods of Mt. Washington," as said range surrounded us, and we figured something along this order had to be the cause!

Phil is laughing his ass off as he slides into the driver's seat, "I bet you sons-a-bitches nearly choked when Coach got on. Jesus Christ, Jesse, I can smell that fucking beer all the way up here, you'd think that you would at least wait until we got rolling," he added.

Actually, by now, all of us were gulping down our first cans, popping them before Phil even finished his speech, as we were all in the mood to get trashed. I figured that with twenty-four beers, I had a legitimate chance to drink at least four of them, depending on how I could keep up with Mark, Burton, Blakely and Joe, all bigger and seemingly very enthusiastic this evening.

"Four would be plenty," I thought, as my low tolerance for alcohol, especially beer at keg parties, was by now infamous on campus.

"T.J. came through for us big-time"; exclaimed Blakely, "let's toast his 'by-now-partying-like-a-motherfucker-ass'".

"YEAH," we all hollered in unison!

"Here's to Bullet trying to figure out what went wrong tonight," I chimed in.

"YEAH," we again shouted.

We all knew that we had not really gotten mentally prepared for Lee this evening, truly knowing we were a better team, but getting caught "off-guard," as so many teams do after a particularly eventful previous contest.

We were fine with ourselves, and knew we would be fine for our future games, almost a "wake-up call," so to speak.

"I cannot wait until Christmas break," Joe mused out loud, which was in a few days; "I need to get away from this motherfucker," referring to school, basketball, and life in general at East Tennessee Valley.

Our school was the host for an eight-team post Christmas tournament, which none of us wanted to play for several reasons: one, it was on our campus, not some exotic location, say, like Miami Beach; two, it was two days after Christmas, which would break-up our holidays at home, as we had to be here for practice beforehand, and the games would total three days, so we'd lose nearly a week of vacation; and three, Lee University was not scheduled, so when was I gonna get a chance to possibly see Sharon?

Oh well, I had to remedy my "Donna situation," anyhow, and I had never in my life acted as a callous, cold-hearted son of a bitch, so this would take some serious thought.

I was soon to find out (actually the very next day) that Donna was more interested in maintaining our harmony: more than platonic but less than romantic, as she was truly an esoteric spirit, and just knew that we would be far better served as real friends, rather than as lovers.

Yes, for me, another lesson in the female super-power of intuition and life! Something I was actually starting to understand and it would make me feel innately stronger and serve me well.

I was now beginning to, and would often later in life, muse on these women of my past, or these "girls of yesterday," as to how each gave me a certain "gift of spirit and prescience"; how collectively I would build upon each and every experience, no matter how seemingly small, or extraordinarily grand, to help me to believe in my life and purpose.

Both of the East Valley vans pulled into the interstate rest stop that was exactly halfway home. All of our beer was gone, and Phil very deftly grabbed all of the empties and discreetly threw them in the trashcans conveniently located next to our parking spot.

I had indeed drunk four, and was high, not trashed, mind you, but intoxicated just the same. So were all of us.

We piled into the bathrooms to take much needed whizzes, and for some strange reason, I had my sunglasses on, obviously unknowingly, because when Bullet asked me "why in the heck would you be wearing sunglasses at this hour," I had to actually feel my face to see what the hell he was talking about.

Most likely I intuitively placed them there to hide my eyes, which by then were a dead giveaway.

"Coach, I have another migraine" was all that I could muster, and he accepted that, which completely impressed my travel-mates, as they all knew that I was quick-witted, but this response was more than your average comeback!

The other guys, in Bullet's van, could tell something was up, but no one gave any impression, as we were a "warrior-family," and some things were just sacred!

We pulled onto the East Valley campus, and parked behind our basketball arena. Each and every one of us was expecting the "okay men, get changed and be on the court in ten minutes" statement from Coach, but such was not the case this evening.

For some strange reason, and I attribute this to Melling's having three hours of drive time to think about everything, let us go to our dorms.

"Be back here tomorrow at 8am," he firmly said, "no excuses"!

None of us had classes on Saturday, so we would all be here, ready to go. We were not scheduled to leave for the holidays for another couple of days, and we had to contend with another few practices, which we knew would be brutal.

T.J. would get to miss this morning session, lucky bastard, but have to be here for the others starting at the beginning of the week.

I went to my dorm house, popped six aspirin, climbed into a very hot bath, and drank another beer.

"Sharon McGee," I mused out loud, "Holy Christ, what a beautiful girl"!

# Chapter Ten

"Oh wise father, I pray of you,
Is there not anything, you can do,
Cast a spell,
Play your flute,
Wave your wand,
Make me a prince, will you..."

The Magic King

# X

Jess had arrived to stay with us for a couple of days, and Loretta was just thrilled! He was going to return in less than 48 hours, Christmas Eve morning, to be with his family, and we wanted to make the most of his visit.

Loretta and Jess were definitely in love, or at least at its threshold, and I knew in my heart that she was starting to heal, ever so slowly.

"I really wish you guys could stay through the holidays," she said to both of us, knowing that my team's tournament started December 27th, and I had to be on the court for practice the previous afternoon, as per coach Melling's orders.

My teammates all assumed that we were going to have a marathon workout, as our illustrious skipper still tasted the bitter defeat from Lee, and we had only one day to get ready for the first round of this tourney. Who the hell schedules these things, anyhow? I would find out that every single player on the East Valley Hornets, that did not live within an hour or so from our school (a few matriculated from very nearby high schools) would be equally perturbed at having his Christmas holidays interrupted by this silly-ass tournament.

Mom, Loretta, Jess and I are all sitting in the living room, bantering back and forth; some talk being about our college activities, some about Loretta's senior year, with which she was quickly growing dissatisfied, almost as if she was "beyond" high school and anything that was associated, which I directly attributed to her recent bout with "real-life's" extreme perils. Quite possibly her evolving romance with Jess contributed largely to this, as well, and Loretta was never one to shy away from a new adventure. This was yet another of her endearing qualities, another of my numerous lessons of life, with my baby sister as my mentor.

Dad was coming home later, and very much looking forward to seeing Jess again, as he was equally enamored with my best friend, although I thought slightly being "behind the curve" in recognizing his own daughter's infatuation.

Mom went into the kitchen to check on the turkey she was cooking, as this evening we were going to have our pre-Christmas celebration, due to everyone's scheduling conflicts.

"God, does that smell great," Jess commented the moment mom opened the door, letting the amazing aromas escape, wafting into the living room where we were sitting.

I was about to add my own comment when Loretta, very steely-eyed, whispered to both of us "Reece is throwing another party tomorrow night, at his house".

Both Jess and I were immediately somber, looking at each other with a cold determination, instantaneously calculating our respective retributions.

My stomach started to turn, knowing that people were going to get hurt, especially me. Jess was such a force and, even never seeing him in action, I just knew that he would be fine, with just about anything life threw his way.

I, on the other hand, have always hated street-fighting; loved the contact of boxing, martial arts, football, etc., but this was an entirely different matter. Knives had a way of presenting themselves, as did baseball bats and chains. Plus, Reece was a genuine badass, and had the experience to back-up his reputation.

Still, I meant to honor the sanctity of my sister's well being, and this was now the time.

I looked at Jess, with obvious stress written all over my face, and immediately knew that this person was put on this earth for Loretta and myself to love and cherish, as all it took from my indominatable best friend to give me peace was the most beautifully timed wink, smile and statement: "brother, tomorrow, we win!"

I thanked God for Jess and Loretta, mom and dad, and felt a previously unknown welling of pride, from very deep within my guts.

Loretta looked equally tranquil, and I realized that she would soon be able to free herself from whatever demons were still residing within her own depths. My sister was a survivor, this I truly believed in my heart of hearts!

An hour or so later, in walked my dad, whistling Edith Piaf's "Mi Lord," one of his all-time favorites by the renown French singer. He looked at my mom, with a very obvious gleam in his eye, and said, "You sure do look fine today honey, and God, does that smell wonderful," nearly quoting Jess' earlier statement to the letter!

Then he very mischievously looked at Loretta while stating "why darling, if not for the trance that you were currently residing, I would not have even guessed that our Jess was already here," and waltzed over to hug and kiss my sister with as much love and caring as I'd ever witnessed from him.

My dad was seemingly becoming more and more attuned to what was happening around him, and I would later know that he was as brilliant intuitively as my mother and Loretta. What a bonus for me, to have this kind of "genetic boost"! I was never a scholar, but always felt like I had an edge when it came to quick decisions that really and truly mattered!

"Why Jess, we might as well adopt you; first Thanksgiving, now Christmas," he grinned and continued, "Welcome home son"!

Jess is smiling, and I swear that his mocha-colored face flushed, obviously feeling my dad's heart-felt greeting.

My dad shakes his hand, and then proceeds to give me a kiss on my cheek and whispers, "I really miss you, Jesse".

I felt a lump in my throat, and my eyes starting to well with tears.

"Me too, dad," I countered.

Since I had gone off to college in the south, Dad had started to noticeably mellow, or at least cool down with that hot temper of his. Maybe it was the fact that his son was gone for most of the time, and there was no other "male-vibe crossing swords" occurring within this household, but I rather suspect that he too was growing, and starting to further appreciate from where he came, and where he was headed.

His job as a commercial artist was going well, and his passion for soccer was starting to subside, ever so subtly, just enough so he could still enjoy playing, but not get so passionately consumed by his game of choice.

"Let's have a glass of wine before dinner," mom announced, furthering her treatment of us as the young adults that we were becoming.

Dad counters, "how about something a little stronger now, and then wine with dinner?" even raising mom's ante of the respect that they were giving ourselves.

"Yes," the three of us chimed!

Then dad very ceremoniously goes into the kitchen and returns with two bottles of very good champagne that had been chilling all day.

"These, I've been saving for a special occasion, and today's the day," he announced.

Having poured each of us a flute, he continued, "to family, and to the real meaning of Christmas".

We all drank two glasses, and were buzzed and primed for the finest meal I'd ever eaten in my life.

Maybe it was the champagne, maybe it was the fact that my emotions were on "full-tilt boogie," and maybe it was the fact that mom can indeed cook her ass off; but I am more inclined to think that I had taken yet another step ahead, into what the real meaning and value of our short time on earth meant in the "big picture," and yes, sometimes this is as simple as the taste buds we were all given, with which to taste God's countenance. This is what I truly believed!

Later that evening, as Jess and I were falling asleep, I felt my body shiver, just once, but very violently, almost as if my dear departed grandfather's soul, or maybe even some other long-gone relative's, traversed my entire self, in less than an instant. I felt immediately flushed, but in a very comforting way, almost as if I had attained an awareness and enlightenment that quite possibly soldiers do on the eve of a particular impending battle. I did not feel afraid, but rather crystal clear in my belief, duty and faith. No matter what tomorrow's outcome would be, I would carry myself with honor, dignity and very importantly, skill. I was itching to get to this monster that hurt my most beloved sister and soul mate; I was determined to really hurt Reece Davis!

\*      \*      \*

I awoke to the laughter of Loretta, Jess and Mom in the kitchen, all eating scrambled eggs, toast and hash brown potatoes; drinking some of mom's deliciously brewed coffee, and just basically lounging around.

"Why, look what the cat dragged in," mom teased, as it was nearly 11am, and I was usually an early riser.

"Good morning," I replied, "sorry I slept so late, but I do feel like a million bucks," and winked to Jess, with that kindred warrior-bond of which we were now so astutely blessed.

Jess and Loretta were another day evolved into their blossoming love-affair, and they were starting to become even more comfortable with each other in "public," which as of now just meant my parent's home. Still, it was progress, and a most beautiful thing to observe.

Mom was obviously totally in accord with her daughter's romance, apparently giving them her blessing, simply by the way in which she was behaving.

I was ever so slightly feeling touches and pangs of jealousy, because of my sister's now divided attention, but had enough spiritual awareness to toss this aside almost immediately, in favor of my own support and love for my treasured sibling.

You see, I believe that real love for someone is simply doing what one can, to enhance the quality of life for said object of affection. There is no "scorecard," or accounting; and, if one is lucky enough to have someone return their love, then this is what our God in Heaven truly desired for His children of Earth. Now this is evolution in one of its highest forms, and hopefully very contagious.

Later in life, I was to be blessed with the most profound awareness and "total consciousness," if you will, on the ultimate joy and wonder of holding my newborn baby in my arms, next to my heart, and truly, inside my heart!

In my case, and with my sister Loretta, I knew that her happiness was going to be contingent on her ability to somehow make sense of her horrific past, and to be able to find trust in a man that would never let her down. This man was my beloved Jess Butkus.

"I understand that there's a party tonight," mom stated, which succeeded into startling me back into the reality of the present.

I sheepishly mumbled something to the effect of casually being interested, but mom knew better.

Mom then gently grabbed my arm and pulled me aside and said, "Jessie honey, you are a very sensitive young man, and this is the quality that I most admire, but this evening you most likely will have to be a very tough young man. You will know what to do, whatever it is, and I will trust you with making the right decision."

I am dumbstruck, wondering from where all of this was coming, especially since I had no clue as to what mom knew or did not know.

She then looked me dead into my eyes, with as much steely strength as I'd seen to date, and softly spoke the words that would forever remain in my mind, and indelibly etched upon my conscience: "tonight is not for Loretta, not for me, and yes Jesse, ME; tonight is for your very own baby girl that someday you will bring into this world!"

Apparently Loretta's therapy with mom included more than I, or Jess, had realized. But to be fair, I always knew that my mom had that killer instinct for justice, something with which would have served her very well in any time and place in history.

Things she did or said in the past were starting to make even more sense to me, and I guess this was part of her legacy and gift to her young son growing into being a good and decent man.

She was actually giving me, and Jess, her blessing; never mind the law. This was more than that, this was anger, this was healing, and this was retribution!

"You two have a good time tonight," mom bade us very cryptically, as Jess and I backed out of her driveway.

Loretta, at her side, arms wrapped around each other, placed her hand on her heart and whispered "I love you both".

Christ, you'd have thought we were going off to war. Well, in a sense, we were.

Fortunately, dad had just gotten home from work, and was inside making a phone call, so he did not have the chance to quiz us on our plans without Loretta that evening, as he would have been sure to wonder, with Jess leaving the very next morning.

Mom and Loretta had concocted a mild lie as to our whereabouts, and regarding our time getting back home.

We drove in silence, me steering mom's Plymouth Valiant, with Jess slowly stretching every part of his body, almost as if he was in pre-game football mode.

I too, knew the value of being limber, and "warm," having trained, off and on with my dad, a lightweight boxer during his Navy days; plus, I was rapidly becoming an adept kick boxer.

True, a street fight is nothing like the gym, or being "inside the ropes," but I always had heart, and this is what my beloved Jess saw in me. This is what made him proud. Heart is also the quality that made Jess Butkus one of the most formidable middle linebackers East Tennessee Valley College had ever witnessed!

Reece's house was just ahead, and my adrenaline was peaking. I took several deep breaths, pulled into the driveway, facing out, mind you, and looked into Jess' eyes.

"I love you Jess," and kissed him on his cheek.

"Right back at you brother," he responded.

How quickly two young men grow up! How utterly fantastic life can be for those who need to right a wrong. How fucking scary!

The house was already at "full tilt boogie," with music blaring and seemingly half the county in attendance.

We both realized instantly, that this was probably the very scene that Loretta had experienced, which made it seem even more surreal.

The front door was ajar, and we walked in. The next twenty minutes were a blur, and it would take me days to actually sort out the livid details.

Nevertheless, here are the exact events that transpired; a most cherished episode of my life, and one that would even bring a brief smile one day to my dying sister's lips, and one that would help me with life after my beloved Loretta!

*     *     *

Reece was over in a corner, back facing us, talking with a stunning blonde with large breasts (why do I notice these things even under duress?), wearing a black t-shirt, very tight jeans, and black biker boots; almost as if he too was ready for battle, as this was not his normal preppie attire. His roommate Butchie was hanging out nearby with, apparently, his same girlfriend, as Loretta had very accurately described her and Butchie to us earlier that day.

There were many I did not know, and I guess Reece's time spent so far in community college garnered an entirely different set of those he chose to hang with.

Many were, even at this early juncture, well on their way to intoxication, including both Billy's, his other roommates; equally described to us by Loretta's remarkable recounting of such a horrific event. I vaguely knew these guys, even though they were from another high school, but appearances can be deceptive, and we all do physically change, sometimes quite a lot, at this point of our lives. Very obviously Reece was undergoing some sort of genesis himself; changing from redneck preppie hard-ass, to something even more sinister and crazy.

I am very anxious, but Jess calmly, but forcefully squeezed my arm, and said "let's get a beer".

"Are you kidding," I replied, "we need to be sharp!"

"Jesse, what we need to be is inconspicuous; so just sip slowly and try to maintain as if we are here for no reason other than to party. Reece doesn't know that we know, only suspects so. Once his guard is down, we move. He's a powerful guy; you need to stick him quickly."

"Did you notice Butchie," I whispered, "he's over there," as I nodded my head.

"Yes, and Billy number one, and number two," he countered.

At that moment six or eight new guests came barging through the front door, which was very good timing as Reece had just now noticed our own arrival, and had given his own nod to Butchie in our direction.

"No black people," Jess said. "Are there no brothers or sisters in this county?"

"Of course, many of my teammates were black…," then noticing the smile on Jess' face, realized he was once again fucking with me, and it did make me smile.

We grabbed two beers and walked through the house, which had several rooms on this main floor.

Loretta had given us a brief description of the layout of Reece's house, as well, but even she was starting to reach a precarious point of re-living too much of that horrible night, and we had left it alone.

I went into the bathroom to take a wiz, as I guess my adrenaline was sending my body into "over-drive," very much like my pre-game ritual in basketball. I also slugged down my beer as I was starting to hyperventilate.

Thinking about fighting is the tough thing, not the actual fight itself, and any warrior will concur. Once it's on, it's on!

Jess continued on through out the house, and eventually found Reece's master-suite bedroom.

I never knew at the moment, and Jess was later to tell me, but, in visiting the actual scene of Loretta's nightmare, Jess came to his own "reality," as I was soon to witness.

I came out and headed back to the kitchen, and into the living room, where I was met by the formidable Reece Davis.

"College boy, home for the holidays?" Reece sneered, half-jokingly, half maliciously.

He was very glassy-eyed, and I knew this look well. It was the look that bullies get when they have drank just enough to get real mean, and not too much to affect their prowess.

Reece had recently gotten tattooed, with two incredibly large eagles, one on each of his massive biceps; obviously pumping iron and gaining even more strength and weight, and I guess contributing, even more so, to his wicked demeanor.

He looked to be around 210 pounds, and was a good six feet tall; and if we were professional fighters, would be at least three weight classes above my super-welter weight status.

No matter, this was real life, not the ring; no weight limitations, no specified glove ounces, no groin protectors, NO RULES!

I looked for Jess, too obviously, and did not see him.

"Looking for your nigger friend?" Reece asked.

Again, I knew that this was happening rather quickly, and wondered where he was.

I looked straight into Reece's eyes, and said "fuck you," not letting my eyes drift whatsoever.

How this escalated so quickly, I had no clue; other than for some reason Reece's knowledge of my sister's and my close relationship would have undoubtedly led to me facing him at some point.

Immediately he threw a left jab at my face; with my reactions saving me, it only glanced hard off of my right eye, not a direct shot, which might very well have knocked me out. He was very fast!

I immediately countered with a straight right hand, blasting him in his face, and was about to throw another when I was very violently yanked from behind and thrown to the floor, landing hard on my back.

The next thing I knew, Butchie was standing over and choking me, with extreme hatred and intent.

The only thing I could do was to tuck my right foot in, and I kicked upwards as hard as I possibly, sending his balls back up into his stomach with the heel of my cowboy boot.

I jumped up immediately, and saw that Jess was pounding the life out of Reece Davis.

By then Billy number one jumped onto Jess' back, and I kicked him into his side, with the pointed toe of my boot, hearing his ribs crack, and he howled in pain.

Billy number two was running toward us with something that looked like a small billy club, and yes, the irony of his name and weapon choice was not lost on Jess and me, when we later recounted our battle.

Billy two was about to strike a blow, but I startled him by moving directly into him, and not ducking away from this type of attack, as is human nature and response, grabbing his hair, bending back his face, and head butting him for all I was worth, cracking his nose, and nearly scrambling my own brains in the process.

I staggered but remained upright, and punched him just below his throat. He was absolutely finished.

I then looked at Billy number one, with the cracked ribs, and with such malevolence, that he threw his hands up with the "no more" gesture.

Butchie was puking his guts out in the corner.

Jess was killing Reece, and I mean killing him; punching the ever-loving life out of him, and re-arranging his face in the process. I had to pull Jess off of his foe, and in the process almost got my own ass knocked out, as the look on my friend's face was nothing like I'd ever witnessed.

Jess Butkus was in his "trance," similar to what he used in his football games to evoke the fear of God in his opponents, but this was even more. This was war, and Reece Davis was going to die.

I screamed "Loretta," as loudly as I could, to him, and he immediately broke his concentration, focusing on me, his best friend.

There were tears in his eyes, and I just bet that my Jess Butkus has just experienced the catharsis of his life.

The entire house was in a hush, as someone had very thankfully stopped the music amidst this entire trauma. Everyone had indeed witnessed something horrific and unsettling, from two apparent strangers; an event that took less than three minutes to unfold.

Reece was groaning, as he had propped himself up, sitting against the wall of his kitchen counter.

Jess looked at him with such hatred, and leaned over to whisper in his ear: "You ever fuck with Loretta, Jesse, or any of their friends and family, this nigger will come back and hurt you so badly, you will want to die. You know that I can, you know that I will. Tonight for was Loretta, you white motherfucker; and one more thing; Jesse would have killed you tonight!"

Jess stood up and we both looked at each other; my face was starting to bruise on the right side, eye blackening from Reece's left punch, and my neck was bleeding from the scratches and fingerprints of Butch's attempted strangulation. My right hand was also starting to swell, and my forehead was sliced open, a direct result of the head-butt I had administered. Still, I was in fine shape, just didn't look so.

Jess, other than his mildly scraped hands, and slightly torn clothes, look like nothing had happened.

We looked at the others, by now gathered in the living room and kitchen, but did not say anything. It wasn't necessary. Some had witnessed the fact that I was initially attacked, and many would eventually know the truth.

I then said very plainly, very simply, very quietly, "anyone want to call the cops?"

No answer, just the shaking of heads, in quiet agreement.

We walked through the front door, and hopefully out of Reece Davis' life forever.

*     *     *

The next morning found Jess taking an extremely long shower.

Having arrived home the previous evening and needing an immediate therapeutic cleansing, especially with my various cuts and bruises, I had nearly exhausted mom's hot water supply, so as to require Jess to settle for Loretta sponge bathing his face and hands, which in truth, were actually quite fine. I, on the other hand, was the one that needed the "make-over," and had let the hot water completely take over my senses, until I found myself starting to fall asleep while standing.

Jess was leaving before noon, so as to be able to spend Christmas Eve with his family, and we sure were going to miss him. Nevertheless, he had promised to come down to East Valley for the tournament, so I actually would see him again in three short days.

Mom, Loretta, Jess and I had not discussed any of the previous evening's events. This morning was no exception. Dad was at work, and even though mom's public school system was on holiday break, she had opted to leave the three of us alone to say our goodbyes for now.

Loretta would, I'm sure, fill her in on the various details in due time. For now, though, mom was very content; almost as if she and her daughter, and any other woman so violated in her past, had some sort of vindication.

Physically I was very sore, definitely looking the part, but fine. Mentally, I was much better, and was actually now mildly anticipating our tournament, as I thought it would be a nice diversion following this particular Christmas holiday, which, of course, was "one for the books."

Also, there was the matter of my newfound love, Sharon McGee.

After holding Loretta for several minutes, Jess left for his own family celebration.

Two days later, I followed him back down south.

# Chapter Eleven

"My love, is running 'round,
My love, is coming down on me,
Your love, is haunting me,
Your love, won't let me be..."

My Love, Your Love

# XI

I strolled into the East Valley locker room Friday afternoon, an hour before our scheduled "December 26th - 2pm sharp" practice time, as Coach Melling had so adamantly inscribed on all of our brains, as well as the chalkboard, before we had gone home for Christmas.

"If any of you are even one minute late, you will be benched for the entire tournament, and I will remember this for year-end evaluations!"

At the end of every year, all players were actually under a review, relating to our individual scholarships, and there were no exceptions. Usually these player examinations went without a hitch, as ultimately our skipper, as most coaches, wanted to maintain continuity from year to year. It was bad enough losing players to graduation, transfer, or even grades, and I really had not heard of any of my previous or present brethren ever having scholarship money taken away, at least for something this minor. Still, there was always a first time for everything, and I wasn't taking any chances, being precariously perched at the 5th guard spot of our illustrious East Valley Hornets squad; knowing that we were losing just Kelly, our only senior guard, never mind the incoming freshman or possible transfers.

My team mates started to trickle in, one or two at a time, with all of us present a good half hour before practice was to begin.

"Holy shit," T.J. Cooper exclaimed when he first laid eyes upon me, "what in the hell happened to you!" He was genuinely shocked by my appearance.

Even though I had well over two days to heal, and I was notoriously very quick to recover from various maladies, the right side of my face was purple with discoloration; and unknown to me that evening of the fight, I had actually suffered a decent sized cut along my eyebrow ridge, as well, which by now had transformed into one of your better looking "boxer" injuries, held together by the miraculous "butterfly bandage." Jesus could Reece punch!

I started to smile, with a momentary "lost in trance" look with this interesting afterthought on the power of Reece's left jab: Jess had informed me that Reece was actually left-handed, so his supposed jab was really his power-straight cross. Not only had my reflexes saved me, but I could also take a bit of a punch.

"Jesse, you alright," T.J.'s voice bringing me back into the here and now.

"Yeah, I'm actually a lot better than I look, and I'll give you the details later, but Jess and I got into a wild-ass fight with four redneck motherfuckers over Christmas break, and kicked the shit out of them."

T.J. and nearly all of campus, for that matter, knew well of the ubiquitous presence of Jess, and our friendship, and I further realized that it was redundant to even state the outcome of any fight that featured the indomitable Jess Butkus!

My neck was still vivid with Butchie's "handiwork" and my right hand was still swollen along with several bruised knuckles. My forehead was tightly bandaged from the stitches Doc Samuel had sewn into me, courtesy of the head butt that I threw on one of the Billys.

Doc, who had most graciously been there for Loretta's horrific night and subsequent treatment, had understood mom's cryptic phone call as to why I needed his attention early Christmas Eve morning, and readily agreed to see me. He had the most benign smile on his face, while he gave me my Novocain shots, into my wound, mind you, and having figured out the real reason behind my and Jess' battle; was misty-eyed whilst patching "his son," as he more than once referred to me that morning, as my proud mother looked on, while holding my hand.

My only body parts that had not suffered from any blows thrown or received were my right foot and ankle; components of maybe the finest, most precise and technically executed roundhouse kick I'd ever attempted, with the real beauty being the scenario for which it was conceived. "Fuck Billy's ribs," I thought to myself.

In other words, it was painfully obvious to all of the East Valley Hornets players that I had gotten into something most magnificent, over the holidays.

"Goddam Jesse, it looks like someone tried to strangle you, "Joe Smith chimed in, with his beautifully resonant North Carolina cadence.

"Someone did indeed, my esteemed black brother, and he most assuredly failed," I replied in a very soft voice, as my throat still burned from the physical trauma and cuts inflicted upon my countenance.

I knew that I would have to give all of the details to some of my team mates at some point soon; otherwise, I would forever be questioned on the event.

I chose to do so at that very moment, at least with the attention of T.J., Joe, Blakely, Mark, Kelly, and Burton.

Interesting, that all four of our other guards, plus Joe and Burton, were there for my story, as these were the same players I rode with on our infamous "beer-swilling" return to campus from the Lee game.

My team mates all knew that I was scrappy, as every so often trouble did seem to "find me". Still, I was never one to seek out a battle, like some do. As I've earlier stated, I have always been appalled at destructive behavior, whether it is exacted upon property, or an attack on a fellow human being. Nevertheless, I would "rise to the occasion" when necessary, and coach Melling was witness to this with some of the minor skirmishes that would inevitably arise in our heated East Valley practices.

"Shit, Jesse, remind me not to get up your ass in practice anymore," Mark intoned jokingly.

His place at starting guard was very secure, as Blakely's and Kelly's (we started three guards, with Blakely playing the perimeter at the small forward spot, because of our great speed on this particular squad), but I always matched-up well with Mark in practice, and sometimes kicked his ass, and then sometimes was made to look like the rookie that I was. Still, his maturity as a junior was far superior to mine, and he, Blakely and T.J. still had another year to play; also, with Kelly graduating this year, I was potentially looking at a starting spot my junior year.

Christ! That seemed like eons away!

Melling's whistle pierced the hallway outside of our locker room, causing all of us to nearly jump out of our skins.

"Ten minutes men," his cracker voice descended upon us, "not one second later!"

We all hustled into our practice gear, me more gingerly than the rest, and my mates all could see that I was hurting.

"Fuck this shit," Joe whispered, "I am so tired of hearing his redneck voice."

This being Joe's last year, and having the "star-status" he deserved, and being black, kept him in a sort of "protected zone" with Melling, Never once did I hear Melling growl at Joe, never once at Kelly (also black).

Joe and Kelly were our team captains, adored by all of us, and they were nearly always stellar at game time, occasionally slumping only to "very good"!

To be fair, again, with Coach, I must say that he genuinely regarded my black teammates with respect, and considering the environment in which he was raised, showed a true understanding of racial equality; something that many of his peers did not. In fact, coach most likely was a bit over-sensitive with this, hence his never bitching at them.

Still, Coach's voice could grate on your nerves, much akin to the proverbial "fingernails on the chalkboard"!

Joe did not have anything "personal" against Coach; and to be sure, there was the recognition of Melling's respect for his players. What Joe did not care for was Bullet's abilities as a head coach, plainly and simply; something that bothered many of us!

We all hit the floor running, trying to get psyched up for this tournament most of us cared little about.

The remaining few of my team mates, having seen me for the first time, just stared for a moment, then went into their own practice modes, as they seemingly were not surprised that only Jesse Mouchebeau could go out and get his ass mixed up with something special during Christmas break.

Melling looked at me for several seconds, started to say something, then thought better or it and just smiled to himself, and slightly shook his head. I took this to be a favorable sign.

As I've earlier put forth; Coach was a very serious scrapper in his youth, and with his size and fortitude, could most likely take on any three of us.

We practiced long and hard, and in fact so intensely that several of our East Valley players puked their guts out during the three solid hours of non-stop hell.

"That's what too much drinking and partying will do! Some of you fellas need to take a good, hard look at what's important in your lives. Basketball will not be here forever for you, so you might as well give it your all, while you can," Melling cautioned, as if he truly needed to say anything.

Jesus, throwing up your guts is rough enough, without having a sermon piled on the occasion!

Bullet was indeed still pissed-off at the way we "threw" our last game away with Lee, and was sending us a message, loudly and clearly.

This tournament did not feature any of our conference foes. It was an annual event held in different parts of Tennessee, with only teams from the state. The interesting thing was that it featured NCAA divisions I, II and III, and even a ranked junior college team; with the participating schools selected at random, and bearing the very apt moniker "All Tennessee Classic."

In truth, it was an extremely unique idea; a chance for any lower level school to step-up and compete with our various Southern brethren. As it was the chance for the Division I big guns to remind the rest of us of how inadequate we were, and how futile it was to actually think that we could compete. In the five year history of this tournament, only one real upset had occurred, with the losing division I team having been subject to its previous night's infamous drinking/swimming binge; hence our own Coach's strictly enforced curfew.

It was also an opportunity for our respective coaches to be seen by the press, and other schools' athletic directors and alumni, who were the real power in college sports.

These A.D.'s all knew each other, and congregated on an annual basis at this event. Coach Melling was all too aware of this fact. We, on the other hand, could give two shits about this tournament, and would rather be hanging out with our families and friends. Literally very few of our East Valley faithful would even see us play, as the alumni fat-cats of our regarded institutions were all given first choice for the precious few tickets available, especially this year, as our gym did not even approach the seating capacity of some of our bigger rivals'.

Also, when was I going to see my beloved Sharon again? I had spoken with her only three times since the Lee game, and her face was starting to slightly fade in my memory. All I wanted to do was drive to her and T.J.'s hometown, and just cool out.

Instead, I was physically hurting more than ever, as a result of the workout we had just completed.

After practice, coach informed us of the tournament bracket match-up, with the eight teams represented. There were to be four quarter-final games played on Saturday, two semi-finals on Sunday, with the championship event on Monday.

This was to be the last year for this particular number of teams, however, as the attention given to this unique concept had forced the sponsors to double next years entries, which of course would even lengthen the duration and shorten everyone's Christmas break, even more so.

Every single one of us, sitting in our locker room, had exactly the same thought, or rather prayer, after Bullet let us know that our first game was with Division I powerhouse Tennessee Tech; "could we all go home, after getting our asses waxed by this team?"

Coach then added, "Men, I want you to dig very deep for this first game. We all know that Tech is a great team, but this is when we can surprise them, as they could be looking past us to the second round!"

Again, a Zen-like collective conscious thought with all of my teammates: "Tech could be still hung-over and half drunk from the night before, suffering from the flu, and still beat the crap out of us!

They were very, very good, much akin to our nemesis Southern West Virginia University, only bigger. That was the deal with Divisions I, II and III; almost all of us were good players, and fast. In fact, speed was East Valley's greatest attribute, and our shooting, plus we were a surprising good defensive squad, despite our lack of height.

It was size, though, that separated our respective divisions, and all one had to do was look at the rosters to see that there was a direct correlation to support this. Our biggest guy, who did not even start, was 6'11'. Tech's frontcourt averaged that height, and their guards were 6'5" and 6'. Yes, they were also very quick. Shit, were we in for a tough game. Hell, even the pro scouts were interested in three of Tech's players; both their guards (naturally), and one of their forwards, all being previous high school all-Americans!

Melling was giving us our game-plan, with a couple of new concoctions of his, and again nearly all of us were "zoned-out" with his rhetoric.

We all knew how to play these guys, and that was with constant full-court defensive pressure, so as to keep them from setting up into their renown half-court offense, which was to "pound it inside," especially on smaller teams, such as ours. Plus, it's dangerous to do the "last minute tango" with regards to strategy; it never works. I am not talking about minor adjustments that the best and most creative coaches do at half-time; but rather the alteration of "flow" that teams develop, their "6th sense". Same as being in the ring, you "dance with the one you brought!"

So here our squad was working on new plays and a general "philosophical change in identity" the night before our big game, most of us realizing that we would simply throw this new state of confusion out in our collective sleep that very evening.

Practice mercifully finally ended, and even Melling did not have us do his famous suicide drill, as this was the day after Christmas.

T.J. was getting dressed next to me, grinning like the Cheshire Cat.

"What's up brother," I intoned, "you look like you have something to say!"

"Guess who's coming to the game tomorrow?" he quietly asked.

I am thinking, because of his legendary resourcefulness, that he had copped a ticket for Barbara, his wife, with whom he had also remained best friends, since their high school days.

"Barbie?" I asked which was his wife's childhood nickname.

"You got it, but she's bringing someone with her," and now T.J. is broadly smiling.

For the life of me I cannot put this scenario together, until it hits me like a ton of bricks. Realizing that T.J., Barbara, AND Sharon had all come from the same high school, I start to "flip into adrenal overdrive," with my heart slowly picking up steam.

"Sher?" her own nickname, was all that I could muster, nearly choking on the word.

"You win the prize, little brother," his affectation for yours truly.

Jesus, was I now more than excited.

"She's staying with us for the entire tournament, and I just thought that you might like to know!" Now, T.J. was playing with me.

"How did…?," then letting my thoughts decrescendo, as I knew that T.J. had a habit of getting things done, much as he had with the "Lee game case of beer," and his "pass" home thereafter.

"When does she get here?" I ask.

"Well little brother, you and Sher are having dinner with us this very evening!"

I shrieked, nearly ruining what was left of my sore throat, and then quickly catch myself, as Bullet is next door in his office.

"Damn, T.J., thanks!" And I am nearly in tears.

"Hurry up, Barbie wants us there in an hour". T.J. and Barbara lived in the married housing section of campus, which was actually very beautiful, and idyllic. I guess that even East Tennessee Valley knew that if you were married AND trying to get a college education, you needed some support.

I race home with Burton and Joe.

"Jesus Jesse," Joe and Burton chime in collectively, "where's the fucking fire?"

"Remember Lee's stunning blonde-haired cheerleader?" I respond.

"Are you kidding me?" Joe replies, "She could be the cover girl for 'Pretty Face Magazine'".

Burton adds: "perkiest little thing I've ever seen!"

"Well, my roundball brothers; T.J., Barbie and Sharon all went to the same high school, know each others' families, and she's coming down this weekend for the tournament. Somehow T.J. copped tickets for both of them."

None of this surprised either Joe or Burton as they were also all too aware of T.J.'s legendary prowess at getting things done.

"Damn, where's she staying?" Joe and Burton miraculously asking this probing question at exactly the same time.

"With Barbie and T.J., at their apartment," I reply.

"Holy Christ, Jesse, you staying there as well?" Joe asks.

"You kidding?" I answer, "With Bullet's curfew, hanging over our asses?"

I knew that my roommates could, and would cover for me, if I was so bold as to stay out all night, but I just could not chance another run-in with Melling. I was simple too expendable. I had zero room for screw-ups in our coach's collection of "do's and don'ts," never mind that Joe was always pushing this particular "envelope," simply because he could!

We all had to absolutely be in by 11pm, and Coach made the point to all of us that he was calling each and everyone of us at precisely this hour, which we then wondered at how in earth, scientifically speaking, was he going to accomplish this?

Of course we knew what he intended, with yet another example of his own wit; still it made several of us chuckle at his screwed up facial expression the moment he had uttered those exact words. Bullet had a habit of doing this on a fairly regular basis, and all of us appreciated his momentary confusion!

"I gotta call Loretta, guys, anyone need the phone?"

"It's all yours, Jesse," Burton says.

"Later tonight, though, you gotta tell us again about you and your partner Jess' fight; you still looked like you got your ass kicked, Jesse!" Joe added, jokingly.

"You got it," I reply. "What are you guys up to this evening?"

"We've got our own little party to see to, now that our little Jesse is leaving us." Burton responds, grinning at Joe.

"See you later," I add, and go into our living room to call my beautiful sister, barely able to contain my enthusiasm.

\*          \*          \*

"Hi gorgeous," I immediately say upon hearing my beloved soul mate's voice.

"Jesse, what a surprise," she answers, "I thought that you were going to call us in the morning, must be VERY important," she added, all too cryptically.

"I had to call you now babe; guess who I am having dinner with this evening?"

"Sher, of course," Loretta answered.

Jesus, did my sister know EVERYTHING?

"How the hell…," and then I just faded, with the immediate re-affirmation of my beautiful sister's unique "powers".

"She's staying with T.J. and Barbie, and coming to the tournament; how cool is that?"

"Well big brother, guess who else is coming to see you play tomorrow?"

I have absolutely no clue; having just seen my family and Jess, immediately ruled them out, as these tournament tickets, as previously mentioned, were nearly impossible to attain.

I am thinking that maybe my high school coach, whom I adored, was making the trek, but somehow that did not make sense at this time of year.

Then another "thunderbolt" lit up my brain; "you Sis, how on earth…?"

"Jesse, my beloved champion, your best friend and my new love are also invited to attend, courtesy of your very own T.J.!"

I cannot believe what I am hearing; I mean it is so difficult to make something like this happen, and even T.J. had surpassed his now legendary ability to "get it done".

"Four tickets," I am thinking, "how in the hell did he do this?"

"Sweetheart," as she interrupted my mental wandering, "T.J. told me the night of the Lee game of his plans, but not to say anything until it was a reality. Well, it became just that Christmas Eve, and I had the hardest time not giving this away. I even talked with Sharon!"

I could definitely detect Loretta's impeccable smile, as she unfolded this rather unique story and surprise for her brother. Several had obviously planned this, and I just came to the realization that Jess must have already known, as well.

Before I could ask, Loretta led with "yes, dear Jesse, he was in on this, too!"

I was absolutely bursting with happiness, when I suddenly realized that Sharon had not seen me since the fight!

"Jesus Loretta, Sher has not seen me looking the way I do. I may give her the wrong impression; she might think that I am just another one of the red-necks she grew up with!"

"Sweetheart," my sister cooed, "she already knows; I thought that would make it so much easier on you."

"Thanks, babe; as always, you are too aware of me, and I adore you for that ability."

"Jesse?" Loretta whispered. "I am so excited for you, as Sher seems to have fallen in love at first sight with my most magnificent big brother, and I sense something very special with you two!"

Christ, my head was starting to swim. There was no finer girl on the planet than my beloved sister, and yet I was starting to experience a similar, albeit different, yet just as powerful inner awakening of the feelings at the depths of my soul. This was the genesis of something most special!

"Honey," Loretta interrupting my momentary mental hiatus, "Jess and I will see you tomorrow at the game; then we all are going out, if your coach doesn't ridiculously curfew the team."

"Who knows with Bullet," I answer, "maybe he will give us a break!"

"Jesse, you are my heart and soul, and whatever happens in this world, know that you have made my life so meaningful; I will never, ever forget our relationship."

I am thinking that, because of Loretta's new found love with my best friend, she is starting to become more philosophical with me; to assure me of the very special place in her heart that I've always resided is secure.

Later I am to find out that it was so much more than just that.

"You too, sis; I cannot wait to hug and kiss you tomorrow," I reply.

Yes, our relationship was extremely unique, and I never more appreciated that fact than just at that particular moment. I too, was becoming so much more acutely aware of things in general; Loretta was educating her big brother in ways that were so removed from the "norm". I was entering into another realm of spirituality, and somehow was beginning to see this clearly!

"See you soon honey, now get going to your dinner, and be sure to kiss her for me!"

"Bye sis," I whisper.

After hanging up with Loretta, I realized that she had not given me any details of her staying down here with Jess; and again, I was coming to the conclusion that my sister and Jess were moving into that extraordinary place where some relationships can only dream, and that theirs' was becoming a reality.

\*　　　\*　　　\*

I knocked on the door of Barbie and T.J.'s apartment, with my heart pounding. I was lamenting the fact that I really wanted to get flowers, but literally had only enough time to arrive still ten minutes late!

When the door was opened, I was so caught off-guard by Sher's presence, that I about fainted!  She was magnificent, and my heart dropped seemingly a mile.

"Hello my dear Jesse," she intoned, "I've been so anxious to see you!"

We kissed right there on the spot, and I have to tell you that in all of my young years, that was the most sensitive, yet passionate thing I had experienced to date.  We kissed again, and again, completely oblivious of the giggling emanating from Barbie and T.J.

"Jesus guys, get a room," T.J. groaned.

Barbie was smiling, holding T.J. around his waist.  They were indeed childhood sweethearts of "storybook" quality.

T.J. adds "let's eat, I am famished!"

I am so in love, immediately, that I cannot even think about food; neither can Sharon, as obviously dinner proved to be the case were neither of us barely touched a most excellent meal.

The next few hours went by in a blur, with the four of us chatting about life in general.

Sharon was very excited to meet Loretta, and Jess, having already been given an adequate synopsis by my wonderful sister.

Tomorrow was going to be very special as, once again, T.J. had been able to make reservations for six of us at a good local restaurant, even during this tournament's infiltration of the masses, which was yet another one "for the books" in the T.J. Cooper hall-of-fame memoirs!

Win or lose, we were going to enjoy ourselves tomorrow evening; and even though no one truly enjoys losing, I was thinking of how utterly stunning a night with Sharon could possibly be, with no curfews, no distractions, and only her gorgeous countenance with which to focus.

T.J., Barbie, and Sher all walked with me to my house, and actually got to meet Burton and Joe, and their departing dates for the evening.

"I am so looking forward to spending time here with you," Sher whispered in my ear, and I felt a stirring in my guts that was again beyond anything heretofore experienced.

She then added something I was to never, ever forget my entire life: "Jesse, I know this sounds crazy, but I love you. I absolutely knew it the moment you walked over to me after the game that night, and smiled so charmingly, yet so boyishly. Your eyes Jesse, your eyes told me everything!"

"See you all tomorrow," I said to the departing trio; then grabbed Sharon by the waist, kissing her with all of my heart's intent.

"Sher, I truly love you, too!"

*     *     *

Later that evening, Joe, Burton and I talked and talked; about nearly everything under the sun: girlfriends, love, basketball and our teammates and coach, life after college, our families, and how fortunate we were to be able to play this magnificent game with some measure of above average abilities!

We also unanimously agreed that none of us wanted to really lose tomorrow, and maybe, just maybe we could surprise Tennessee Tech.

I mean East Valley could "ball" pretty well, and sometimes life affords one the opportunity to pull-off the stunning upset.

Could we actually make history, at least in a small, yet most meaningful fashion?

Possibly, but we still found it necessary, and wanting, to split a bottle of very good red wine, and thank God for our lives!

# Chapter Twelve

"I can remember, that look in your eyes,
And I could feel, something unreal,
When I held you in my arms,
My child..."

Child of Mine

# XII

Saturday morning arrived earlier than expected as Burton, Joe and I had "miraculously" found a way to justify a second bottle of wine before falling asleep the night before. Apparently the "Gods of College Basketball" saw fit to subconsciously twist our arms for a pre-game ritual of sorts! All three of us were mildly hung-over, which was nothing to worry about, as we had previously on occasion "been there, done that, and got the t-shirt, thank you very much"!

"Goddam Jesse, you and your fucking red wine," Joe moaned, obviously more affected than me.

"I feel like a million-fucking dollars," Burton sarcastically replied, apparently just slightly less affected than Joe.

"Both of you can kiss my ass, nobody twisted your arms (save for the previously mentioned "Gods"), and besides, now we can look forward to breakfast at Coach's house," which elicited even more groaning from my roomies.

Melling had offered/suggested/implied/ordered that this was a 7:30am get-together, for team-spirit and whatever. ALL of us, to a man, on the East Valley roster, would have much rather slept the extra couple of hours, rolling into the first game of the day, whilst digesting our egg sandwiches and fries, a specialty of the campus cantina.

Still, it was extremely magnanimous of Mrs. Melling to cook for an entire basketball team consisting of young men that could all eat like horses.

We three arrived at coach's house just under the deadline, and were very surprised by the unbelievable spread, furnished on our behalf! I mean, Mrs. Melling must have started preparing food at 5am, and I was starting to salivate.

I, once again, reflected to myself, coaching ability aside, that Coach and his wife were very good people. Years later I would often muse, with regards to this very moment, as to how generous and nice people could truly be.

Mrs. Melling was raised in the same red-neck environment as her husband, and here we were, black and white kids, all sitting at their dining room and kitchen tables, being cared for, as only a mother and father could. Very touching indeed!

Kelly and Blakely were the most appreciative, as their moaning while chewing obviously delighted our hostess, to no end.

"Jesse, my Lord what did you get mixed-up with," Mrs. Melling offered me, in her wonderful southern cadence; so unlike her husband's cracker delivery, having seen me for the very first time since our Christmas break.

"Truthfully maam, I was defending my sister's honor, and I had no choice," I answered.

By now, all of my team-mates, and even Coach, were starting to understand the unique relationship I possessed with Loretta; and most had even mentioned a very positive thing or two, with regards to this; especially in light of my recent battle-royal!

Michael André Fath

"Well my dear Jesse, sometimes 'honor' is the only possession we have, in recourse, and I am very appreciative of young men like you that see and understand this."

Mrs. Melling was an extremely astute and beautiful young woman, college educated, with two young children, and going through life with her husband gave her an insight many did not have. As I have said earlier, Coach was a legend of sorts, and most likely she had witnessed a thing or two, first-hand.

She then winked at me, and fluffed my hair. "You're special, Jesse, this I truly know!"

"Thank you maam, I really appreciate you saying that," I replied, my complexion starting to slightly redden.

I felt yet another "emotional stirring" of sorts, deep within my guts; this one, of course, different from the recent thunderbolt of love thrust upon my countenance, by the lovely Sharon McGee.

Still, I wondered what in the world was happening to me, in light of recent events, and felt, again, this "spiritual-awakening" of sorts, and oddly enough it was being triggered by women!

Breakfast was magnificent, and all of us expressed our gratitude to Coach and his wife.

Sometimes we are indeed "educated" in manners previously unknown and we should most definitely take note; as these "opportunities" many times are very few, and very far-between!

\*     \*     \*

Our game was a 1pm start, the second one scheduled, which was fine by us, as, win or lose we would have most of Saturday afternoon and evening off, provided we could sneak out of the arena. Things got very hectic when four basketball games were in succession, every three hours, and Bullet would be so pre-occupied with other coaches and A.D.'s that he would hardly miss us, amidst the packed gymnasium.

The Tennessee Tech players, already on the floor, were methodically going through their drills, looking like a pro team, especially in light of the competition in this year's event, save for West Tennessee University, another invited Division I team that had absolutely crushed Faulkner College, a D-III school, in the first game; and yes, these match-ups do support the survival of the fittest theory much more often than not!

As customary with our home games, our cheerleaders would erect a "paper-wall," at the entrance of our gym, that we all would burst through, while listening to the deafening sounds of Sly and the Family Stone, our teams' this year's voted winner as our pre-game music. Since we were this year's hosts of the "All Tennessee Classic," by pre-arranged sanction, we were going to run the same drill, with me leading our team onto the court of our arena.

As "Dance to the Music" was blaring over the P.A. system, I yelled to my team, as we all gathered in the atrium outside the gym, "lets' go kick their big fuckin' asses" (yes, I always seemed to curse, especially making use of the "F" word, when hyped before a game), and upon hearing our cue, took a couple of steps and took off, with my teammates right on my heels.

Normally, everything goes smoothly with our charge, and coupled with our beloved R&B music pounding everyone's ears, makes for a very lively introduction.

This time, au contraire, Mon ami!

Jane Covert, our head cheerleader, was so entranced with Tennessee Tech's awesome display of power and ability, not to mention one of their forwards that looked even better than Namath and Elvis, had her troops just inside the doorway, milling about, obviously forgetting the time-honored ritual of yours truly crashing through the gates and into the valley of our East Tennessee "Babylon".

I came flying through, and there she was, looking at me like a deer-in-headlights, still having the presence of mind, though, to open up her arms and gather me in as we both tumbled onto the floor. Of course, all of our Hornets followed suit, with those few immediately behind ending up in precisely the same manner, arms and legs entwined with our various sisters in battle, spread about the floor like a Caligula imbued Roman orgy.

Those players lucky enough to have not fallen, resembled some new drug-induced tribal dance, side-stepping on their toes, so as not to break an ankle, or worse, look as foolish as we sprawled about.

All in all, no one was hurt, save for our supreme embarrassment stemming from the deafening roar of approval from: the boys from Tech, applauding most vociferously; the many students and fans from ALL eight schools represented; and, the media, extensive as it was with these storied tournaments, with uncannily clear video showing up on the local news that evening, further adding to the day's festivities, and my apparently rising star status!

I think that the only folks not laughing their asses off were the coaches, who most likely unanimously thought of yet another example of a team's not being 100% focused.

Melling, who normally would still be in his office during this pre-game soirée, was of course out and about milling with his coaching brethren, and glared so intensely as if to fry us with his heat sensor eyes.

We all gathered ourselves and proceeded with our own warm-ups, actually looking very sharp, as we did believe at least in ourselves, and our speed.

Funny thing happened, though, and I started to giggle right as I sunk a 15 foot jumper, to lead yet another drill. This trickled through my teammates, and before long, all of us were laughing hysterically, unable to control ourselves.

I glanced at the Tennessee Tech players, and some were smiling while shaking their heads as if to say "Jesus, these guys are indeed out of their fucking minds, but it sure looks like they know how to have a good time"!

I glanced up to try and find Sharon, Barbie, Loretta and Jess, though tear-filled eyes, finally locating them not far behind our bench. I blew all of them a kiss, as they too were laughing, and graciously bowed, not even caring if Bullet witnessed this. As luck would have it, he did not, as he was yakking it up with Tech's infamous coach Sommer Sanders.

Still, I would not have cared on this day, as for some strange reason, my love affair with basketball was evolving into something substantially different, and unique, and I could not put my finger on just exactly what!

Of course, Blakely and Joe would have even another of their fabled high school teammates on the Titan's roster; this time, one of their all conference players, Jet Parks, a gifted and smooth shooting 6'6 forward, and previously mentioned high school all-American!

"Shit, Jesse, these guys are fucking huge," T.J. opinioned to me; as we took our seats on the bench, both looking up at the small and beloved contingent of our own specially invited guests.

"I think that Coach's game-plan sucks," I countered; both of us, rather ALL of us, knowing that our only hope was to run Tech's asses into the ground.

For some reason, Bullet felt that our half-court offense would do the job, as we were superior shooters, whilst our defensive scheme being predicated foolishly on hope and prayer, would follow suit!

Each of us wanted to press from baseline to baseline; harassing their superior guards and forwards, and run the moment they scored on us, utilizing our own very gifted speed and the "full-court concept" to its fullest. Of course, Melling would have none of this, and it would show.

Tech immediately starting pounding the ball inside, and pretty much all we could do was hope for an errant rebound.

Joe, Blakely, Mark, Kelly, and especially Steve, being our center, were much too early approaching exhaustion, being physically roughed up, due to the nature of Coach's game plan. Even Burton, playing pretty well, had his chest nearly caved in by their power forward muscle-bound freak, Isaac Newsome.

Jet Parks was crushing us with his superior shooting touch (damn, Blakely and Joe's Rocky Gap coach was a basketball-player-developing-genius), and both of the Titan's guards were methodically cutting us to pieces with their ball-handling skills.

Only six of us played the first half, due to Coach's neurotic belief in "non-adaptation of game-plan," and when the buzzer sounded, mercifully ending the first 20 minutes, we were down by 27!

In our locker room during intermission, something extraordinary happened, never before witnessed, at least by me, as I was just a freshman.

Before Coach could start in on us, yelling about how we lacked the necessary intestinal fortitude to achieve victory, Kelly and Joe asked for a private audience with our Coach Melling, and off they went into his office.

We all sat there in stunned disbelief; but, Mark and Blakely were smiling, with their obvious knowledge of what was then transpiring.

Apparently, our beloved captains had had quite enough of this ridiculous embarrassment out on the court, and were simply going to try to persuade Bullet, in the private confines of his office, to let us run and press Tech, utilizing most of our players to keep up an unyielding pace, and maybe, just maybe, wear their talented asses out!

We were in very good shape; this we knew, this we were intensely proud of, and again, we could shoot "lights out," on any given night.

I could hear some of their heated discussion, although it was not on par with an actual argument, as we did have respect for our Coach, all of us being reverently appreciative of our various skippers in our collective and previous playing experiences.

We all could just barely make out the conversation: "You gotta play Jesse and T.J.," Kelly stated; "you know Jesse is our best shooter, and T.J.'s defense can harass their point guard into some turnovers".

"Coach, we need to be fresh to keep up this pace," and it's going to take all of us, running their tails off, and pressing the hell out of them," Joe emphatically stated.

As I have said, these two players were very respected by Coach, and only these two could have pulled off a coup such as this; at least until next year, when Mark and Blakely would fill their shoes becoming our senior co-captains and leaders.

Melling came back into the locker room, with Kelly and Joe following.

"Jesse, T.J., be ready to play; David and Burton, same thing; in fact all of you, be ready to run," were gonna go after 'em!"

"Jesus," I whispered to T.J., "you believe this?"

T.J. was smiling; in fact all of us were grinning from ear to ear.

Coach left, and we all collectively cried out in the most awesome war whoop heard since Custer's fabled and very unfortunate experience with the fabulous Sioux Nation at Little Big Horn!

We were going to jab, counter punch and take it to this Division I beast, or at least go down with some dignity!

From the moment the buzzer sounded to start the second half, our

East Tennessee Valley College basketball squad played like we'd never played before.

T.J. and I were in and out, as a guard tandem, to spell Mark and Blakely, from the extremely taxing full-court pressure we had implemented.

As soon as we would score, we would "jump into their guard's jock-straps," so to speak, harassing the ever-loving shit out of them; switching defensive assignments, almost at will, and "going for broke" with regards to intercepting passes, and gaining positions for offensive charges.

When Tech would score, we would, in an instant, race up the court, with full abandon, to quickly score ourselves.

My first shot, though, would also be featured on the later evening's sports TV highlights, as their aforementioned all-conference forward Jet Parks, seemingly a safe enough distance away from me, closed his space from me so blindingly quickly to block my shot three rows deep into the stands, eliciting a most stupendous roar from the entire Tech crowd, and most of the others witnessing this amazing athletic feat!

Still, I had enough self-esteem and confidence to keep shooting, and shoot I did, hitting my next three shots, and sinking both of my free-throws.

T.J. was also "in a zone," hitting six out of nine floor shots, and four from the charity stripe.

In fact, all of us Hornets were in a Zen-like state of consciousness, very likely due to the fact that for the first time I, and many of my team mates, had ever experienced playing for Coach with such freedom of restraint, and reckless abandon! Every single time the buzzer rang out, we would substitute a player or two, just to keep up the unrelenting pressure.

If indeed Tennessee Tech had an Achilles heel, it was the fact that their squad outside of their first seven players was not as battle-tested; the Titans simply were not that "deep"; still, in reality, their last seven players could very well have been on a par with our first seven. The difference this afternoon being, though, that we caught them by complete surprise.

We tied this fabled powerhouse, with fifteen seconds to go, and our fans were screaming beyond human capacity. Bullet was sweating profusely, yet we were fairly calm, as subconsciously we always knew that this was a "win/win" situation for our Division II team, once we got close.

Sommer Sanders called time-out, and gathered his troops, blistering them with profanity that all of us could hear. Even the TV crews were gathering ALL of this, as once in a great while, albeit rarely, another "Cinderella Story" could manifest itself in this storied basketball classic, giving hope to all of us "lesser than D-I schools" for future encounters.

"Get the Goddamn ball up the fucking court, and shove it down their fucking throats, for Christ's sake," Coach Sanders screamed, "you sons-a-bitches will be the laughingstock of all of Goddamn Tennessee if we lose this. We are Goddamned nationally ranked and are about to lose to these little sons-a-bitches, and I am not gonna have it."

Then, as all great coaches do, Sanders calmly and, unbelievably while smiling, softly spoke as he diagrammed their play, pointing to certain players for emphasis, not caring if we, or the entire arena, for that matter, could see, assuring his players that they would indeed succeed.

They did!

Just as if Tennessee Tech was playing a high school team, their all-conference-pro-scouted guards, pulled the ball up court, with such grace and passing with such profound efficiency, getting the ball to their behemoth center.

Their off-side forward, "King Kong" (Mr. Newsome), then freed Jet Parks with a viscous screen, and with .3 seconds to go hit the most gorgeous 18' shot ever seen is this classic; sending our hopes and dreams back into our own reality as the final buzzer echoed within our own home court walls.

The entire arena erupted, saving the collective sigh and deflation of our East Valley fans, and most of our team just took a seat on the gym floor, wherever we happened to be at the final gun, in our own moment of final exhaustion.

I looked up into the stands and Jess, Loretta, Barbie and Sharon were all headed my and T.J.'s way.

Both of Tech's guards pulled me up and off of the floor to congratulate me, in only the way we warriors truly know when we've been in a real fight; and, I momentarily drifted in thought to our earlier in the season's disappointing loss with Southern West Virginia University!

I really did not know these guys, as they were in a "different league"; but sometimes basketball is just basketball, no matter who's involved, and talent is talent, no matter what level one happens to be.

"Awesome game white boy, you really had us. Shit, if you guys would've come out like that in the first half, we'd be gone," their 6'5" guard implored.

Something everyone of our East Valley team would mull over many times in the remaining months of our season. No shit! If we would've, could've; but, most definitely, we should've!

Anyhow, this was one of the truly memorable compliments I would get in my brief college career; along with SWVU's Chick Washington's accolades, a couple of pro players' comments during summer pick-up games, and the few others sporadically bestowed in the near future.

What is it with these amazing Black players? What are they seeing in this small white boy's game? Maybe I am indeed "onto something"; maybe I will someday be great! Who really gives a shit? I'm fucking in love!

"Damn, you get mixed up in something serious?," their 6' point guard, Damian, inquired, referring to my fight injuries and reminding me of my not-too-distant-past altercation.

"I survived," smiling as I responded."

"Yes, I suspect that you did," Tyrone, his backcourt mate, added.

"Thanks guys, it was an honor to be on the court with you, and good luck the rest of the tournament!"

"Later brother," both intoned, as we "soul-gripped" our conclusion.

"Later, brothers," I replied.

They similarly congratulated T.J., and spent even more time with Kelly and Mark, as starting guards do have their "bonds".

Joe and Blakely were in embrace with their former high school teammate and game hero Jet Parks, acting only as those, having previously experienced those most sacred and fabled childhood experiences on the field, or in the gym, can possibly imagine.

Jane Covert had cornered their "movie-idol" forward, chatting it up in a most vociferous manner, and it seemed as if everyone on our team, their team, our cheerleaders and theirs, were in some sort of post-game ritualistic splendor; all happy to be alive and well.

Maybe this was yet another of God's lessons about competition: *unless it's war, it's not war!*

So, enjoy the moment, live the dream, and thank you very much!

Losing never really "destroyed" me, as it seemingly did with many players and all coaches. The coaches' consequences were, of course, more serious in that their very jobs depended on their won/lost records; however, I somehow always felt that if I gave it my all, as well as my team, then there was the next game to focus on, not a post-battle depression syndrome yanking one down into its abyss.

Bullet was yakking with Coach Sanders, and the media was swarming, but not towards yours truly, but rather to the more deserved Tech players.

No matter, I was in love, was loved; and, loved my sister, best friend, ball-mates, and family. Life was indeed very special, and I was going to enjoy all of this.

"Jesse, Jesse, Jesse," my already-approaching-infamous-status best friend Jess Butkus hollered, voice booming above all of the cacophony.

"You guys were great," he continued.

Loretta whispered in my ear how proud she was, tears welling in her gorgeous eyes, throat nearly hoarse from screaming, while hugging me intensely.

Sharon just stood by, and then embraced me in only a manner fitting of newfound love; that of something so sensual, and sexual, that I could barely contain myself.

She pushed my sweating hair out of my eyes, carefully grabbed my face with both hands, and kissed me like there was no tomorrow.

T.J. and Barbie acted in like manner; and how cool was that; after several years of going steady in high school and then marriage?

Jess and Loretta were equally, if not somewhat less "obvious," filling each others eyes with laughter and heartfelt adoration.

Splendid behavior indeed! Some of us did, in fact, get this "life-thing," and we were so very much alive!

All of us wanted out of there, sooner than later, and agreed to meet in the lobby after Coach either praised or chewed us out; one never having a clue as to which way his pendulum would swing.

Turns out, he had gotten such high regards from Coach Sanders, and a few others, as to how his "half-time re-adjustment game plan strategy" was so brilliant, that he apparently believed it was indeed "his" idea, and was rather polite in our locker room.

Even with this loss, it did help to enhance Melling's reputation.

"You boys played your hearts out, and that's what I'm talkin' about," Bullet monologued.

"Cooper, Mouchebeau, nice shooting," Melling continued, "Strong, way to get after Parks; hell, all of you played your guts out, and I am real proud!"

Then, as if a miracle, heaven sent by those previously mentioned "Gods of Basketball," Coach uttered those fabulous words we were all secretly hoping for: "you boys are welcome to stay and watch, but I am giving you the rest of the day, and tomorrow off, but you gotta be here for the final on Monday, as this IS our home gym, and we need to be here for the closing ceremonies," which was not only the trophy presentation, but the announcement of the all-Tournament team, which none of us could expect to make, having gone out in the very first round.

Jesus, none of us gave a shit as to how this tournament would play out, and truly wanted to go home, now! We had had quite enough of this college basketball precipice, and were mentally fatigued with another such close call.

Still, Coach was not going to take any chances, whatsoever, of suffering the embarrassment of not having his players there if indeed something extraordinary happened.

Lastly, he bade, "we are going to have practice Tuesday morning, and then you all can go home until next Saturday, before we start back up!"

Once again, the Sioux, no Cherokee, no Apache, no Comanche (they were the meanest?) unanimous war-whoop!

We ALL, would be home for New Year's Eve; how simply grand was that?

I had not even expected time off from the games at hand, much less all next week's projected grueling practices, as we did have the rest of the season with which to contend!

Bullet pulled me aside, and squarely held both my shoulders: "Jesse, keep working hard, listen to what I say, and maybe we will have more time for you in our system!"

"Thanks, Coach," was simply all I could say, as I knew again, in my heart of hearts, that Melling did not really care for my, as he so often derogatorily put it, "playground style," and I always could feel that he, if given the chance, would have me remain in a supporting cast for my entire college career!

Also, I was slowly transforming into something other than a gym rat; evolving into a role of more import than previously imagined. This I TRULY KNEW!

*       *       *

The Mountain View restaurant was very cozy this cold evening. Tucked away 10 "mountain" miles or so off of the interstate that ran right beside our campus, "The View," as we affectionately labeled her, was not only a stunning tourist spot, facing Mount Washington, but a very popular "hang" with not only East Valley students, but several other schools in our proximity.

More importantly, however, was the fact that this was one of the very few places possibly available in our entire region, as it was "off the beaten path," due to the tournament's provincial demands on its infrastructure.

Again, as so many times proven, T.J. had impossibly come through with reservations for the six of us.

"Jesus, T.J., remind me to hire you for my agent once I graduate," Jess laughed, while affectionately referring to his true love of opera, and his real desire to do just that, upon matriculation.

All six of us were a sight to behold; sitting by the stone hearth, fire crackling, sipping our wine (again, T.J. to the rescue, as Loretta was still under age, and I had just turned 18), and truly enjoying the very sweet moments of new love.

Sher was stunning in her simple, yet elegant black jacket/dress, which glorified her blonde hair immeasurably.

Loretta, equally enticing in her chartreuse cashmere sweater and skirt, playfully would nudge up against Jess, much as a she-wolf with her trusted alpha male, nuzzling each other, epitomizing the oh so fine art of affection.

Barbie, in many ways still resembled the high school cheerleader that had fallen in love with her sports hero classmate. She seemed several years younger, even at 20, and I strongly suspected that she would look like she had "just walked out of her senior yearbook," even at her 30th class reunion. Her white turtleneck sweater was nothing shy of perfect, and I was blessed to be witnessing young marriage, seemingly healthy and very much alive, and hopefully eternal!

All three young ladies were radiant, never mind gorgeous, and the glances from various patrons, male and female, were too numerous to ignore.

Yes, Jess and Loretta were a "mixed couple," and in this part of the South (I still maintained that was behavior everywhere; North, East and West!), one could not help but to notice the furtive, if not downright obvious countenances of disapproval; but tonight this was not the case. Our voyeurs were truly benevolent, and this made us feel even more special.

"A toast," Jess intoned, raising his glass, with ours following suit; "first to real and lasting friends; and secondly, what we fight makes no difference, but how we fight is surely what matters most; so may this be the beginning of a most remarkable life for each of us!"

I knew that Jess was alluding to several recent events, not just ballgames, with his few, yet very memorable words and we took them as truly solemn!

We ordered dinner, and basked in that youthful glory of the wonder of life to be, without the painful distraction of so many later adult problems each and every single one of us would encounter, in the course of our day to day lives.

To further enhance what he had already miraculously achieved, T.J. then stated: "I've got a surprise for us," grinning like the bastard tomcat prowling down his favorite female alley, in the height of their springtime heat cycles.

He simply unfolded his hands, and out fell three room keys, obviously belonging to The Mountain View Hotel.

"Not only for this evening, but tomorrow's as well," T.J. gleefully sang!

We sat there in stunned silence, and then the laughter flowed forth, much as it had when our team had its school-girl giggling fit in our pre-game warm-up earlier that day.

Then all of a sudden I started to feel slightly embarrassed, not knowing if Sher or Loretta would feel compromised by something in which they were not yet ready to participate.

Of course, the three girls, and T.J., were in cahoots; and most probably like so many more manifestations of similar behavior would evolve, let us know so.

Then just as quickly my discomfort faded away, knowing that Loretta and Sharon were comfortable with this.

The singular most important reason, however, for my personal happiness, was the fact that Loretta, love aside, and not yet ready to sexually involve my best friend Jess, was still willing and longing for the strength of a male's embrace again, sleeping peacefully, trustfully and soundly; and, upon reflecting with this very thought, my eyes started again to well with tears, for the second time today, for a decidedly different, and much more important reason!

My spiritual connection with my beloved sister was not only powerful, but more than obvious to anyone that simply paid attention to detail.

When Loretta and I kissed or embraced, it was more than the normal brother/sister affectation, but less than something abnormal. It was OUR kiss, OUR dual connection to the universe, our feelings of undying love for one another that made those surrounding us feel equally passionate and sublime.

I could tell that Barbie and Sher knew of Loretta's horrific encounter, at least to some degree, because they both immediately knew why I was reacting as such, and joined in with my tears of joy; and, it's these types of sensory collusion that I always would attribute to these various girls' powers of perception and divine countenance.

I would forever marvel at this skill, and constantly work on building my own!

We then all held hands and bade each other a good night, collectively agreeing on our next morning's breakfast rendezvous.

Monday morning would be here in no time, but it still seemed "miles away". In the course of these next two days I would experience love, intimacy, growing friendship from an already established base, and see my beloved sister once again regain her sense of worth, her unbelievable yet stately sexuality and confidence, and her re-affirmation of her older brother's sacred bond with her.

T.J. and Barbie would yet again fall in love with each other, something that they just "knew" how to achieve.

Jess would evolve as my "brother," and would hopelessly be ensnared within my sister's being; something that would affect him the rest of his life.

Yes, our final time here would be upon us before we would want, and our lives would simply move ahead at that very point.

Loretta and Jess would go back home Monday, but I could not. I had to, as Coach put it, "be there for the championship game," and of course we had practice the very next day.

Yes, we were entitled to our brief New Year's Eve mini-break, but I would blissfully stay on campus, catching up on schoolwork, with Sher staying at T.J.'s and Barbie's; eating dinner with them and sneaking Sher into my room for one of the most memorable weeks of my life.

Campus was nearly desolate, but I was surrounded by wonder.

Even in these very few days, I would improve as a basketball player, letting myself daily into the gym, with our trainer Phil's keys; but more importantly I would grow as a young man, having experienced some very "grown-up" things.

Loretta and I would talk every day, twice a day, with Jess' occasional butting in to check up on his soul mate brother.

She was progressing, and that was a miracle!

I would dine, drink wine, kiss oh so very often, and make love with Sharon McGee, as only those willing to die for their girlfriends can truly know!

Is it possible to fall in love, after falling in love, after falling in love?

# Chapter Thirteen

"My son you must learn now
Of what can be your power so true,
Never will an Old Man's magic
Change what only love can do."

The Magic King

# XIII

It seemed as if the two games with Tennessee Tech and Southern West Virginia University had taken more than their toll on our young squad, as for the rest of the season we struggled to finish third in our conference. We did have our moments, though; and yes, we did beat Lee University the second time around, at home, which was some sort of vindication I got for the grief that Sharon took at her school, all good natured, as to how she could be involved with "one of the enemy". In fact, although I played sporadically in that contest, I played well. It seemed as if this was Coach's standard pattern for me: if we needed some points, he yell for me to "get in there," but that was it; and this was apparently my role for the remainder of my rookie year.

Yes, I was very disappointed, as I knew that I could help the team; so did a majority of the other players. Still, Bullet kept reminding me of my inadequacies as a "disciplined" (read: *his system only*) ballplayer, and I would just have to change my approach if I was going to be any integral part of future East Tennessee Valley College teams.

This was very perplexing to me, as I truly was an unselfish player;

who thought that the beauty of a well-timed pass was equally as gorgeous as a 25' shot touching nothing but the bottom of the net!

Jesus, I was a natural shooting guard, however though, residing in a point guard's body; and I could handle the ball under pressure, but Melling never really saw my potential. I honestly thought that his mind was made up that very first time I whipped the ball around my neck (a stunning pass by the way) in practice, and something I am quite sure that he had never witnessed; never minding that many times I would sometimes absolutely kill our starting line-up in scrimmages.

Why do many in power have these obtuse tendencies to make "final judgment calls," so extremely early, never seeing and experimentally yielding to those innately defined skills we all possess that if not nourished and abetted, hinder our God-given natural abilities?

My team mates were all grateful for this season's close, as it was time to move on. We would so miss Kelly and Joe, both as players and leaders, but mostly as liaisons with our skipper, who simply was not yet ready for College head-coaching. Bullet many times treated us as if he was still in High School, coaching his red-neck local boys against other similarly provincial teams. Well, this was "the next level"; many of us were from different backgrounds, philosophies, etc., and needed to be treated accordingly.

Maybe Mark and Blakely would fill Kelly and Joe's shoes admirably, but I somehow doubted we'd have the same results, regardless of these two players' great floor and leadership ability and potential.

Melling would be into yet another year, with his antiquated system further notched into the East Tennessee Valley College basketball program's philosophy.

"Oh well, maybe Coach will come to his senses over the summer, and things will miraculously change," something I sincerely hoped that

I would not find myself saying in exactly the same fashion after my sophomore run!

*     *     *

That spring was without a doubt the singular most glorious time of my life. Jess and I were asked to join a very unique fraternity; special in that its members very obviously traveled "ALL walks of life": thespians, jocks, scholars, nerds, Blacks, Whites, African, Asian, etc. We were a collection of sorts that would later define a direction of where this amazing country of ours was indeed headed, excepting that this was still The South, and there still were all-white frats, such as the jock one, with which we would have a sometimes healthy, sometimes not so, relationship!

Sher and I were becoming an "item" on campus, as she was frequently there on weekends, staying with T.J. and Barbie.

I had yet to meet her parents, though, and she mine, as we were both still being cautious with our love-affair.

I suspect that Sharon and I had similar high-school backgrounds with regards to her boyfriends and my girlfriends: having several, if not many; as falling in love was oh so sweet, but such a double-edged sword when one grew tired of their partner and vice-versa, or became smitten with another, too soon, too fast.

I remember Mom telling me that she was getting very weary of becoming close with some of my girlfriends, and then seeing them just "go away"; although, she ALWAYS welcomed my latest with open arms, with the hopeful attitude of "maybe finally Jesse will see that this young lady is truly the one"!

Ditto with Loretta; she would be such a blessing in making my paramours all feel quite at home, and even also in a "sisterly way," calming those around her, within the confines of our family's domain.

That spring Coach Melling brought in a 6'1" transfer sophomore guard, from Great Smoky Mountain State, to compete for my (or as he said it, "someone's") next year's slot on the team; not to replace me, mind you, but this could keep me back on the depth chart.

Jesus, did this shit ever end? I mean what the hell? I had a fairly good freshman year, and yes, we were losing one of our starting guards in Kelly, but we did still have T.J., Mark and Blakely, all seniors and extremely experienced, not to mention outstanding ballplayers.

I figured to be the 4th guard next season, freshman coming in, or not, and I was not going to sit back idly and let Melling dictate more stupidity with regards to my playing time. Plus, my intentions were focused on a starting slot by my junior year, if all went well. Somehow, though, my gut instincts told me now, and as stated earlier, that this would never be, regardless of how well I performed.

"Mouchebeau, this is Mitch Flowers, who's transferring here this spring. I want you two to play one-on-one, so I can look at him more closely," Coach intoned.

A majority of our squad was there that afternoon working out, in one of those "unofficial" sessions that the NCAA (and our school) did not sanction, but that served a "practice" purpose none-the- less.

The team all looked at Bullet like he was crazy, when he pulled Mitch and me aside, because we were scrimmaging and generally having fun, Mitch included, getting "auditioned," so to speak; but, Coach HAD to have me play him.

"Hey, I'm Jesse, you look real good out here," as I offered my hand, referring to Mitch's play so far in our pick-up games. We had been going at it very intensely.

"Nice to meet you, you're an unbelievable shooter," Mitch replied.

Both of us were being polite, but full well knew what was at stake here, and it was PRIDE, plainly and simply!

We started our one-on-one contest, "playground rules," which was: "first one to score ten, by ones, make it take it," which in lay terms meant that your opponent could actually beat you 10-0, if he kept scoring; because you kept the ball on shots made, rather than turn it over to your opponent, after a score.

I let Mitch have the ball first, and stopped his drive by stealing the ball.

Then, I proceeded to score ten in a row, interrupted only by Mitch's comment of "shit, you're quick as a cat," remarking on one particular move I made to more or less make him look silly.

I had no remorse whatsoever that game, as my reputation was on the line.

Mitch genuinely congratulated me, which let me truly know that he was a good guy, and whispered "why does Coach Melling have it in for you?"

I had no real answer for that, other to shrug my shoulders and quietly mumble "beats me!"

Coach just walked away, and after he left the arena, my team mates all, with no disrespect to Mitch, congratulated me, while welcoming him into our family; small victory for me, but in the big picture and scheme it would most likely remain a "non-event"!

Shit, I probably just accomplished more in my own personal East Valley basketball demise by completely demolishing this new, and quite good, prospect, right in front of Melling's own eyes.

T.J., grabbing my arm, just said "fuck Bullet, he'll never get it, let's get the hell out of here!"

Mitch was here to stay, at least for two years as he would be a junior, and I knew that he would most likely play in front of me next year. I found out that he was an outstanding player in high school, and that Melling had coached against him in some previous district or State tournament. Coach had actually recruited him for East Valley two years previous, with Mitch opting for said mentioned junior college in North Carolina that had a great track record for developing their teams and placing their matriculating two-year players in high profile programs.

Still, I could improve and improve, working on my game, so as to let Mitch, and any other guard on our team, know that I wasn't going anywhere, and that it would be foolish, and maybe really obvious, for Coach not to play me!

*   *   *

I called Loretta that evening, just on a whim that she needed me. It was one of those eerie and slightly psychic premonitions that were just now starting to make their presence known to yours truly.

Again, I had a disturbing feeling in the pit of my stomach, which I knew was not due to any intestinally-related cause.

"Hi love," I greeted her when she answered the phone.

"Hi babe," my beloved sibling responded, "how's life in the big South?"

She sounded stressed.

I recounted the entire afternoon's basketball drama, and to her credit, Loretta listened with interest and responded with compassion, as these "Coach Melling stories" were indeed starting to get very tiresome, for ALL of us!

"You know, sweet Jesse, you just may have to transfer to play on a regular basis," something that had crossed my mind, oh, maybe a thousand times this year.

"I'll give it another year, darling, besides, my Jess is here to stay, and I need him as much as you do!"

"Amen to that dear brother,' she replied, in her wonderful and very sultry voice.

Yes, if someone on the outside had ever listened to nearly any conversation between my sister and me, they would think that we were lovers. As stated, though, we were beyond unique, we were soul mates!

"Jesse, listen to me, and please do not interrupt," her cadence and intonation immediately grabbed my attention, "tomorrow I am going to a specialist that Doctor Samuel suggested I see; I've got a small lump in my right breast that has not gone away since discovering it three months ago. Mom and I have discussed this with Doc (Samuel), and we all feel that it is nothing, but we need to truly know. If it is something serious, then we'll take care of it immediately, and I will be fine; are you still listening to me?" she politely, yet firmly questioned.

It took a couple of seconds to respond, as I was crying quietly, so as not to piss her off with my weakness with this sort of thing.

"Yes," I barely audibly responded, "I am.....," and could not finish.

"Honey, I will be fine, I promise you, I am not going to get sick; you know me, you know what a fighter I am, and from whom I learned how to survive," referring to me as she often did, when echoing her appreciation of her big brother's life-long mission to care for his sister.

I am just now starting to catch my breath; "is this why you've lost weight?" I asked quietly.

"Maybe, Doc seems to think that it could be related; but also from the stress of my 'battle' (as she referred to her rape)."

Loretta had reduced said horrific encounter to benignly calling it her "battle". This way, her way, she treated it simply as an "incident," terribly tragic to say the least, but just as so many in our world experienced in one form or another; to be handled in much the same way as say a soldier would, having his best friend die in his arms, or maybe like a Mother losing her child to some horrible disease.

One would HAVE to recover, and get on with living, if one was to survive!

Life would continue to offer us these events, and Loretta felt that this was simply one of hers: to bear, and to recover, to continue to live, and to help someone else overcome a similar situation, so as to have "new life and hope," as she so often stated.

What a treasure my sister was! How so very lucky I was to have her in my life!

"Sweetheart," she continued, "I promise to let you know how everything turns out, and will never keep anything from you; you are my trusted hero, dear Jesse, and we will fight this, if necessary, together!"

Just then I heard a knock on my door, and I mentioned that to my sister.

"That will be Jess, honey; he already knows, as he had called just before you, and I had to tell him."

God damn, I thought to myself; when I was lamenting over Bullet's bullshit, my sister was possibly dying of cancer.

Fuck, sometimes I really let my own self down, with trivial shit. Jesus, I need to get my priorities more so in line!

"Alright babe, we'll win, you and I always win," I mustered," we're the best doubles partners ever"!

"Amen to that, dear Jesse, now go let your best friend in, and we'll talk tomorrow; I love you more than anything, sweetheart," and she truly meant every word of her proclamation!

"Goodnight darling," I responded, "YOU, are my absolute hero!"

"Yes, I am, and do not forget that" she chuckled.

What an amazing spirit!

What a perfect guardian angel I had!

What was I going to do if I ever lost her?

\*         \*         \*

Jess walked in.

We held each other in our arms, tightly, and it was Déjà vu, recalling the time of my sister's story of her rape.

Not caring whatsoever that we were two young men; and again as before, the infamous, tough, football and opera-singing powerhouse Jess Butkus and his best friend Jesse Mouchebeau cried, and cried, and cried!

# Chapter Fourteen

"Sometimes I look at you and feel so fine,
Wanting to hold your skin against mine,
I close my eyes, your image I see,
So quickly you have captured me."

Looking Through Tear Filled Eyes

# XIV

Loretta's right breast had been removed as the tumor was indeed malignant!

My sister was in unbelievably great spirits as Jess and I stood by her bedside in her room at our parent's house that late April evening.

"Alright boys, so I will get another," she whispered, and started smiling when I winked at her. I was starting to lose it but she squeezed my hand and amazingly I felt that everything was going to be alright with her.

Mom had told me that just before her operation the doctors had been visibly relieved as my spirited sister had apparently, and so eloquently, relaxed the entire staff with her matter-of-fact wisdom and humor; rarely existent in someone so young!

What a girl!

Still, my heart was broken and I could only imagine how Jess felt, as this had brought these two soul mates even closer together!

Dr. Samuel motioned to my mom to follow him into the living room, and she, in turn, nodded for me to follow her.

"Loretta is indeed a fighter," he said to no one in particular, "she's got remarkable recovery strength; still, she's got quite a few acres to plow!"

Doc often spoke in "country witticism" using time honored expressions of both the South in general and his own creations in particular.

"Her body has suffered a physical trauma to be sure," as his eyes met ours, "but what we need to watch for is post–op depression, as her mental recovery is just as important, maybe even more so."

Mom seemed to know exactly what Doc Samuel's intent was, as she immediately and obviously seemed resigned to a certain fact; something of which I was still yet unaware.

"You mean the trauma of her rape," she intoned to Doc, her eyes now clear, dark and focused, "we need to see if she really can clear her mind, rid herself of her memories of that horrible….," and here mom completely lost it.

Doc held her in his very powerful arms, as my mother sobbed and sobbed.

"She's been through so much, my little girl…" mom cried.

I felt helpless, as I too started to cry, tears streaming down my face, as I realized Loretta's rape was never going to go away; it's ugly head would still rear up at any given moment's notice, and my beloved sister would continue to suffer, through her entire life.

And, my beloved Jess would most likely have to deal with Loretta's continuous mental battles, never mind his own!

Goddamn, I wanted to go and kill Reece! I wanted him to suffer excruciating pain, and then die! I wanted to rid myself of this overwhelmingly helpless and paralyzing feeling that had so suddenly consumed me, and permanently damaged my soul mate and sibling!

Still, Reece was human and could suffer any one of many hard shots that life had a way of tossing, sometimes out of left field and oh so unexpectedly; but not cancer! You cannot grab it by its throat, cave in its ribs, and punch the ever lovin' life out of it. You had to sit there and take it, and hope for the best with your God-given abilities to internally fight this dreaded disease.

Internal strength and commitment was something that I knew Loretta possessed, but just how much could one person take?

Mom took notice of my prickly skin and wide eyes, now clear with rage, as I must have been a dead giveaway for rampage and vengeance at that precise instant.

"Jesse honey, we will get her through this, but you and I mustn't do anything stupid," she softly spoke, "and for God's sake we promised Loretta not to let your father know," referring to her tragic attack.

I started to react to this, as my own personal feelings were that dad should know, but mom had vehemently rejected saying anything to her husband, as I am sure this had to do with her very own similar occurrence. Plus, she had only seen my father truly angry a few times, and it had really scared her. She knew that his war experience left him forever scarred, and his all too powerful capacity for destruction, albeit somewhat in check for so many of their years together, might create something with which they would all be sorry.

What was unknown to mom at that time was that Loretta and my father had started to "re-build" a relationship, lost years ago in childhood, and that now had begun to repair itself, ever so gingerly, laying a future foundation for trust and strength, as only a father/daughter's union could hope to accomplish!

Loretta had clued me in on a couple of her loquacious meetings with dad; that she was actually making real progress with someone that she realized she needed in this life, and a male figure that she wanted apart from Jess and me.

I was happy for her; I always wondered how my father could not worship the very ground that his beloved daughter trod upon, and as it was turning out, my dad was "coming through" with regards to Loretta. He was actually falling in love, all over again; with the little girl he held in his oh so powerful arms, as an infant, so many, many years ago.

This made me very happy, to say the least!

Yes, you may have guessed; Loretta was indeed gathering her beloved, and gracing them, one and all, with her spirit; something that she felt all would hold dear, in their very souls, for eternity.

Loretta would let dad know of her horrific encounter, if and when she needed; she would embrace her father in ways so far unbeknownst to him, and continue to develop their own personal bond, never minding mom, and really, the rest of us. She had that capacity for connection!

I snapped out of my obvious trance, thinking all of these developing scenarios, when mom stated "Jesse honey, Mr. Samuel is getting ready to leave."

I thanked the good doctor, and his eyes and mine, once again, connected on that "father/son" plane that I was now beginning to realize had been occurring for much of my young life, on several occasions, and not just when he was stitching me up after my fight with Reece!

He left, after placing his hand upon my sister's forehead, and quietly offering his own innermost invocation.

This definitely did not go unnoticed by me, and once again Doc Samuel had recaptured my most profound respect.

Mom truly felt that Reece would "get his" someday; I on the other hand, was dedicated to exactly making that happen, in the right time and right place, with the results very possibly affecting my life, as well.

Poor Jess. He had also started to lose weight, since Loretta's diagnosis, something of which my sister had duly taken notice and was committed to reversing, as she always did seem to pull those around her into her spiritual umbrella, for whatever recovery was needed, no matter what the circumstances dictated.

Jess sauntered in, making it obvious that he needed to talk with me.

"Jesse, is she gonna make it?" tears welling up, yet again in both of our eyes.

"Of course, brother," I whispered, "she's such a fighter; makes you and me look like a couple of New York City chorus line dancers," which as also a running joke of ours as we both were very much into musicals and theater, and knew all too well of the strength and agility of our Yankee dance artists, even though at least 100% of them were more than likely gay!

"Jesse, I know this sounds unbelievable, and you're gonna think I am crazy but I want to marry your sister!"

I was not shocked in the least; did not think Jess was crazy; and, as a matter of fact, thought that I would do exactly the very same thing, under these circumstances.

My beloved Loretta and my beloved Jess; what a pair!

I could only respond with "well brother, you gotta ask her; probably be a great idea to talk with mom and dad, don't ya think?" winking and smiling at him.

He was starting to relax, ever so slightly. I was trying to imagine the stress from his point of view. I loved Loretta more than anything on God's earth, but she still was my sister; she was Jess' obvious true love and potential life companion, and I was starting to get yet another glimpse into this magnificent friend of mine's very being. Jesus, I could not have imagined a more astounding person for my sister.

Still, they were awfully young, and most of the time, even with unbelievable commitment of the hearts involved, these unions do not last. I knew mom and dad would think the same, however much they were starting to love Jess.

"Jess, let's talk later, and I take it, you've not said anything to Loretta?"

"Not a word, brother; this is something that hit me hard while I was holding her hand a few minutes ago."

"You know, Jess," I continued, "my sister is rarely concerned with herself; it's everyone around her that she loves, and you gotta be prepared for the 'let's wait until I recover, and see' speech, as she will not want you, and me, and my mom and dad to get too wrapped up in our emotions; I know her, she will react this way, if only for our own well-being."

"You're right Jesse," he resigned, "maybe I ought to wait."

"I didn't say that, my dear brother; I think she will be very impressed and incredibly happy if you ask her," and this brought the grandest smile on my friend's face.

"You think?" he responded.

Jess was visibly anxious to go be with his girlfriend, and I could read this a mile away.

"Go on back in there" I motioned, getting up, "I'm going to call Sharon; she really wants to come up here and see Loretta, and God do I miss her."

"I hear that dear brother," Jess whispered.

*　　*　　*

"Hey babe, it's me," I whispered as she answered the phone, "Loretta's doing fine and asked about you – just her style, isn't it!"

Sharon was getting used to my Loretta stories, and sometimes I questioned myself if this was too possessive of her time with me, but never once did Sher give me even a glimpse of not truly caring about my sister, and while I loved her intensely, it was an even more special kind of adoration, for that very quality. Hell, I was in love with two girls; how simply and marvelously wonderful!

Double-edged sword, though; but, hopefully I'd be one of the very few exceptions in history to survive said situation!

"Oh Jesse, I feel so sorry for Lori," she whispered.

Apparently at some point after our magnificent week together following the Christmas tournament, Sharon had bestowed this sobriquet upon Loretta; and my sister, most surprisingly, welcomed her new friend's affectation.

Loretta had repelled a variety of nicknames over the years, most staunchly shooting them down, and steadfastly remaining with her proper and given name.

I recalled her verse, of several years ago, and I heartachingly began to smile, ever so slightly:

*My name is Loretta, my dear…*
*Loretta is what I only hear…*
*Should one try to change, to something so strange…?*
*Their face I shall gladly smear!*

"Jesse, Jesse, are you okay?"

"Sorry Sher, I spaced out and was thinking of Loretta and me, laughing together, in one of our late night escapades just a couple of years ago. I so miss those days."

Sharon could hear my throat catching and again I started to get teary-eyed.

"Jesse honey, I know I've not met your parents, and under these circumstances this would be an awful time, but I so want to hold Lori's hand and say a prayer with her; does this make any sense?"

"I could drive up there and stay in a motel, so as not to get in the way," she continued.

Of course it made all the sense in the world, and I replied "I've got an idea."

"I'm going to come back up here from school again next Friday morning, so why don't I either get you at Lee, or if you go home, I could pick you up there, meet your parents, and we could be at my house that evening?"

"You would stay here with us, I am sure mom and dad would be fine with this," I continued.

"You really think so?" she countered.

"Absolutely, babe; mom has heard Loretta talk about you often, and she did actually see you the first time we played Lee. She's very much looking forward to meeting you, so see if your folks are okay with all of this, and I'll tell Loretta once I hear back from you."

We small talked a bit more, but Sharon, very astutely, was learning that I could only hang on the phone for so long, in stressful situations, without starting to mentally "check out"; a foreshadowing of things to come!

*          *          *

Jess had indeed talked with Loretta, mom and dad, and had apparently most graciously stated his unselfish and utterly respectful reasons for his proposal to her, from the very bottom of his so tender heart!

He was treated with such honor from my parents that it helped to cushion Loretta's later response to him, which was pretty much verbatim from my earlier and said "warning".

Still, Jess felt reassured from my sister's "temporary rejection," and departed for school that afternoon, football spring practice being in full swing; heart heavy, but full of hope and faith!

I left the next morning, with similar pangs in my chest and soul, and drove the several hours back to East Valley, with someone else obviously "guiding" my car, as I could not remember the actual drive.

Scary, but sometimes maybe we do have our own guardian angels, caressing us through our collective strays and full-on departures from this physical earth.

\* \* \*

I picked up Sher at Lee University the following weekend; she made it obvious that she did not want me to meet her mom and dad, and older sister Sheila, just yet.

On the rest of the way to my house, she filled me in on her parents' impending divorce, and the depressed state with which her home was currently embroiled.

Her father, an attorney, had "found" another woman, and this did not bode well for me, or for any male persona for that matter, in a household full of vengeful women.

"They'll come around," she said, holding my hand, "but now's not the time!"

"Do they know you're coming home with me, "I asked, and staying at my house, for two nights?"

"Only Sheila does, and that's for an emergency;" adding, "she gets it Jesse, she knows how much I love you, and of Lori's crisis."

We small-talked the rest of our way to my parents' house; anxious, to say the least, but hopeful in spirit.

Mom and Dad greeted Sharon as a long lost daughter, and Loretta was evidently more than happy to see her new "sister," as she most affectionately referred to many of my previous loves.

With Jess playing that weekend in the annual spring football game, I had, with Sher, Loretta's undivided attention and affection.

This was good for the soul; this was magnificent for the heart!

# Chapter Fifteen

"One day I will catch you,
As you glide through the night sky,
Holding so tightly, you won't leave me,
Don't bother to ask me why,
Just take me falling star, so very high."

The Nightrider

# XV

The New York Military Academy was as breathtakingly compelling in person as every single brochure had suggested! Being that it was the "sister – prep" school of West Point, it contained much of the regal/ martial stature as her older sibling's institution. The Hudson River flowed with magnificent royalty past this fine facility, giving everyone that came in contact with her, an ocular and scent-filled glimpse into this great country's Yankee history of said Valley!

We had just left our initial staff and counselor introduction and orientation, meeting many fine athletes from all over the country; Joe, Burton and I were all unpacking in our respective assigned sections. I was still thinking that eight weeks would be a very long time to be counseling these same kids, even though Joe, being a veteran of the previous two summers here, had said that once we got into our routines it would fly by!

Joe was here, even though he was "technically ineligible" having officially graduated college, because of his own unbelievable rapport with other counselors; in other words, keeping us all in line. I was later to discover that summer just what this meant, and was accepted here partially due to his personal recommendation to the New York Military Academy in general, and its commandant, in particular.

Plus, he had secured his first career placement with a company back in his native North Carolina, and was not due to begin until September; he was going to enjoy one last round with some of the previous counselors again working here and with whom he'd developed friendships.

This particular summer camp was unique in that its said length indicated a "dropping off" destination for many well-to-do black, Jewish and Italian kids in and around the New York City locale. Many parents looked at this event as their own particular two month getaway; even said, they and their children were very much aware of the stellar reputation and high standards that The New York Military Academy's summer program had to offer, both in its hand selected athletic counselors, and with the facility's esteemed history.

The director of the camp, and Commandant of the Academy, Jimmy Napoli, had also pulled me aside to speak of three kids in particular that would be in my section; in other words, their safety and well-being were, of course, my own responsibility as all of my other charges, but I was to pay particular attention and keep a watchful eye over them!

Eddie and Clarence Franklin, the god-mother of Soul music Aretha's very own boys, were assigned to me, and meeting them with their mom was especially meaningful, as I (and who doesn't?) greatly adored her voice and songs!

They would prove to be, throughout the summer, and with a couple of visits from Aretha to "remind them of their manners," very well-mannered, intelligent, and funny kids; simply put, we had a blast and their mom was very generous to me when we finally said our good-byes eight short weeks later.

The "third kid," previously mentioned, was quite another situation.

Mr. Napoli, in an unusually low volume for his infamous and projecting baritone voice, pulled me aside.

"Son, Joey Caruso will be arriving with his father tomorrow morning around 10am (along with all others throughout the day, as we counselors were there early to get acclimated), and if there is any one kid in particular that needs a 'big brother' here, it's him and he will need you," as he affectionately plopped his huge index finger on my chest.

"I cannot go into detail, but once you meet his dad, I suspect you will figure everything out; let's just say he's an important man in our Italian community!"

I am looking at director Napoli's granite face, with obviously a quizzical expression, as he continued; "Jesse, you'll be fine, and always come to me, if you need anything. Capite?"

"Yes sir," I replied.

"One more thing," he intoned, "Joey, due to a severe and life-threatening childhood illness of which he has mostly overcome, is a frail little boy, but with the heart of a lion; even though he has a genius IQ, his dad wants him to develop his physical skills as much as possible, but his body can only take so much and his father is well aware of this fact. So, please keep an eye on him: limit his stress, body heat, fatigue levels, etc., without being too obvious, as the little guy will want to do exactly as all of the other kids; he's got unbelievable determination!"

I was truly beginning to understand, and I looked our Commandant into his eyes and promised him everything he was asking of me.

"Yes sir!" I replied, once again.

"I know son, that is exactly why I chose you for his counselor," he added.

I had also found out later from Joe, that Coach Melling had also put his "2 cents" into my resume to director Napoli; emphasizing not so much my basketball prowess, as Coach would never truly abide by the way I played ball, but by extolling my "stand-up to the plate" virtues and promising the Commandant that I would not hesitate for a second to "rescue" any one of my kids, in a crisis, even filling him in on my "Christmas escapades" with Reece Davis, and some of my minor skirmishes with teammates in practice!

Apparently Coach had said exactly what Jimmy Napoli (and Joey Caruso's dad) needed to hear! How interesting, especially coming from my college coach nemesis? I could never figure him out, other than the fact that maybe, just maybe, there was more to life than basketball, and Coach possibly held a special place in his heart for me; just not on the court!

Later that afternoon, several of us played a very intense and spirited full-court game in the gym. This was an all-sports camp, featuring some of the nation's very best lacrosse, baseball, football, tennis and swimming talent our Division I, II and III schools had to offer, and most proved to be fantastic guys. Basketball was the "theme" choice background of our camp counselors, but several of these other sport athletes were phenomenal roundball players, as well.

Yes, the screening process was very particular, and rarely did someone "slip through the cracks," with regard to character!

Later that evening, many of us went to a local neighborhood bar for sandwiches and beer. While we had to behave ourselves, Jimmy Napoli knew we were young men with wants and desires and actually was quite liberal with our privileges. He just did not want us to fuck-up; and for added measure (another big lesson in life here for yours truly), was well connected with the local constables, who always were keeping a benevolent and watchful eye on us all!

I also that evening made a new good friend of Michael Pisano, an unbelievably gifted all-American junior forward from the New England Division I powerhouse Stoneybrook University. He had commented to me, over a beer, of how much he admired my shooting and ball-handling skills (keeping in mind that he was the leading scorer in his college division, which was made very apparent previously in our game), and actually had earlier called his coach to possibly recruit me for Stoneybrook!

Michael was the only one of us talented enough to later go on and play pro ball; something that was very evident that summer when we would scrimmage with various players from the NBA champion New York Knicks; he would match well with their speed, power and technique, and I would get my "education," with this very high caliber of the professional game!

\*     \*     \*

I called Loretta and Sharon that evening, whispering on yet another institutional hallway pay phone. Both of my girls seemed in fairly good spirits, but I obviously was feeling a major withdrawal from my loves, with each reassuring me that these eight weeks would fly by.

I was not so convinced; still, I knew this was a great opportunity for me, and the summer would prove this exactly to be, several times over!

I just wanted to be with my paramour and my sister, I was more in love with them at that moment, than even the day before; plus, relationships at our age tended to "stray" with separation. Even though I felt that Sher was totally committed to me, I was well aware of how instantaneous love's "thunderbolt" could be; exacting upon its victims Cupid's most lethal arrow!

I was also beginning to feel severe and intense premonitions with regards to Loretta; anxiety so deep that every once in awhile would trigger the worst of migraine headaches.

I told not a soul, not even my beloved sister, as we shared everything; this was my battle, and no one else's.

Later in life, a much decorated Vietnam War veteran and Doctor of Psychology was to most profoundly say to me: "Jesse, battle is easy, love is hard!"

I would find this to be so accurate, throughout my life, by of course the much ballyhooed "hard way!"

*     *     *

At precisely 10am the next morning, everything director Napoli had earlier discussed with me came to light.

Little Joey Caruso arrived in a small caravan of black stretch limousines, three of them to be accurate, with an entourage of not only his father, but eight of the toughest looking bodyguards one could imagine; every single one of them obviously Italian!

Yes, little Joey Caruso was the only son of Giovanni Caruso, the God-father of one of the New York Mafia's five families.

Can you believe this shit? Me, Jesse Mouchebeau, having the responsibility of watching Don Caruso's only child. Jesus Christ, I was nervous that sunny summer morning.

Mr. Caruso was a very calm and seemingly nice man, and looking into his eyes one could just guess the intelligence that lay there. He put his arms around me and suggested, "let's walk a little while, son."

We strolled around the parade grounds, small-talking about life in general; asking me about my family, girlfriend, etc., and me filling him in on Loretta's all too serious battle with cancer.

Not surprisingly, Don Caruso already knew much of this, and

as genteel as humanly possible, offered his unsolicited help, if ever needed.

I thought about mentioning Reece Davis, but my better judgment allayed that reflection; I simply did not want to come home and find out that he had "disappeared"; THAT was my job!

"Jesse, I am trusting you with my son, this summer. Joey has had a tough go of it, but the little guy is fearless, and that makes me so proud of him, how he has battled against all odds, much like your very own sister! His mother worries too much, and I have to listen to her, but I do know that a boy needs to trip, fall, hurt himself, and get right back up and go again. You know of what I am talking about. I know of your reputation as a young man that will take care of those he loves, that will 'go to war' for those he loves, and this willful honor is absolutely the quality in a person that I most admire, save nothing else, in this entire world!"

I listened acutely, feeling his words permeate my entire body, and surprisingly I felt very comfortable with this most formidable man. I somehow knew, in my heart and soul, that Don Caruso felt truly good about his only child's "big brother" that summer.

"Mr. Caruso, I understand, and you can absolutely count on me," not small words for an 18 year old to say to a New York Mafia Chief!

Don Caruso patently was convinced because he then, and being raised with European cultural mores this did not phase me in the least, kissed me on both of my cheeks, and I could swear there were tears in his eyes.

"Young Jesse, you have made an ally of me, forever," and added, "let's go meet your little brother."

Heavy words for anyone of any age!

We then went to meet and have lunch with little Joey, and this entire Mafioso contingent, with Commandant Napoli's blessing.

Can you imagine the other counselors thought processes, witnessing this event? Evidently I was already making my impression on this new group of acquaintances.

Michael Pisano, pulled me aside, whispering "go get 'em kid, I know Mr. Caruso well, he's a good man."

Jesus, my new friend was "connected," as well. Hell, he was raised in a New Jersey suburb of New York City, and was a high school basketball sensation, so maybe this did make sense, in some wacky way. Plus, the Don had, most astutely arranged for Michael to watch my back.

How deliciously diabolical?

Joey and I hit it off very well; he was an extremely funny, sensitive, and very prescient young man. Maybe my never having a younger male sibling had something to do with this effect, but I dare say that my love for my sister had more than anything to do with my noble skills in this department.

Each of Mr. Caruso's "friends," in turn, bade me farewell; each benignly punching me in the chest and stating their individual appreciations.

The Don just winked me a goodbye.

Christ was life amazing?

Life was heartbreaking!

Life was to appreciate and treasure!

After meeting the rest of my section kids, and talking until the wee hours of the morning, I quietly prayed to God for Loretta's recovery, saturating my pillowcase with my tears!

# Chapter Sixteen

"As you break unto the sands,
And sift through my hands,
I can feel your presence in this ocean"

The Gypsy Queen

# XVI

L oretta sat up, as I quietly stepped to her bedside that late August evening; the sun's departing rays filtering through her bedroom draperies as golden as my sister's countenance.

I was mildly shocked by her apparent weight loss, but she still looked divine, and as fearless as the day I first truly realized the awesome depth of my then very young sister!

She smiled at me as I pulled up and straddled her pink padded bench, covered with favorite Disney characters, that she had kept since childhood; a totem of my sister's and not to be taken lightly, and placed my head in her arms, caressing her slim waist for a good five minutes.

No one said a thing; I felt her warmth, and she mine. This particular moment I will cherish the rest of my entire life as looking back, I can plainly see that something miraculous occurred that evening.

Whether or not one believes in extra sensory perception, spiritual connection, or even the "direct current" from God, does not even matter to me. I know that this happened and felt an energy flow from my soul mate into my very being; something I had really never experienced, and noticing all too lucidly its pure and serene calming effect.

"Hello beautiful," I softly said, likely with the very most affection I had delivered to date, to anyone ever.

"Hello back, my hero," she cooed, "tell me all about this amazing summer you had up there," she added. "I want to hear every single thing that happened."

Even though we had talked once a week while I was gone, we had promised each other to share everything in detail once we were again reunited, with no distractions.

She did not mention Jess, and I did not Sher. This was not the time and place for our other passions, this was our time; much like when we were very young kids whispering and giggling to each other into the wee hours of the night and early morning so as our dad would not yell at us with his patented "go to sleep, goddammitt, I've got to work in the morning!"

"You first," I said to her; "tell me how you feel, you getting surgery any time soon?"

"Right now, no babe; I've seen enough of hospitals for quite awhile and Doc Samuel wants me to gain some weight before I doing anything so drastic."

This did not surprise me, for my sister, as beautiful as she always would be, she was never vain, and if her left breast seemed a bit lopsided from her right, well that was just too fucking bad for anyone that even thought something was amiss!

"I feel tired sometimes, dear Jesse," Loretta continued, "but I know I've got to eat and keep up with my daily running," with which she was religious.

My sister was the singular most determined and focused person I had ever known! I can only imagine how difficult it was for her to maintain the several miles a day she raced throughout the countryside of our youth. It had been a little more than four months since her mastectomy, and she was out there, in her self-imposed and all too rigorous regime, of course, sooner than the six weeks her physicians had suggested.

Since her high school graduation, Loretta had put aside any ideas of college, at least temporarily, as she somehow knew that wasn't necessary at this point in time. She would tell me "Jesse, I've got matters of consequence much greater than Philosophy 101, or Introduction to Western Civilization!"

Thinking back, she knew, even then! Every single time in my life that my thoughts return to that evening, I get so emotional that I truly need to be alone. These are good thoughts, however; these are my "go to for self-preservation forays" with which I would continuously place myself within said grasp, whenever I needed her, especially after she had departed this dear earth!

Apparently, my sister had set the course for her remaining life; a mission of preparation for all of us that she so dearly loved and that she was going to leave. As said, she knew clearly, and was not afraid. God, if I had had the same thoughts as her that evening, I simply could not have maintained.

Sometimes I thought of myself as so fucking weak, that it truly pissed me off. Those of us that have known so dramatic an event should have the intelligence and fortitude to shake off the minor bullshit; but alas, we are human, no? We easily forget the pain of others and focus on ourselves to the point of triviality many times.

She was truly my guardian angel, and with regards to all of the wonderful things I would see and do, and all of the amazing events that would directly affect me, she would stay solidly imbedded as the most important, with her countenance and vision etched upon my heart and soul!

I knew that she and Jess were starting to ever so slightly fade in the amorous aspect of their relationship, through her various hints during our summer phone chats, but they still talked every day, and their love for each other quite apparent.

Of course her physical condition had much to do with this, but quite possibly these two extraordinary young souls were already maturing into the next phase of existence with each other, much like many serious relationships do post first passions, and which usually was reserved for couples much older; but again, these two were beyond special.

"Okay big brother, tell me the 'tale of my Knight's New York adventure,' everything. I want to close my eyes and travel with you for as long as it takes."

I then kicked off my tennies, and slid onto her bed, tucking her head upon my shoulder, and recounted the events of that most amazing summer.

*               *               *

*I told her all about Mr. Caruso, and his son Joey. How we became fast friends, and how the "little lion," my sobriquet affectionately bestowed upon him when we said our good-byes, had transformed his frail body into something to behold; his father placing my head in his hands that last day and saying to me "Jesse, you honor my name and family, as I do yours!" His bodyguards again, one by one, all looking me directly into my eyes, giving me their individual modes of esteem, and offers of grace and support, if ever needed. They were all well aware of the extra hours I'd spent with their Joey, and this had not gone unnoticed. Don Giovanni had made it clear to me, non-withstanding his most generous "envelope," that if I, or my family, ever needed help, to let him know. I told Loretta that I absolutely believed him, and his men!*

"Am I boring my beloved girl?" I asked sarcastically, knowing that my story seemed too fantastic to be true.

"God no," she replied, "this is amazing, not even YOU could make this up!" she giggled, making me feel even better than before.

*I continued, with my sister, of how I had befriended the resident boxing coach of the New York Military Academy; that all counselors had a two hour break each day, mine being 1-3pm, and how I spent the entire eight weeks training with a former middle-weight champion! God, I had learned so much from this magnificent warrior. Coach DiSorrelo had schooled me in the sweet science's methods of those that had fought during boxing's "golden years"; how these fighters were of a special breed, and not to be taken lightly. I told Loretta how much I had improved in the first month, and of how I had asked coach "Di" to escalate his intensity with me in our daily sparring sessions; of how he had warned me that I was not ready for his "real" efforts, and of how I was too full of myself to listen. Yes, coach Di had literally knocked me out with a left hook body shot to my liver, which maybe the most painful of all punches in this glorious sport. Of course, I recovered and apologized profusely to him for my immaturity, and continued on with an invaluable education to be treasured my entire life. I did at times show great defensive and countering skills, and even nailing coach DiSorrelo with very good combinations, sometimes getting a rise in his anger, but to his good credit, he always smiled and acknowledged my advancement. I told my sister that when we said our goodbyes, Coach Di had promised me an open invitation to train with him at any time, and of how he was going to miss my intelligence and will to fight. He could not have complimented me any more perfectly.*

Loretta was, by now, entranced, and had turned sideways to face me; "tell me about Michael," referring to my closest friend of that summer camp's adventure.

I easily learned more about the game of basketball from this one extraordinary player and person, than any one coach I'd ever had; including my wonderful high school mentor!

Michael Pisano was simply fabulous. His intelligence was his greatest asset, and I am talking of a competitor of the very highest caliber. His shooting skills were legendary, as said; his defense good enough, but his court vision and perception were "off the charts". This is what made him an all-American as a sophomore; this is what turned him into a professional player.

*I looked into Loretta's eyes, smiled and told her of how Michael Pisano and I hung out every evening in the gym. After 8pm, all of us were released from our duties, having assistant counselors (aspiring high school athletes) to watch our kids and get them to sleep; all we had to do was a 10pm final check in our sections and we were free to go out. Mikey (his affectation from his Italian youth) and I would often get in a solid 90 minutes of one-on-one, shooting drills, defensive work, and if others joined in, several furious full court games as well, which kept us all in excellent condition. I continued to my sister of how many fabulous ball players there were, and of how this was THE BEST way to truly improve. Michael was 6'6", and very, very quick, but I could actually "hang" with him, to his immense delight, and I told Loretta of how much he wanted me to transfer to his school that very summer; of how his coach would do all of the paperwork necessary for a "hardship" reason, so I would not have to sit out one entire year. Still, I continued to her, Burton was always there to remind me of East Tennessee Valley and of how I would be starting my junior year, notwithstanding our sometimes ridiculous coach, and how he wanted and needed me on our team. I told her about the annual camp counselor game, which by now had grown into a provincial event of such stature, that it was always sold out, filling the New York Military Academy's rather large gym to capacity and beyond. All of the local papers, and even a reporter or two from New York City's premier sports pages were on hand to cover this festivity; and that her own brother was favorably mentioned in several, along with Michael Pisano, as well as a several other ball players. Michael and I would also, once a week, go head to head with various New York Knicks players that would drop by and test their skills against us mere mortal college talent. God, the pro game was so far elevated from the college game that it wasn't even funny. Mostly it was the sheer physical power of these remarkable athletes that kicked our collective asses. Our speed and skill were almost on a par, but the pure strength and brutality of the pro game was what impressed me, by a great measure! I finished my "Michael" tale, telling her of how he had taken me home one Saturday to meet his family, especially his mom, and of how I had gotten a glimpse of the "real Italian way"; something most definitely to be treasured!*

"Had enough, or can I wrap this up?" I whispered to my best friend. "There were a couple of weird and tragic events, and I did not necessarily want to upset you, but I figured that you would give me shit if I thought, for even a second, that my beloved sister was incapable of the truth."

"Jesse darling," she answered, "I have cancer, and will beat it, but not by those I love 'tip-toe-ing' around my feelings; you know this, you know me. Promise me you will never do this," she added with a tear in her eye."

Looking into the windows of my sister's soul I said, with a matching tear in mine, "on my soul, on our souls, word to God!"

Her returned smile caressed my very heart, massaging my innermost feelings with such tenderness, a genesis and confirmation of only life's greatest friendships!

*I finished my story with Loretta snuggled even closer, alert but with her eyes shut. I told her of how Joe Smith had to deal with a very tough and unruly counselor that had gotten "into his ass"; of how he had later gone to see this guy, concealed pistol by his side and later pointed at his head, and had said in no uncertain terms to him that either he leave camp that very moment or by God he would be "mother-fucking dead." The counselor left and no one ever knew why, save for Burton and me, not even Jimmy Napoli. Damn, Joe was something else, remembering how he had gotten us all off from our now infamous homecoming party's transgressions! I ended with the events of one of our kids' father, a well known jazz trumpet player, being murdered in the City; of how sorry we all felt for this poor little boy who would never see his daddy again; and, when his aunt came to get him, how every single one of us lined up and down the Academy drive, somberly cheering for our little mate, all of us crying our eyes out.*

Loretta was ever so quietly sniffling, but it was one of those good cries, those that cleanse the soul.

She caressed me and kissed me on my forehead and said to me: "Jesse, you will for all of eternity, be my greatest love, and I thank God for you every single day!"

I could not speak, and slept with my sister, once again united as the children we once were.

# Chapter Seventeen

"Your thoughts, taking me,
Is love just a tragedy,
Looking out, for the one,
Finding out she has come and gone..."

My Love, Your Love

# XVII

I was extremely anxious to see my girlfriend as it had been nearly ten incredibly long weeks since Sher and I had laid eyes on one another, much less anything else! The summer position with her city's parks and recreation department and my journey to the "other side of the earth" both prevented us from getting even a day together, and romantic letters, while very nice, just do not cut it!

This was going to be interesting and quite possibly disastrous, as while I had been gone, her father had moved into an apartment, ostensibly to accelerate her parents' impending divorce. Even though Sharon, Sheila and their mom all knew this was coming, it seemed that the estrogen induced stress levels in their household had risen so high that it was hazardous for any male to be around, including Sheila's boyfriend and now fiancé Chip.

I guess this is assumed to be normal, under these conditions, but that did not help my insecurity in the least! My only hopes, as made sense to me, were: 1) Sher was obviously in love with me, and had professed so to both her mom and sister; 2) she had made it very clear of

Loretta's life-threatening disease and of our relationship that obviously went far beyond a normal brother and sister's; 3) Sheila had gone to bat for Sharon, informing their mom that I was "one of the good guys," which was yet another dichotomy in that their father used to be "one of the good guys," as well.

I could only wish for the best, but truthfully, I was more concerned if our relationship had stood this recent test of time.

I had behaved in New York, another "first" for me, but really it was not hard; I would close my eyes and remember that game with Lee University, when I first was struck by her simplistic yet awesome beauty, and those icy blue, yet sometimes sea green eyes that would just melt your soul. God was she gorgeous and I started to greatly anticipate kissing her, caressing her and yes, sleeping with her.

Jesus, I was a young and passionate college basketball point guard, about to begin his sophomore year, dating a gorgeous cheerleader from a rival conference school; how dramatic, yet how normal, could this possibly be? Were not some romance novels written thusly so?

I pulled up to her house, a very charming abode, situated in the heart of River City, a glorious southern town cradled and tucked amidst God's hand-carved Blue Ridge Mountains and the churning Roanoke river.

"Wow," I am thinking to myself, "I could be happy here," caveat though, only with Sher, as my city instincts and love, as well as my infatuation with our nation's coastlines and beach municipalities, all too often precluded me from paying close attention to so many of our Lord's presentations of these rural and awe-inspiring picturesque gifts.

My adrenaline is rising and I am now very nervous, as my first impressions literally never let me down; and lately it appeared as if my instincts were somehow becoming faithfully sharper, almost to the point of being ridiculous.

She walks out, green sundress (here I fucking go again) accentuating her very deep tan, hair cropped even shorter than before, and that smile; well, you can bet I just about melted.

Her reaction to me, and mine to her, immediately alleviated all of my doubts and fears. I had forgotten the fact that while I had been in camp all summer, I had conditioned myself, even beyond my normal stature, into something resembling those more notable great light and middleweight physiques, with much credit due to my boxing coach DiSorrelo's exhausting regime; and, presented just as bronze a summer picture, just as fresh a countenance to Sharon, as she to me.

We kissed just long enough to once again reaffirm our young love, and ended just in time to greet her mother and sister.

I was immediately struck by the genetic beauty of this family's women! Mrs. McGee's red hair was overwhelming in its sheer intensity, and her eyes were the direct conduit to her daughter Sharon's, maybe even more so on the green side, looking not a day over thirty, even though I had been told forty-five, and only so by swearing on my oath under the possibility of a most severe penalty!

Sheila was quite possibly the most stunning of all. Her hair's length even more abbreviated than Sher's, with an auburn richness that rivaled our most ravishing models and movie starlets. Her eyes obviously came from her father's side, being so dark brown as to appear black, absorbing as opposed to reflecting any surrounding light.

Holy shit, were these girls something else! Still, I could not help feel something amiss, deep within the recesses of my sometimes much too analytical mind, and furthermore, I was thinking of what Mr. McGee's paramour must be like, walking out of this seemingly Utopian household, all the while knowing full well that there were always "three sides to every story".

I dismissed all thoughts instantly, as I needed to relax and be at peace, even temporarily, as leaving Loretta back home to return to my East Valley sophomore year completely ripped out my heart, even though I would be coming home that very first weekend after classes had begun.

My sister's pangs of separation were also evidently heightened due to Jess' current absence from her due to his summer football practice which had started a full month ago, and unless Loretta came to see him play, and was well enough to make this journey, there was simply no break in the East Tennessee Valley schedule until the middle of October. I felt very sorry for both of them, and promised my sister an in-depth synopsis of our school's first week including: 1) the football Hornet's chances in general, and Jess' stature in particular (as the first two games were "away" ones, I would not see him play in a real contest for several weeks); 2) Coach Melling's reaction to my playing in our unofficial practices and scrimmages; and, 3) my detailed description of the McGee family, and my on-going love affair with Sharon.

"Jesse honey, are you alright?" Sher whispered, nudging and waking me from my momentary lapse of consciousness, immediately bringing back into focus.

She had noticed, during our recent phone conversations, of this escalating habit of mine, and had fully given me my space and forgiveness, knowing of my internal crisis with Loretta's health issues.

"Yes Sher, just 'went away' for awhile; sorry."

Mrs. McGee added, "Well, it sure is nice to meet you Jesse, after all we've heard, Sharon has talked quite a lot of you."

"Yes, she most certainly has," added Sheila, in seemingly more of a sexy tone than I was prepared for. I dismissed this though, due to my personal acknowledgement of my own mental state as of late.

"Let's get in out of this unbearable August sun; I've made some fresh lemonade, and I am sure our Jesse is thirsty," Sher's mom offered.

"Our Jesse," I thought to myself. What a nice thing to say! I smiled in response, capturing Mrs. McGee's attention, and I could swear, Sheila's momentary affection.

"I am really losing my fucking mind," further thinking to myself.

Sher, once again, rescuing me; dispelling my wacky reflections by grabbing my waist from behind, and kissing me, very slyly, on the back of my neck.

God, was that ever needed! Sometimes the simplest of all loving gestures are the most profound, and when couples discover these, administered thusly, they can heighten, even more so, an already exploding sensual awareness of each other.

How awesome a concept, yet how often ignored a principle!

We all sat at their kitchen table talking about the various things going on in our respective lives.

Sheila was a senior, majoring in education at Bridgetowne, a small college nearby. She and her fiancé Chip had met there her freshman and his senior year. Chip was now in his last year of law school (also somewhat local) and they planned on getting married after Sheila's impending graduation, next spring. After their honeymoon, Chip would take his law boards next summer and begin his practice here in town; Sheila would very likely get a job teaching one of the elementary grades, with both living "happily ever-after," or so was the grand scheme.

Sher had confided in me her distrust of Chip, something she could not exactly put her finger upon, but knew that Sheila was a force to be reckoned with, and could easily handle herself. I was also seeing signs of this, as I oh so briefly caught Sheila looking at me, by way of reflection in the mirror next to their back door, with what I thought was a most inviting of stares, all "under the radar" mind you.

"Jesus," I thought to myself, "watch your ass, young Jesse."

Sheila was a complex young lady; obviously gorgeous and smart, but there was a diabolical and dramatic nature to her, as many attractive women have, and I did not wish to get caught in her cross-hairs, even for a second. Many times history has shown this to be absolutely lethal for young and inexperienced men, of which I most definitely was still a charter member. Still, she proved to be extremely charming (this trait very evident in all the McGee girls, including the mother), and indeed captured my attention.

"How's Loretta, Jesse?" Sheila offered, knowing that my sister's welfare was literally eating me alive.

Sharon had informed me that the three of them had sat down the previous evening, at her request, to ostensibly discuss withholding their tongues around me regarding their father's recent collapses in morality, mainly to ensure a little peace and quiet while I was visiting. Their "talk" had also migrated to Loretta's current and dire health condition, and past traumatic events, and it was then that Sher had openly given her version of me and my sister's most profound of relationships, even detailing the now infamous fight with Reece Davis.

Seemingly, Mrs. McGee and Sheila were both touched, and sadly so, by said events, and promised this younger sibling their graciousness and respect. Sharon had confided that this had apparently captured both their hearts.

"Loretta says she feels well," I replied to Sheila, "but it seems that she is unusually tired at times and is ever so slightly losing weight, which truly scares me."

I continued with describing her indomitable spirit to these women, information they had previously received from Sharon, but not in those telling words of a brother who absolutely worshipped his remarkable sister, and had the real life wisdom of many years of acute involvement.

Mrs. McGee offered that she would say a prayer for Loretta, as did Sheila, and I have to say that this touched me to the point of catching my throat.

I thanked all three of these girls for their real concern and spirituality, and we moved onto lighter moments and current events, quite possibly to alleviate each of our own internal and conflicting dilemmas.

I was to be there for several days, and could not help my thoughts from drifting to if and when Sharon and I would have some real alone time together.

Young men are nearly all singularly and collectively cursed by God with respect to the tortures we bear when involved in a sexual relationship. The mindset, intelligence and stellar intuitive traits of those young women we adore many times is simply too much to handle, no matter how smart we think we are. Fatalities often occur my friends, when we, innocuously or not, give ourselves too much credit, no matter what the circumstance.

I recalled a line from one of my assistant coaches during the first weeks of practice last year, when he uttered those words that would briefly scar then enlighten me for many years to come: "if I could only buy Jesse for what he's worth, and sell him for what he thinks he's worth!"

Harsh words? Not really! This coach, who also had the experience, ability and accolades to validate anything he offered, was just motivating a young and brash athlete. I knew that coach Houston genuinely liked me, as my game reminded him somewhat of his, but I still had too high an opinion of myself then and he directly wanted to catch me before it was obviously too late.

"Let's make reservations tonight at the Magnolia Tree," Mrs. McGee offered, "I do not feel like cooking, and we can put it on Mr. McGee's tab," she not so cryptically offered.

"Mom, let's not talk about dad, please," Sharon requested, "you promised."

"You're right, sweetheart," she replied, "still, we should, and *can* (winking most wickedly at me) really enjoy ourselves and celebrate Jesse's arrival."

God these girls were too much!

Sheila then added that Chip could also be available, as his apartment was only an hour away; convenient to his law school, and easily accessed by his fiancé, without the scrutiny of either set of parents.

Growing up in the next county, he had "fortuitously" (his expression) picked the undergraduate school as Sheila eventually would, and following his matriculation remaining in said county each of his graduate period's summers, interning with a local law practice. Together, he and Sheila had decided to live their lives in the same provincial atmosphere of their youth, with Sheila winning out in the selection process with her beloved River City.

"Absolutely, darling, call him immediately," Mrs. McGee requested.

I was struck by the intimate affection these three women afforded each other, and on a very constant basis. Obviously they had always been close, but now, even more so. I assumed that I would meet Sher's dad at some point, but this most certainly had not been discussed. Still, it was very unsettling to witness said father's "non-existence," even if temporarily so.

Moms with their sons, and fathers with their daughters, have for time immemorial established those bonds of trust, faith and hope with their offspring's opposite sex relationships. What I was witnessing was potentially a serious breech in said reliance, and many of us could very well suffer future consequences if these transgressions were not resolved in some way or another.

My thoughts once again skirted to the recent development of Loretta and our dad's connection. Since her surgery, something had struck a chord deep within my father's soul, something remarkably and spiritually profound. His affections for his daughter were most rapidly developing and growing, completely impressing and gladdening my mother, albeit inserting an ever so slight hint of jealousy within her! Still, mom was astute, and accepting this new relationship was not even questioned.

Loretta had mentioned to me of this genesis in their existence, and the more that I thought about it, the more it made me smile. Truthfully, I knew she would need each and everyone of us; we were in her fight for survival as a family, Jess included.

Chip arrived a short time later and after our introduction and small talk, we all piled into his Cadillac, with Mrs. McGee riding up front, and Sheila, Sher and me occupying the backseat.

Chip was an extremely good-looking guy; six plus feet in height, maybe 190 pounds, and one-time high school football star, also playing two years in college. He was now an avid golfer and tennis player, still presenting a very formidable athletic image.

I sensed the same veiled discomfort as Sharon had previously mentioned to me; almost an underlying "being on guard" feeling, and did not discount this, filing my intuitions away for future recall, if necessary.

Chip's physical presentation was also apparently appreciated by Sheila's and Sharon's local friends, as simply walking into the Magnolia Tree, on such a popular evening, caused a minor ruckus with a few of them, each making it a point to come by our table later, just to say hello.

I did notice Chip's revolving attention to each girl during the course of the evening, and picked up on the fact that this guy was most likely a real player with the opposite sex, witnessing his obvious experience and demeanor; and, not discounting Sharon and Sheila's very own "moth to flames" bearing on the young men in this town.

"Christ, this is unreal," again listening closely to my inner voice; "powerful family, indeed!"

Dinner was excellent, and Mrs. McGee's earlier offer of her estranged husband's generosity proved to be the case, which was appreciated by all.

During the evening I had found Sher's mom to be extremely eloquent, and with a couple of glasses of wine relaxing her even more so, very funny. Chip had also ordered himself a couple of cocktails during the course of dinner, and I noticed Sheila's ever so slight displeasure with this as Sher and I were too young to legally imbibe.

I also could not help but observe Chip's general reluctance in noticing his fiancé's signals to him, something that I sensed might later ruin this relationship. Still, one could always hope for the best, as numerous scenarios historically had survived much worse.

Was there a pattern here, with each of these women seeking out their father's image in their mates, only to be later disappointed?

I surely hoped not, as I felt far removed from this type of behavior, and did not think that Sharon or even Sheila, being as intelligent and confident as they were, would suffer too long said transgressions.

Mom McGee gently, yet firmly, offered to drive home, as she too noticed Chip's alcohol intake, and to Chip's credit he agreed most readily, initiating a very loving kiss from his adoring girlfriend.

He was a smart young man, and would most likely become a successful attorney. He also knew that Sheila and Sharon were very independent souls, as their mother, and just might be dangerous to truly cross.

"Chip, please spend the night, you and Jesse can share the guestroom," Mrs. McGee stated, after arriving home.

I am immediately thinking my plans to sneak Sharon into my room were obliterated instantaneously, and caught Sher's disappointing eye contact with me.

"Thanks, mom," he replied, with Sheila again kissing him affectionately.

My thoughts are now evolving, and I am wondering if somehow the four of us can collaborate and somehow concoct a clever plan to switch roommates for the evening, or at least find some time in the wee hours of early morning for our respective trysts?

Alas, I underestimated Mrs. McGee, but not in the likely obvious manner.

"Girls, I am going to bed; I've got a big day tomorrow, so please show our young gentlemen their room, and I will see you in the morning," she stated.

Was this possible? Was this beautiful woman, with goddesses for daughters, feeling all of our collective pheromones?

"Goodnight mom,' both girls answered together.

"Goodnight Mrs. McGee,' both Chip and I echoed.

Goddam, was I a happy camper!

Sher later told me, whilst wrapped together in adoring embrace, that this had been normal for Chip and Sheila for quite some time there, but was very surprised at her own fortunate turn of events. She also furthered that her mom, being a very passionate and young woman ("no shit" I tell myself), was trying, best as she knew, to ease the impending pain of the apparently unavoidable and forthcoming divorce.

"Sher, I love you so," whispering in her ear, "God did I miss you," I added.

"Me too, Jesse, me too," she cooed.

My eyes are wet with tears, and sensing why, she most lovingly offered: "Loretta will survive this, my darling; we've got to have hope."

Holding onto my most precious friend, I allowed myself another half hour of caressing, and quietly slipped back into Chip's and my quest room.

With Sheila having left awhile earlier, and Chip fast asleep, I knelt in prayer for my soul mate and sister offering my own hopefully telepathic goodnight to her.

*　　*　　*

"Hey babe," I whispered to Loretta the very next morning, using the phone in the McGee den.

"Hey yourself," she answered back.

I am quiet for a few moments and then hear "well Jesse, how are the McGee girls accepting my most beloved champion's presence; I am sure they've got to be very impressed with you!"

"Yes, I guess so, although I have to tell you that it is a bit weird, with everything going on, you know."

Loretta was aware of the impending divorce of Mr. and Mrs. McGee; still though, she was very curious as to how I would be made to feel amongst all of the women there, and she was truly concerned for Sharon's well-being, as they had talked several times over the summer.

"That's to be expected, Jesse; all of a sudden these girls' lives are being disrupted and that's got to be incredibly painful for anyone!"

My thoughts were drifting again as to how Mr. McGee could find someone else as lovely as his soon to be former wife; and the daughters, wow, how could anyone move away from them?

Later in life I was to learn a very hard lesson; one that would almost destroy me with this very same scenario. When we are young and naïve, everything must end in "fairy-tale fashion"; Disney movies tell us so when we are children, our teenage romance novels describe in detail of how amazing true love can be, and later there are always the inevitable "grown-up" films we gravitate towards depicting storied relationships winning against all odds.

"I know babe," I answered, "they are actually doing quite well, and Sheila and Mrs. McGee are just a beautiful as Sher, no kidding, I was floored!"

I can hear my sister smiling and taking in her brother's all too familiar infatuation with the female sex in general, and now these girls in particular.

"You behave now dear brother," she responded, "if Mrs. McGee and Sheila are as smart as Sharon, and I suspect so, they've most likely already figured you out, and have their antennae on alert," she finished, chuckling deep within in her so sexy voice.

"We're all fine, sis; Sher wants to talk with you after we finish, and her mom and sister both are praying for your recovery."

"Please give them my thanks, and I will tell Sher myself after we finish," she answered.

We talked for another five minutes or so, and then Loretta caught me with "Jesse, before you hand the phone to Sher, I've got to read you this letter I found on my nightstand this morning; it's from dad."

Once again alarms are started to toll in my head as I was supremely "gun-shy" by now, with any new tidings, and sensing my apprehension with this, and of course yet another beautifully telepathic example of my beloved sister's incredible mind, Loretta quickly added "it's just wonderful, babe, you will love it!"

Now, I am imagining her smiling; that stunning countenance of hers radiating from within to without, which was legendary in my storied sister's effect on all men, young and older!

"Tell me sis," pausing momentarily, and then adding "I can tell you're happy, and you have no idea of how much that means to me."

"Of course I do, dear Jesse, remember with whom you've shared nearly your entire life!"

Truth; what a powerful entity!

She then read one of those singular and most magnificent bodies of prose, with which I was ever to experience. This, I would carry in my heart for my entire life:

*My dearest daughter,*

*It was just eighteen years ago, that I held this wonderful and sweet smelling little bundle in my arms; a most precious little girl that opened up the kind of heart-aching yet most elegant love that daughters forever have been credited with giving their fathers, and took me to a place far different from even your beautiful brother Jesse.*

*I could not have been overwhelmed any more so, as you were clearly returning anyone's stares right back to them; almost as if you were taking it all in and sizing everyone up, right from the start. Later, sweetheart, we all found this to be absolutely true, did we not?*

*You had jaundice, and to battle the yellow pigmentation of your skin, you were placed in an incubator for six days, only leaving it to get fed by your mother. Every night I slept right next to your "little home" in the baby ward, and would watch you sleep, in your little diapers fashioned out of surgical masks.*

*God you were just gorgeous, and I fell in love so truly and deeply that when the good nurses needed to prick your little heels for blood samples, your crying would end long before mine.*

*Well, of course we all survived that, but that was when you captured my heart forever, and to this day I can clearly see that little newborn miracle jumping headfirst into all of our lives, announcing to the world, "here I am!"*

*You were such a difficult little baby, but in a good way, expressing your restlessness and outgoing personality, even then, by not sleeping through the night for the first eleven months of your life; I would either wrap you up in your baby harness strapped tightly in front of me and walk throughout our apartment complex, carrying you until you fell asleep, or would sit with you lying on my chest, rocking you for hours on end, sometimes far into the early hours of the morning.*

*Your mother and I were so tired, and thank God your brother slept soundly by then, but it was so worth our love and effort.*

*One particular night you seemed very out of sorts, and your crying told me something slightly different was going on within your little body, and even though it was a very cool fall morning, I decided to take you outside thinking the brisk air would calm you. Well, we walked and walked, and every few blocks I would pull you away from my chest and glance to see if you had fallen asleep; your tears would then begin again and I would whisper my words of love to hush you. Finally you stopped, but I did not want to take a chance on waking you, so we strolled for another full half hour, through the various pathways, sidewalks, and autumnally scented trees that landscaped your very first home. Finally, I decided to take a look at you, and under one of the street lamps I saw what I will forever cherish; you were as wide-eyed as humanly possible, awake and alert, staring and smiling at me but remaining quiet, and I absolutely knew telling me you loved me, in only the way your little newborn person could. I will never, ever lose that vision; one of the very most overwhelming moments of your dad's entire life!*

*I watched you grow up, and I must confess much too long, from the "sidelines," into the most beautiful young woman I've ever seen. You appeared to carry the loveliest features of your mother, yet re-shaping them into something extraordinary, something magical. You took it upon yourself to fly by your older brother, and all others for that matter, with your God-given instinctive abilities and intuition, never minding all of those awesome physical skills you exhibited (remember the "swimming incident?"), and I must confess that seeing you so in control of yourself, I felt a sort of relief in not having to watch over you so closely.*

*That was wrong of me, and I cannot ever get those years back, and even though my little girl was kicking ass in the world, I needed to reassure and reaffirm my daughter of the love her father carried for her, and give her credit the hundreds of times she excelled in whatever she took on!*

*I sometimes truly wish I could go back in time, and start with you again, but life does not allow us these desires. Your brother Jesse is to be commended for his watching over you, and in my eyes he has exhibited many of those same life-saving and inspiring qualities as my Navy mates did back in the war. Your relationship with him just might be the singular most impressive accounting of true love I have ever known, and your mother concurs most readily. You two have made both of us so very proud!*

*Now my baby girl is very sick, and I feel powerless to fight it; this breaks my heart, and brings tears to my eyes whenever I think of you, and nowadays that is all of the time. I know your brother and mother feel exactly as I do, but there's something more with me, and it is the fact that you are the daughter I always dreamed of having.*

*Even as a teenager, I would dream of someday holding a beautiful young baby girl, and promising her the world, safely tucked in my arms, and kissing her little eyes and cheeks.*

*This miracle occurred for me, just eighteen very brief years ago, and I thank God for my most profound good fortune.*

*I want to tell you, my most precious Loretta, that I will be with you all of the way, and we will battle your disease together. You are so strong and your will-power can save you, this I know.*

*God knows what he has in store, but in the meantime, we attack and win this fight, united in our faith, compassion and pure love for each other.*

*I was very angry with Him when you were first diagnosed, and cursed Him for not using me for this dreaded disease. I have lived enough life, and you and your brother are just getting started. Your beautiful mother knows of what I say, but life does not work this way.*

*I think God is testing you, my sweet daughter; why, I do not know. I sometimes get so angry that I want to shove this right back into His face. Still, He knows of my grief and fear, and apparently has allowed me a small catharsis seemingly on a regular basis.*

*Your have always been my heart and spirit, sweetheart. I just needed to tell you directly, even though I've neglected both you and Jesse for all of these years.*

***Never in this world has anyone so embraced my soul, and never have I loved one so deeply!***

*Daddy*

\*          \*          \*

I was speechless, and Loretta was softly crying.

We both remained silent for several moments, and I said to her, "you okay?"

"Yes, my beautiful brother, I am more than okay, I am very, very happy!"

I was thinking that my dad was echoing those exact feelings and thoughts that I had possessed seemingly my entire conscious life, and I most startlingly realized that I was my father, or becoming a very close facsimile of him.

Loretta, sensing precisely my reflections, offered "Jesse honey, I am so blessed; I have so many to look out for me: your best friend and my love Jess, our most awesome mom, and, two angels disguised as my father and brother!"

"Yes, I am so very glad in my heart," she finished.

We both offered promises of eternal affection and softly said our goodbyes for now.

I handed the phone to Sharon and went for a stroll throughout her neighborhood, gathering my composure to be sure, but also giving my sister and my girlfriend time to be just girls, with no opposite sex interference of said freedom, intuition and intelligence.

Sher and I would spend the next few days laughing with her mom and sister, going out to dinner, and sneaking in, whenever possible, our romantic interludes, with every single time throwing me more deeply in love with this gorgeous young lady.

I did not meet her father on this trip, and that was just as well, and the more comfortable Mrs. McGee became with me, the more I recognized a slowly fueled and most passionate hatred for her soon to be ex-husband.

I was too young to witness this adult shit, but hell, as I've said and we all know, many have seen much worse.

We left for our respective sophomore years in school, both excited and yet fearful for what lay ahead, especially being apart.

Love is a double-edged sword; it can save you, but it can also kill you!

# Chapter Eighteen

"Someday soon you will see,
Only the dreamers are just like me,
You see I can fool them,
Use and abuse them,
I am a dreamer don't you see,
You can be like me..."

Only the Dreamers

# XVIII

Jess had hit Western Carolina's tailback so hard that our entire stadium collectively gasped and held our breath seemingly forever. After laying there on the turf for a good minute, he finally got up, cautiously and ever so slowly shaking the cobwebs from his brains, and then commenced to deliver yet another of the finest examples of sportsmanship I've witnessed to date; he trotted over to Jess and patted him on his ass while nodding his head in acknowledgement, and then ran to the sidelines with all of us cheering this remarkable warrior!

Football is such a magnificent game to watch, and even more wonderful to play, and on this simply stunning September afternoon, with "Indian Summer" warmth and bliss permeating each and every one of us in attendance, I was reminded of my high school days as an all-conference defensive back, and just two short years ago.

I absolutely loved football: the damp smell of the locker room, with all of our uniforms far beyond need of laundering; the collective male and almost tribal scent of young boys all fearful and yet excited at the same time of what lay in store out on the gridiron the very next time we entered that hallowed zone; the sound of our cleats clacking on the tile floors, creating quite the military cadence; the grab-assing, the taunting, the jokes, the updates on our girlfriends, the coaches up our said rear ends constantly, and pretty much just the general knowledge of belonging to that hallowed and time honored tradition of knocking heads and kicking ass!

*My thoughts drifted to one game in particular my senior year, on an early November afternoon, yet eerily similar Autumnal palate, complete with the very best Mother Nature had to offer that particular time of year.*

*We were playing St. Paul's, from Richmond, VA, and they were the highest ranked Catholic team in the state. As if this wasn't enough of a challenge for our very mediocre team (my senior year was filled with numerous and disappointing losses in basketball and football, as our high school being brand new, could simply not recover from the division and subsequent depletion of all of us senior athletes from our now rival school, where we once belonged), their 6'3," 200 lb all-state wide receiver, Denny McCarthy, would be my personal challenge this entire game.*

*Denny had numerous major colleges scouting him in this his senior year; he had been selected to play on St. Paul's varsity team three years ago, while only a freshman , an exceptional honor, and the university scholarship interest for him had been there even as a sophomore for this luminous wide-out!*

*This was our next to last game of the season, and White Oak High School was still winless; yet I could not contain my excitement preceding each and every game we played, as I always found a way, deep within myself, to appreciate just participating in these contests and getting up for them every single week, as I loved them so dearly.*

*Not only was I leading our conference in interceptions, but I had not, in our eight previous games, given up a single touchdown pass, and for any of those that have ever played football at a high level, will truly understand how remarkable a feat that was; being isolated on that "island" as a cornerback many feel is the most difficult task in all of sports!*

*I had watched enough film of Denny to know that he was just marvelous; he was not afraid of going across the middle, but his "flare, out, and fly" routes were unparalleled, leaving many a cornerback and free safety chasing him into various end zones throughout the state.*

*One of his favorite moves was a "square-out," looking over his shoulder at his quarterback for a split second hesitation, and then racing up the sidelines, usually for a score. I studied his move, and he was particularly adept when he was flanked to the left, and usually later in a game when he had already abused said defensive backs with the first half of this patented technique.*

*I would be ready for him!*

*St. Paul's was kicking our asses, as to be expected, but I had held this wonderful receiver to just two catches in the first three quarters. He was very pissed, as he had not been "skunked" in a game since his junior year, and his two touchdowns per game average this season was in serious jeopardy.*

*It's late in the 4th quarter, and he lines up, flanked wide left. I knew this was it, as I had also studied his quarterback's particular mannerisms that preceded each of these successful scoring plays; he would look to the right, while beginning his cadence and tap his left thigh, ever so discreetly. I saw it all, and was going to not only abort this play, but just possibly intercept this pass and race down the sidelines to my own glory and team's success!*

*The play begins, and I backpedal with my adversary. Denny cuts sharply out and I slide right with him, step for step; he glances over his shoulder and then breaks up the sidelines. Goddamn was he a fast fucking white boy, but I was right there.*

*As I would later, many times (and now), visualize over and over and over this beautiful play, everything was in slow motion, as it seemingly was in actuality.*

*His quarterback lets it fly, and it was such a beautiful spiral, arcing sublimely throughout this gorgeous November sky. I knew that I could knock the ball out of play, but decided to go for the interception (against my head coach's previous warning) and up I went, reaching for this pass. My outstretched right fingertips brush underneath this football and instead of cradling in my hand, it continues on, sliding off mine and into Denny's, in part due to his awesome leap, but mostly because of his twisted body position blocking me away in mid-air; he was simply that great!*

*He scores, and the St. Paul's fans all erupt, as their glorious wide receiver had once again demolished yet another opponent. Never mind winning the game; as much at stake was the personal integrity of their particular hero.*

*I was shocked at my failure; I was so sure I had the ball. I trotted over to the sidelines and my head coach is screaming at me. I look at him in bewilderment and start fucking crying angrily, and actually shouted back.*

*"Goddamnit coach, I had it."*

*"I told you to knock it down," he yells.*

*"Fuck this shit," I scream.*

*He's about to grab my shoulder pads and shake the living shit out of me (a favorite pastime of his), when both assistant coaches intervened and calmed him down.*

*I overheard something to the effect of them reminding him that I was the very best "d-back" in our conference, and that no one had ever played so well against McCarthy.*

*The game ended shortly thereafter; I had held Denny to just three catches for 50 yards, which was his least successful achievement the entire season, and actually one of my very finest efforts to date (I would surpass this though, the very next week, with our last game of the season and White Oak finally winning)!*

*Still, I burned over the touchdown play, and started to trot off the field.*

*"Hey, number 6," I hear but ignore, "hey, Mouchebeau," even louder.*

*I look over at the source of this greeting, and it's Denny.*

*He points his hand at me, extending his index finger in pistol fashion, and pantomimes shooting while saying "gotcha!"*

*I grab my balls and respond "get this, motherfucker!"*

*We start towards each other, but our teammates intervene, which was really fine by me. I was too fucking tired to fight.*

*He was an arrogant son of a bitch, but what a tough and great player!*

*That was to be the only score I would give up in that entire football season; an accomplishment I would always treasure!*


I am "awakened" by another stupendous roar, and quickly shake my head, bringing me back into the present, and game at hand.

T.J. Cooper leans into me and offers, "shit Jesse, you were 'out on your feet', where the fuck did you go; you thinking of your sister?"

He was also one of the very few in my sacred "inner loop" of trusting and caring friends regarding Loretta.

"Just dreaming T.J.; no big deal! Reliving my football past," I responded.

"I can dig that," he says. "God, did you see Jess hit that running back?"

"Yeah, that's my killer brother!"

We both laughed somewhat nervously; mostly because of Jess' fearless approach to this violent game, but also because their player had not been seriously hurt.

Most athletes have a deep and dreadful and almost superstitious fear of career ending injuries, and most of us are constantly praying for safely surviving every practice and game we encounter!

The game was close, but East Valley had pulled off another win, and even though it was an out of conference match-up, our football team needed the confidence builder from the previous week's thrashing.

Jess had played very well, save for the huge penalty he incurred while demolishing a punt returner during his "fair catch" in the 4th quarter.

Sometime's my best friend got too psyched and his natural instincts would over-ride his judgment! On the field, Jess was nearly uncontrollable, playing just within the limits of reason and sanity, yet somehow still managing to be great most of the time.

This time, however, we all could hear East Valley's head coach reaming him out; some things just never change, whether it is high school, college, and I suspect even in the pros, coaches will be forever up athletes asses for fucking up. It's what we many times deserve, no matter who is privy to said chastisement!

"Let's get out of here," T.J. offers, "Barbie says we've got enough for dinner, and wants you there."

This was T.J.'s senior year, and his young marriage seemed to be, remarkably so, very intact, especially given the fact that he and Barbara had been together since their high school years. Plus, my romance with Sharon, who, as previously detailed, had attended their same high school, gave me an even more familial relationship with this vibrant couple. I always, and even then, prayed for them to be successful in their union, dispelling all of the odds stacked against this manner of relationship. In fact, they eventually would do just that, raising three beautiful children and living back in River City, where T.J. would become his own high school's extremely successful head basketball coach!

"I'm with you, let's go," I agreed. "I will see Jess later; he will want to talk with Loretta for awhile after he showers, and then we can catch-up;" something we had been really wanting to do since school started, as there had not yet been enough time to hang, with all of us getting re-acclimated to the rigors being a college/athlete.

Dinner was fabulous, and Barbie had me call Sharon while there. She looked upon Sher as a "little sister" and was also well acquainted with the McGee parent's impending break-up, counseling my girlfriend whenever needed.

Sher sounded in very good spirits, and I hoped to see her soon, but knew that was a dream. As being one of Lee University's cheerleaders, she was committed to all of their football and basketball games, never minding their own practices, and with me in daily basketball practice, now "unofficially" but very soon full-tilt boogie, there was simply no time.

We did promise each other a romantic reunion the one weekend that Lee's football team had a "bye week," which was still a month away. I was not sure if I could last that long without going out of my mind, as I had reached that so delicate and delicious state of being, where one can actually crave their partner's affections, no manner what mode!

I was "there in spirit," as she was, and hopefully we could maintain our love affair throughout all of our individual distractions. Time would tell, of course, and I would basically have to mark it, day by day, until our much anticipated fantasy came to fruition.

Dinner was great, and as T.J. and I cleaned up the kitchen, giving Barbie her needed time to study, we talked about this year's squad.

Coach Melling, even though having aggressively recruited T.J. from junior college, had more or less given up on him as a starting guard, but still used him in heavy rotation with Blakely and Mark. Our previous "3-guard system," with the now graduated Kelly, was apparently no longer in effect, with our skipper saying that he intended to go back to the normal basketball line-up of a center, two forwards and two guards.

Interestingly enough, though, was that Kelly was now a graduate assistant coach, and T.J. had so hoped he'd be able to convince Melling to continue with our patented attack, using Mark's, Blakely's and T.J.'s great quickness and speed. Plus, with these players all going full out, at the onset of each and every game, they would need to rest occasionally, and this is where I thought I might get more chances to play.

I also had envisioned the scenario of our esteemed "bullet-headed" coach utilizing all six of us guards in two teams of three, rotating in and out; to constantly pressure our opponents, both offensively and defensively. I mean how innovative would that be? We had the tools, but alas, so many head coaches, especially at the high school and Division II and III levels, became so bull-headed regarding their own systems, that they paid little heed to the talent in front of their very own faces. This is, by the way, where literally all coaches ultimately succeed or fail; one needs only to historically look at specific examples, either locally or nationally, of scholastic sports to verify this!

T.J. and I concurred that this season would be a trial for both of us, with neither truly getting the minutes on the court we deserved; T.J., mainly due to the fact that he was a senior and an outstanding player, would most likely be the first sub for either Mark or Blakely, and I would reprise the role of my freshman year, coming off the bench to score points when needed, which was a drag in that I had noticeably improved in all facets of my game!

Playing against those great college players in New York over the summer, never minding the pros, had truly given me a different sort of mental edge, as well; I was simply not afraid of failure anymore, and T.J. was one of the very first of my teammates to support this. I did not think that any of the other players on my team, save for Burton, worked any harder to excel.

I mentioned to T.J. that even though Mitch Flowers, the transfer guard from Great Smokey Mountain State (NC) was not the ball handler and shooter I was, I just knew he would be in front of me on the depth chart, as he was a junior and also recruited by Coach; and, I could also see that freshman Jimmy Childs, local high school sensation and very actively recruited by Melling, just might push me back to number six, which would be one slot lower than when I was a freshman. Jesus Christ, this was really starting to piss me off again, as I had once actually thought that I might be an East Valley starting guard by my junior year!

"You can only do what you do, partner," T.J. offered, "just keep kicking ass in practice, and know that you did; Bullet is an idiot, and nothing you or I do will probably matter to him. You know, this is my last year of roundball, and I'd sure like to go out playing and making it count, especially since I'll be coaching some high school team next year, and missing you guys terribly."

I felt bad for my friend; it was his very last year of scholastic ball, and I envisioned that if this was my scenario, I'd feel pretty down.

"Hell T.J., you'll play a ton this year; if Coach wants to really win he'll have to play you!"

"And, remember one thing, his ass is on the line as far as his job goes, this ain't fucking high school," I added.

"You're right Jesse, he's gotta play me; and you too, goddamn, no one shoots like you, bro!"

"We'll see," I paused for a moment, "I need to get back to the house and meet up with Jess," I continued, "he will have talked with Loretta, and I sense things are very difficult for both of them."

"I can only imagine, Jesse," T.J. answered. "Please tell Loretta that we love her, and smack that black son of a bitch in the head for me, tell him he played a helluva good game" T.J. added, giving me that million dollar grin of his.

"I will do so, and thank Barbie for dinner," as she was very deep in homework study, and I did not want to disturb her.

We hugged each other, maybe tighter and longer than normal; two college basketball players trying to figure out life, and play the dealer's hand!

*     *     *

"Hey Jesse, I'm really glad you're here," my best friend greeted me as I opened the door for him, steering him towards our living room.

I was living in the same place as my freshman year; the very same and now infamous house that hosted the "homecoming party of all times" my freshman year, when I truly thought that I was going to be kicked out of school.

"I think Loretta is pulling away from me." Jess spoke very somberly and I knew he was deadly serious.

"Why do you say that?" I questioned my obviously pained and depressed brother; "something happen tonight?"

"I don't know, Jesse; she just seemed very detached, almost as if she was bothered by me calling her."

Jess' eyes were beginning to tear up; Jesus Christ, I had watched my linebacking hero demolish several players on the gridiron earlier today, and yet here he was, literally reduced to tears, just hours removed from the game.

He should've been out celebrating with his team mates tonight, but that wasn't as important as his love for my sister.

Jess Butkus was a marvelous human being! No question about that, and I loved him dearly.

Without having talked with Loretta myself, I asked him to listen to what I had to say; knowing my beloved sister all too well, I really thought that I might help my saddened and maybe broken-hearted best friend.

I began:

"You know brother, my entire life, or at least what I can vividly recall, has been one of continuous amazement and, honestly, bewilderment as to Loretta's power and energy. She was never 'normal', and I always knew that she would somehow be there for me, and others, it was just her way. God, when we were toddlers, mom and dad said she was talking in complete sentences, way before me, and she was a year younger! She was so coordinated and athletically skilled that she most likely would've been all-everything if she wanted. The same thing for what she achieved in school; her grades were always A's, but she never flaunted that, especially to me, her big and dumber brother. She would just comment at the dinner table on any little thing I would do right, disregarding our parent's lavish praises upon her. Jess, she so adored me and looked after me, in her own special way, that early on I developed a sort of 'serenity', knowing in my heart that I was my little sister's world; how fucking awesome is that? Every time my heart was broken, she was there to help me understand this particular girlfriend's reasons for leaving, and not to hate her. You know something brother, she was always right. Once I thought about why things had happened, I did not blame anyone, and felt so much better! All through high school she would be there for me, every single time, no matter what happened, and you remember the murder/suicide I witnessed; Jesus Christ, what a thing for a 15 year old to see, but I was fine after that, and Loretta most definitely held my hand. Anyhow my dear friend, I now am convinced and firmly believe that my sister and I are one and the same spirit, and now that she's possibly in real danger, she's trying to give away some of that energy, for us to take, even if it somehow 'dissolves' her own; that's how magnificent my sister truly is. Does this make sense, brother?"

I am starting to lose it, and forced myself to regain my composure as Jess would've broken down if I had not.

My friend is smiling ever so slightly, and even with his glassy and solemn eyes, visibly relaxes his entire body.

"Now, what she said to me makes sense," Jess whispered, "I really thought that she was tired of me being concerned, and you know, just bugging her!"

"Let me tell you something Jess Butkus," I answered, "Loretta has never had someone like you, and I've seen them come and go! She adores you, and this I truly know. You were there with me at the big fight at Reece's house, and you will always be with me, whenever I need you. She *knows* this, and this is amazing comfort for her. I gotta tell you that she has said so, more than once my friend."

"Thanks, Jesse," and Jess pauses for several seconds, 'thank you, brother," he added, in his most heartfelt manner.

We small talked about football and some of Jess' team mates, basketball and some of mine, our classes, the cafeteria food, our fraternity, Sharon, Jess' choir repertoire, and even about the classes we were taking; what we did not talk about was what we both feared more than anything in this our beloved Lord's most wondrous world, and that was the very real possibility of my sister succumbing and dying to cancer.

It was there in the pits of our stomachs, a most murderous anxiety, threatening to disable us both.

This apprehension would so affect my dear friend and me our

entire sophomore year; affecting Jess' play on the field and my play on the court, and we would struggle with our grades mightily. God, if we only knew what was in store for us, we might have both collapsed then and there.

I guess it is our Lord's will for us to always hold out for hope; praying for some sort of deliverance from such acute pain and devastation.

Life hands us unbelievably treacherous hands, from time to time, and even though most of us make it through the various barriers and ultimately survive, we can become scarred to the point of simply not caring for our safety, and this is truly dangerous.

Battle has proven this time and again; warriors need to constantly strive to believe in a greater good, and shed themselves of that most easily attainable and available killer that is always just around the next corner; that which is cynicism!

*    *    *

Loretta told me, later that evening, that her happiest childhood memories were of the two of us, just the two of us, talking about life and love and hope and faith, never really moving into any religious dogma, but just being aware of the wonderful things around us; those everyday totems and artifacts, and the simply divine and ubiquitous natural elements that just could not have happened on their own!

She was a wondrous creature, my sister Loretta. I was more in love with her then, than at any time of my previous years. My fears were even greater because of this, and these exponential intuitions were simmering beneath my skin.

Amazingly enough that night, I shed no tears; she would not allow it!

# Chapter Nineteen

"She rises early, adventure on her mind and in
her eyes, no surprise,
Answers to no one, she seeks her fortune and her
fame, life's a game..."

She's a Warrior

# XIX

It is early morning and I am quietly watching Sharon sleep. I lean over and with my ring finger slowly and ever so carefully lightly brush her bangs away from those blissful and resting eyes, noticing just the slightest hint of a smile on her stunning face. She sighs in her deep slumber, breathing in a cadence that suggests peace, at least for the present, but I know that in reality this is not necessarily true. I notice the well-worn sheet draped just over her hips and thigh, accentuating her athletic and even somewhat boyish figure, yet reminding me of the breathtaking woman this young girl was rapidly becoming. I am in wonder as to how I am laying next to this goddess and thinking that someone else should be here, not me, further supporting my insecurity in general and as her one and only love in particular. Still, I do know she adores me, and I most certainly her, and just hope that the turmoil existing in both of our current lives does not seek to undermine and damage this most profound of young love affairs. I gaze at her mouth, knowing intimately its capability of delivering the most sensuous and loving kiss I've ever received, and maybe ever would. Her breath is warm and inviting, her smell delicious, and something that I truly know will never, ever leave my memory, indelibly etched upon those special places most of us reserve for such nostalgic gifts!

My thoughts start to drift back in time, traversing the many years of my conscious remembrance, and I begin to single out those most amazing relationships I was lucky enough to experience. These girls of yesterday each gave me joy to be sure, but I was now starting to feel and understand the true worth and value of said connections; that each on its own was a most special offering, a genesis if you will of discovery, enlightenment and clarity, to be nurtured and developed and used with regards to any future involvement with my most beloved opposite sex!

Mary Jean Lowell again comes to mind, as it's only a little more than two years passed that I let slip through my fingers maybe the most gorgeous young girl I'd ever seen anywhere! I sometimes reflect that she truly was "the one," Loretta thought so, but timing is everything, is it not?

Jesse Mouchebeau back then: too young, impetuous, naïve, insecure, unstable, wild and most definitely too virgin; all characteristics describing an adolescent and somewhat gifted, fairly good-looking athlete and half-decent guitarist ascending into his senior year of high school, bound and determined to actually get laid, no matter who's feelings he trounced.

Asshole, back then? Yes I was; not in that classic sense of someone who just crushes others' passions, as I was honestly always aware to some degree of the deep pain of scorned pride, but jerk based upon what I now knew to be the truth; the truth that is the intense self-respect and dignity each and everyone of us possesses to some degree or other, that is sacred ground!

Emotional crime can be a nasty one, inflicting suffering on someone's feelings, plainly and simply, with the various degrees of such manifested by either intent, miscalculation or ignorance. Recognizing this transgression; knowing, controlling and understanding, had been my proudest growth and maturation since Mary Jean, and I so hoped that I would always carry said proficiency!

Her tears, that summer before our last year of high school, were of such a heart-breaking and intensely painful kind, that I would never forget how God-awful I felt; never mind my precious girlfriend.

She was such a sweet girl and I had hurt her badly, and swore never to do something so injurious again. Never!

There were others before Mary Jean to be sure, many girls, all special in their places and time amidst my growing up, all significantly contributing to my schooling, all loved by me; honestly, passionately and without second thought.

These girls were also privy to my wonderful sister's influence, whether directly or casually, and *all* influenced my adventures to even greater places because of Loretta's spirit.

Jane was my very first infatuation, my little playmate and buddy in pre-school. By God's hand I swear we kissed behind the big oak tree in the playground at recess, and what a most amazing experience, recognized even by a four year old!

I will not forget that initial touch; nothing could ever take the place of something so cataclysmic with regards to setting the wheels in motion of my life's love affair with the opposite sex.

Girls; what a concept, and how wonderful it would always be just to participate, just to be "in the game"!

I look back at my sleeping beauty. She's so peaceful at the moment, and I am glad for her. Even though divorce is not dying, there are those similar aspects of being left alone, without those day to day moments of security.

I have felt Sher's unease ever so gradually become more and more obvious, slowly and surely overtaking her naturally great demeanor; not that she's gotten angry with me or anything, just this undercurrent of anxiety cautiously awakening.

She breathes in a most delightful rhythm, her cadence hypnotizing me as I lay within her very powerful spiritual field.

I am drawn to her radiance, and am thinking sexual thoughts, not so much of the lustful kind, but those of reassurance and reaffirmation.

As if by divine intervention she slowly opens her eyes and focuses for a few seconds, taking the time to assess her surroundings and respond.

Her eyes say it all, and she immediately smiles, once again capturing my heart and soul; I fall in love again, immediately.

"Hello Jesse, how do you feel?"

"I am fine, sweetheart, never better," I whisper, "I love you, babe!"

"I love you too," she coos.

"I've been watching you sleep, God, you are so beautiful."

"Jesse, thank you so much for being there, you make me feel so secure," she answers, obviously gladdened by my presence.

Important words to hear, at any age, due to the profound implications of taking care of those you love, in whatever capacity needed; but alas, the possible and proverbial double-edged sword raising its deceptive head with the responsibility of taking on just too much to handle, many times with emotions finding their way into the most difficult and uncontrollable downward spiral.

She continues, "What's on your mind darling, you look lost in thought."

"Loretta?"

"Not really, Sher, at least not at the moment. I am kind of embarrassed to say that I was thinking of making love with you again."

"Why feel badly about that, Jesse? I am right there with you, babe. Please hold me and kiss me."

I comply, caressing her face in my hands and delivering my sweetest effort to date, lightly touching her eyes with my mouth, ever so slightly, and sharing her mouth with mine, her tongue with mine, literally finding a rhythm of sharing our breaths, staying there in oral embrace for an eternity.

There is nothing better in this world than a perfect kiss!

We then find ourselves, once again, in the throes of passion that early romance suggests: wild and uninhibited as only teenagers or young adults can create, having yet to experience the eventual and unavoidable harsh lessons that the world brings upon us, so affecting every fiber of our very being, and thusly influencing day to day life and even love, many times unfortunately without our recognition!

Later that morning, after breakfast, and after another round of losing ourselves within each other's bodies and souls, we caressed by our cars outside the Mountain View Hotel, complete with its panoramic splendor and now its added and special history for Sharon and me in that it was the original scene for our blossoming romance back in our previous freshman year.

My how time does fly, especially when it's "great time," and for me, that was always a period of loving someone, and in turn receiving said affection. My world operated on this basis, as surely as the dawning of another day.

"Bye, sweetheart, "I gently expressed to the girl I adored.

"Bye babe, see you at Thanksgiving, and good luck with the team!"

\* \* \*

That weekend was yet another chapter in my most significant love affair to date. I drove back to campus thinking of how lucky I was, and how unlucky my amazing sister's life had been in the last year.

As miraculous a person as Loretta Mouchebeau had been so far in life, things were changing for the worse in hers, and I only could hope and pray that there would be a happy end-game with all that was transpiring.

The hardest thing for me was knowing, truly knowing, of my developing prescient gifts, and trying to ignore those signals that spelled tragedy for my beloved sister.

I felt ashamed thinking these thoughts, yet could not stop them.

How does one take in and heed those signals of awareness that will protect, yet avoid those that illuminate disaster?

Another one of life's great mysteries, and I did not like it at all that I was gaining ability with this particular perceptive trait.

Why did I feel so afraid, so sad, and so miserable?

I simply could not survive without my sister's élan, she was my life!

# Chapter Twenty

"The attraction is real, you cannot see,
That something possesses you, intimately,
Your image awaits you, every hour,
Remember Narcissus, a wasted flower..."

The Mirror Awaits

# XX

We are playing Patrick Henry College this evening; highly regarded both athletically and academically, this division III school was located literally minutes from the East Valley campus. This should be a benign contest but said endeavor has all the feel, and obvious hype from the local papers, as something that will actually count in the NCAA projected pre-season rankings, which pisses everyone of my team mates off, as we have yet another one of our Saturday evenings taken from us and committed to the "powers that be," that of the university athletic system, and we have nothing to gain from potentially getting our asses kicked by a real good team!

We are ready individually, as our conditioning and off-season workouts were taken seriously by all of us, to some degree, but are not collectively as a team; graduation had taken our best two players and we were still learning Coach Melling's "new" system, an antiquated one at best, truly ignoring our best attributes and competitors. Also, Coach's recruiting was starting to bear out the fact that high school prospects did not really want to play for him, as witnessed by this year's one and only truly great freshman player in Jimmy Childs.

Shit, this was never going to end, and I was really getting sick of our obtuse coach's "red-necked high school style".

This, coupled with my sister's failing health and my girlfriend's geographic location was enough to put me over the edge.

Earlier in the week, I had nearly gotten into it with Mark at practice simply because he had wise-cracked to me in an intense inter-squad scrimmage; something to the effect of "if you can't stand the heat, get out of the kitchen".

I actually had stopped playing for a moment and given him my fighting glare, which was the wrong thing to do. On one hand, it let him know that I was deadly serious, and on the other showed an extreme lapse in character of yours truly, being disrespectful to not only a senior player, but our co-captain!

I immediately apologized to him and our entire team, and later after practice had taken him aside and reiterated my feelings and to his good credit Mark said that he understood; he and a few other team mates knew of my sister's situation, and all gave me my space when it was apparently needed.

Well, sure as rain, we were taking a beating from this smaller school, and one of their starting guards, Tommy Foxx, was lighting it up.

Coach yells for me to go in and cover him: "Jesse, get in there and play some defense on this guy, he's killing us."

Well, I am most certain that Blakely, Mark and T.J., Mitch and Jimmy all felt wonderful hearing Bullet's accounting of their performances so far exhibited tonight; and, as earlier assessed by yours truly, here I was, Jesse Mouchebeau, number Goddamn mother-fucking six on the East Valley Hornets depth chart for guards, being ordered to pull off the impossible.

I could give a flying fucking damn that Tommy Foxx was killing us; I just wanted my sister to be healthy and happy again, and I wanted to be with my girlfriend.

I also wanted our clueless basketball coach to recognize the unbelievable talent of this year's team, so that we might actually enjoy this game once again, a game with which each and every single one of us had so sacrificed countless hours of our youth to achieve some measure of success and satisfaction!

I could sense my pent-up rage again moving out of control, and I needed to do something to relieve the pressure!

I ambled over to the scorer's table and checked in; we still had eight minutes to go and I was most likely going to play the rest of the game, so I thought that maybe I would actually have enough time to get into a rhythm and see what I could do.

I played very well, wouldn't you know? Tommy must have been tired by then, because I was moving the ball with ease, and actually scored a few times, holding him to a single basket.

He was a cocky son of a bitch, though; one of those black players that seemed to take it personally that I was white, and was mouthing off the entire time. I really did not mind these mental jibes we players used on one another in the past; in fact, I found them very amusing, much like "the dozens" game my team mates and friends played every night at dinner, but at this point of my life, as earlier with Mark, Jesse Mouchebeau was a ticking time-bomb.

I was getting real tired of hearing this player lip-off, and told him so. I then took the ball to the hoop and faked him into the air, leaning in, catching his off-balanced body with my shoulder and "submarined" him, tossing him very hard to the floor.

All basketball players know that this is truly a dangerous maneuver, and there is most certainly an unwritten code of ethics that we religiously adhere to, with this particular move being one of the significantly outlawed, simply because of the potential for serious injury; at this point, though, I had really had enough of this arrogant and very nasty player.

To his credit, he came up fighting, and we got into it, right there beneath the basket, trading a couple of quick punches, with the referees stopping it before all hell could break loose with both of our teams.

Both of us were thrown out of the game, and given a stern warning by the head official as to if this had been a regular season game, we would have been suspended indefinitely.

Bullet screamed at me "get out of here Jesse, go to the locker room, and wait for me, I'll deal with you later."

Tommy's coach acted literally identically with him, and we both walked out of the gym together.

In the foyer of our facility, just beyond the doors left open, we stood for a second, looked at each other, and for the strangest reason smiled. Maybe our innermost sensibilities took the reigns of our subconscious minds, and had us act like the young men we were supposed to be: college athletes with class and character.

"I am so sorry I undercut you out there, I know better," I said to him.

"No problem brother," he replied, "I had it coming to me; sometimes I get carried away with my trash talking, and need to cool it."

We both then shook hands, and lightly hugged, wishing each other success in our respective upcoming seasons, with all of this being apparently witnessed by the coaches and players left in the gymnasium.

I also momentarily wondered if this gifted young player had shit going on in his life that was spiraling out of control, just as mine, hence his behavior.

This was indeed a valuable lesson for me in that I once again awakened to the fact that my existence was not the only important one in the universe; I was not the only person under God's watch suffering.

Later in the locker room, Coach pulled me aside with a surprisingly gentle admonishment; most likely because of the turmoil going on in my life, and partly because he had seen me talking with, and then apologizing to Tommy.

I think that Melling again was feeling the confusing yet very real dichotomy of my existence on his team; Jesse Mouchebeau being an insolent and sometimes very brash player whom he did not truly care for, but a young man with courage, and of whom he respected.

I just knew that this season was going to be a very futile one for me, and it was beginning to play out as such.

I had to accept being the 6th guard on our East Valley roster, and simply adjust to my role; playing as well as possible under these set-forth conditions, retaining my scholarship, and seeing how things developed over the course of the year.

I decided then and there to focus on my sister and girlfriend and Jess; giving them my positive energy, and realizing how they might need my attention; not the East Tennessee Valley Hornets basketball team!

"Fuck it," I would just parlay the cards dealt me, and really try to appreciate and respect the amazing love that was in my present life, thanking God for said gifts!

\*        \*        \*

I called Loretta that evening, and surprisingly my dad answered the phone, as he usually was not one to do so, especially later in any particular day after a couple of Johnnie Walker Red's on the rocks.

"Hey Jesse," my dad began, "how's the team this year?"

"Great, dad," I lied, as I did not want to complain in the slightest whenever I called home, as I had made a pact with myself to act accordingly so!

"We should do pretty well, this year, but you know we lost Joe and Kelly, and they were our heart and soul; still, I should get to play more"

Dad took an audible breath; "son, when one door closes, another opens, and I know you realize that, but think about it for a moment; has your own game adapted anyway whatsoever with the system in place down there? I know you have improved tremendously over the summer, but that's not what I am asking, you understand me?"

I was thinking to myself that dad was onto something. It had not even occurred to me to really try and fit into Coach Melling's system, but rather to elevate my own personal game, never minding that I actually belonged to a system that was already in place; one that was not going to change anytime soon.

"Dad, I think I see what you are saying, maybe I do need to look hard at myself and try to maneuver my skills into our teams' direction."

Not an epiphany, mind you, but maybe a bit more clarity for me.

"Battle changes battle plans, Jesse; always has, always will," dad responded with obvious sentiment.

I felt pretty good, but knew we both were avoiding what was really on our minds!

"How's sis?" I asked, with very real trepidation.

"Jesse, I need to tell you that I am worried sick over her; she's acting on the surface like the little warrior she's always been, but I do know that she's scared, and all I want to do is exchange places with her, take on her cancer myself, but I cannot; I've had a great life, and she should too."

I knew all too well of what dad was wishing. I had also talked with God in the very same manner, about transferring my sister's illness onto me, with her miraculously recovering and helping so many in this world; something that I had no doubt that she would eventually accomplish.

Me, I was just a normal young man; college student and athlete at the moment, going through life not really affecting anything or anyone, as my illustrious sister had, time and time again. I never had any inclination of "shaking up this world" but knew that her influence would eventually be profound.

I was thinking of the letter that dad had written Loretta just a couple of months earlier; the words greatly impacting not only her but me, as she had so elegantly read them, and very obviously treasured them.

"Dad, she's so damn tough, she can beat anything," I replied, with the only words I could muster. I was starting to lose it, but bit my lip intensely, just to maintain control.

My father then proceeded to say something very touching to me; words that I had never heard from him in all of my years, and sentiments of which I had no idea.

"Jesse, when you were born, I was so unbelievably happy; my first child, and a boy at that. I kept thinking of my buddies that died in the Philippines in the war; that never had the chance to find the right girl and eventually hold their very own babies. You were so special, and always will be to me, never, ever doubt that. I felt that I was a new person, and maybe a changed young man for much the better, especially because the world's conflict was still so close to me, still very real within my mind; but, when your sister came into this world, it affected me in a noticeably different manner. I looked at this little girl and all of a sudden I thought of all of my previous girlfriends and loves, and how much they had contributed to my life up to that very moment. I fell so in love with your sister, and it was different than how I loved you."

"This make any sense at all, sweetheart?" he added after a slight pause.

One thing about my dad; he was a hard ass, but never flinched from affection for either of us, whether words, or kisses, or simple hugs; he was most influential to me in this regard.

Wham! It was beginning to startle me as to how much alike my father and I were, and as to how I was evolving in similar fashion. I had many of the very same sentiments for Loretta, only from a "parallel" sibling aspect. God, I could only imagine this profound love I possessed for my sister coming from the very contrasting angle of the one (with my mother) who was responsible for creating this amazing girl!

"Yes, dad; makes all the sense in the world," I agreed.

Dad was truly suffering too, and this was bringing all of us even closer together. We were in a fight for life, and nothing was more paralyzing for the both of us.

I was starting to feel his fear, his helplessness, and I could not find any more words for this man; nothing whatsoever to comfort him, and I just sat there holding the phone for several seconds.

"Jesse," dad whispered, "are you still there, son?"

"Yes, dad, I'm here; just don't know what to say."

"You do not need to say anything, honey; I am very aware of how much you've been in each other's lives, all through your childhood, and probably know a great deal more than you think. Your care for Loretta has proven to me that you are every bit the man I ever was, and even more so; and, nothing has been finer to experience than watching you and your sister look out for each other. I could not have been given a more courageous son, and I should have said this to you sooner."

My tears are now flowing, cascading down my face, and I am visualizing in my mind's eye when, as a kid, I would watch the Shenandoah River squeezing through its narrow, boulder laden parts creating the most wonderful rapids with their magnificent cleansing sounds, all moving towards its greater purpose.

I had also found God on these riverbanks many years ago!

My tears were now an acute metaphor, and I knew this.

My father knows I am crying and lets me do so, not saying anything but letting me know he's still there with me by his signature breathing patterns; something that which I seemingly was always cognizant.

"Let me get your sister on the phone, Jesse, she's right here now."

"Okay dad," I choked quietly.

"One thing more," he continued, "I love you son, more than you could possibly know, never forget that!"

"Thanks dad, I love you too!"

\*          \*          \*

"Hi babe," she said softly.   Her said expression was the most appreciated affectation I had ever received from my beloved sister.

Loretta's words were music to me; her cadence, tone, phrasing and flow were much like those perfect passages we have all experienced from our very favorite instrumental and vocal artists; pieces of melodies that touched our hearts and at times literally brought tears to our eyes.

She and I laughed out loud reminiscing, once again, of our father's infamous soccer parties; way back when he and mom were young and in love and truly living life to its capacity.

A good two hours flew by  as we revived and relived a great deal of our childhood and adolescence, growing up in each other's arms, so to speak; girlfriends, boyfriends, rock and roll bands, her various and astounding feats both in the classroom and on the field, sports teams, dances, and the myriad battles fought by me.

One thing was very evident to both of us that evening; we had truly experienced a pretty good life so far, notwithstanding recent events. Our high school days were great times, and we appreciated them to their fullest.

I was starting, with my second year of being away at college, to realize that many students there were very melancholy growing up, and for the life of me could not understand why, especially if their particular home environments were healthy and sound.

Jesus, how hard was it to be happy; to just enjoy the smell of cut grass in late spring; the ocean's thunderous waves crashing onto the beach amidst the seagulls' cacophonous symphony in the summer; clean autumn air perfumed with the fragrance of burning oak leaves; winter's icy embrace on our collective faces as we skated furiously in our ice hockey games on the numerous frozen ponds in our neighborhoods; and, the warmth of your friends in general and just maybe someone you adored in particular?

For me, it was easy to be thrilled, and I most voraciously sought out anything to contribute to this state of bliss; usually I was rewarded thusly, and rarely did I let the inevitable disappointment keep me down for very long.

For Loretta, it was more than just contentment, though. It was exploring and understanding the meaning of happiness and searching for its boundaries, its depth, its purpose, its varieties and its soul.

My sister was a philosopher even as a child. She would question me with the most profound of topics, ideas and scenarios.

Many times I could understand my most prescient sibling, but often she had to guide me through various stages of foundation toward resolution.

Never, never was she impatient with me; she would just hold my hand, and give me that dazzling smile while saying something to the effect of "never mind that thought babe, let's try it this way."

We both needed this evening's talk. Our communication with each other was absolutely essential; always had been, and always would be!

"I love you sweetheart, you sound great," I said in closing.

"You too, big brother; I cannot wait to see you and my Jess at Thanksgiving; Sharon too!"

Jesus, I thought, it had been a year when I first had brought him home from college to meet everyone.

I was very glad to hear Loretta mention my friend's name with obvious affection and love, as it had been awhile since they had seen each other; and just maybe they would succeed with their relationship after all. I certainly hoped so, especially with the help of God's blessing.

My sister needed to find happiness again, and if anyone with a life threatening illness could muster up the sheer resolve to do so, it was Loretta Mouchebeau!

We said our goodbyes; our spirits uplifted measurably so, even if temporarily.

I felt pretty damn good that evening. These small and seemingly inconsequential victories were starting to become very much appreciated, extremely important, and oh so sweet!

# Chapter Twenty One

"There is power in your stare,
I can feel it, is it fair to me?
I want you there, with me, tonight...."

Dark Eyes

# XXI

Coach Ellen Harding was more than your average jock professor; not only would she eventually make it to the college women's basketball hall of fame, but academically she had no equal as a teacher, that while very tough, was even more fair.

I happened to really like her, although she would admonish Jess and me, without fail, if we happened to slightly deviate from proper classroom procedure, as we were sometimes prone to do. Her kinesiology class was difficult enough without the two of us disrupting, even benignly so.

I just knew that she was destined for greatness, even back then, and every once in awhile I would talk with her after class about things unrelated to either what we were studying, or East Valley athletics in general; she was that compelling! Still in her early 40's and quite active in her own personal health and fitness, she had this unique aspect of wisdom and authority while still appearing to be quite youthful and attractive in a very distinguishable sort of way.

Often she would engage me in philosophical dialogues, sometimes being specifically curious about a young man's perspective. I truly believe this is one of the reasons she was a great woman and role model; she was unafraid and honestly interested as to what men thought, especially college men, which of course affected most college women!

The girls she coached all loved, adored and most importantly respected her. Not bad behavior from my esteemed, if sometimes even crazier, athletic counterparts!

"Well, the great Jesse Mouchebeau is in love," she opened to me after class that first morning following my incident with Tommy Foxx.

I was seriously expecting a tongue lashing from Coach Harding, as my behavior in that exhibition was most abhorrent with her entire approach to "the game," and thusly was completely caught off-guard by my revered professor's initial greeting.

In fact, I was so thrown off kilter that I just looked at her for seemingly five full and "unsure" seconds before reacting.

Coach had a very warm smile on her face, and I sensed she felt just a bit of the inner demons raging throughout me, as it was becoming more known of my sister's battle with cancer, even though I had kept the details pretty much in check with only my inner circle. Still, these things have a way of going public, so to speak, and I can only suspect that this was through the benevolent feelings of those I loved and was loved by, and even my team mates and friends on campus, sending signals of hope to each other, and maybe contributing the much appreciated gift of prayer.

Sharon and I had established our relationship to many that previous spring when we were first falling in love; walking throughout the East Valley campus, holding hands and kissing each other whenever we thought we had a proper moment.

"Yes," I smiled back at Coach Harding, "I guess you could say that."

Before she could reply, I continued, "Coach, I am sorry for the way I acted in the game Saturday; I really, really am sorry!"

Women have so powerfully affected me my entire life, and I am not talking just about romance here. I had gleaned much wisdom from said sex, even at my young and tender age, never minding what the future would allow, and here again was yet another powerful gift from the growing list of females contributing to the higher development of yours truly.

"Jesse, do you have the time to walk with me for a few minutes," she inquired, but more so discreetly requesting.

"Yes mamm, I do," answering cautiously.

We strolled down a corridor and she stopped and turned towards me.

"You are a very special young man, Mr. Mouchebeau. I watched how you handled yourself last year: on campus, in the classroom and on the court, both in practice and during games. I also was well aware of the countless hours you spent in the gym, after your practices ended, constantly striving to improve your game."

She continued, "I know and can see how talented a player you are, and can perceive your frustrations developing with Coach Melling, which in turn are being transferred sometimes to your team mates and to opposing players, such as that guard from Patrick Henry in Saturday's game."

I was listening to her, very respectfully, as I sensed this was more than a pep talk; this was from her heart.

"I am aware of your sister's battle with cancer; and, began to know and understand your very unique relationship with her, probably starting with last year's Christmas tournament, and seeing you battered and bruised from what I found out to be your retaliation in avenging her honor; and, this information given to me by your very own coach, who, believe it or not, does have some very meaningful respect for you as a young man."

"I also, from time to time, would catch a glimpse of you and that lovely young girl from Lee University, walking throughout these grounds, oblivious to the trials current in your young lives, and giving each other moments of hope. Those instants made me smile to myself!"

"This is what life is about, Jesse," she furthered. "Life is not basketball, life is not academics, and life is not so callous. Life is living with each other, for each other, and giving back to those we love, and to those that need."

I listened to Coach, and started to speak, but she grabbed my hand and held it looking into my eyes.

"One last thing Jesse; you need to embrace this, and to continue to nurture your feelings for those around you and be strong, because you will be needed even more than you have ever imagined. I expect great things from you, and not just here at East Valley but later, after college, and truly feel that you will affect many in your life; others will need your trust and faith and guidance, Mr. Mouchebeau, and I suspect that you will be there for them!"

Heartfelt words indeed and I could see my teacher's eyes filling with adoring moisture, and I swear I could've fallen in that "worship/respect kind of love" with her; well, probably I did.

All I could manage was "thanks Coach, I really appreciate you saying this, and again, I apologize for last Saturday."

"No need to apologize, Jesse; I do not condone that type of behavior but that player asked for it; and, I did see the two of you out in the lobby together, which impressed me quite a lot!"

Then she put her hand, most affectionately, on my shoulder and winked at me.

"See you in class, and good luck with this year's team; it looks like it may be a long tough season for the Hornets!"

She could see what was going on with our team, and was also very aware of the talent we lost to graduation, and I suspect was not a great admirer of Coach Melling's system and methods!

"See you Coach," I reiterated, and smiled and walked away.

*     *     *

I sat on the stone wall surrounding East Valley's infamous duck pond just next to the student union building, feeling the warmth of this early November morning's glorious and unabated sun, and lost myself in thought.

I reflected on how my life had evolved to this very moment, but from the perspective of many of those singular episodes specifically affecting me, those that involved women; whether they were friends, paramours, older sisters of friends, teachers, parents, cousins, etc., and of course my beloved Loretta.

My sister had always contributed to my well being, and of this there was no question; but lately, especially these past two years, there was an extrasensory connection far beyond what we always both knew existed, and it was growing even more so.

I was deathly afraid of this though, as I suspected, no I *knew*, that there was a developing "transference" of Loretta's most profound abilities to me, and the reason for this was her doing; to protect her most beloved brother for the rest of his life, which would not include her, at least in the physical sense.

I was scared beyond comprehension, beyond what was fair for an 18 year old boy seemingly just getting started in life.

I thought again of Coach's words, and while they did give me a momentary respite from my pain and anguish, I also derived from our conversation the very definite signal she gave me regarding my sister's needs; and promised myself, then and there to be strong for Loretta, mom and dad, and of course Jess, swearing for God to not only witness, but hold me accountable for my actions, as I feared failure if things got very bad, and discerned they indeed would!

\*          \*          \*

Early that evening I got a call from my mother, and I knew something was very, very wrong.

"Jesse honey," she began, "Loretta collapsed at dinner, and we took her to the hospital. She's doing fine, but Doc Samuel advised us to have her to stay there overnight, so they can run some tests tomorrow and she can rest."

I was stunned and remained silent, waiting for my mom to continue.

"We have no idea of what's going on, but she has lost a little more weight, and has been so tired lately; your father and I stayed with her until she fell asleep. She made me promise to call you and said 'please tell Jesse not to worry, I am just run down, and will be fine, I promise.' I believe those were her very words honey."

Mom was scared and obviously trying to protect me, remaining very calm with her demeanor and I decided to try and do exactly the same. I knew she and dad were going out of their minds with grief, yet they would be very fearful for my collapse and I was going to spare them of any concern; they would need their thoughts and prayers for Loretta, not me.

"Mom, I am okay, but I am coming home, I gotta be with her."

She started to say something, and very quickly I continued.

"I will wait until tomorrow to drive up there," I lied, "so don't worry, I'll be fine. Please tell Loretta that I love her and will be there soon."

"I will Jesse; your father and I will see her tomorrow, and let her know that you'll be home soon."

"Bye mom, I love you."

"Good evening Jesse, we love you, too!"

*     *     *

Again, Jess and I held each other.

Again, we cried like babies with each other.

Again we promised each other love and support and faith.

Again, we were collectively crushed by life!

I drove home that very evening, after calling Sharon, and after leaving a note taped to both Coach Melling's and Coach Harding's office doors, letting them know I would be back in a few days.

I would not miss anything important, but Jess had a game in a couple of days and just could not leave, which pained him to no end. Football was still in full swing, wrapping up its season, but we still were a week away from our first game.

I could give a shit about basketball at the moment, yet somehow knew that Loretta would be disappointed in me if I neglected my passion (not to mention my scholarship).

I would be there for her, early that very next morning, and drove very cautiously, feeling my beloved and most adored sister's presence, guiding me home to her side.

Sound's crazy, but I cannot to this day remember any details of that ten hour drive; only getting there, at her hospital bedside by 6am, to have her awaken, focus her eyes on me, and smile.

I once again fell head over heels in love with my sister!

# Chapter Twenty Two

"Her sight, can turn a heart around,
She fights, might just knock you down...."

She's a Warrior

# XXII

Every single one of us handles peril, trauma, grief and tragedy in our own specialized manner; with each of us concocting whatever resolve we can muster to cope!  It is human nature, and it is most necessary.

In my sister's continuing battle with breast cancer, never was this more apparent to me.  Mom, dad, Jess, Sharon, our friends and relatives all seemingly had very unique approaches with Loretta, with one very important factor in common, and that was the heartfelt love for my sister!

Each of us had a "different Loretta" to lose, and every single one of us would feel this unbelievable pain in so many different fashions, with so many different reactions.

All of us would be impacted dramatically in our lives, collectively bearing this anguish and trying, and failing, to make any kind of sense of all of this.

The most despairing thought for me was that I and all others were losing one person, but Loretta was losing us all. Whenever I tried to think of this from her perspective, it completely paralyzed me and I could not even swallow, immediately tearing up and wishing that I could die right along side of her, holding her body and departing at just the very same instant to our greater reward, together, holding hands and skipping onto God and His realm!

How does one, though, bail on the rest of the world for a single person? I knew in my heart that this was not to be, but just the same I wished for some kind of way to accomplish this very thing. I simply could not bear to be without her; I did not think that I would survive and really did not care to.

I could only imagine what others felt, especially my parents; I mean how does one say goodbye to their very own child? That has proven to be the most traumatic experience known to mankind, and carrying the pain I felt while at the same time realizing that it was even greater with mom and dad was incomprehensible to me!

Loretta had collapsed due to the cancer reappearing in her other breast, and then invading her lymph system, with no regard to its ugly purpose, other than to destroy this wonderful young girl; never minding her more than courageous fight, mentally, physically and most definitely spiritually.

The holidays, both Thanksgiving and Christmas were very somber affairs to say the least. We did celebrate them, at Loretta's insistence, inviting Jess and Sharon for both, and we did collectively manage to grab a few smiles, laughs, but the tears that were shed by all of us far outweighed their happier counterparts.

My basketball season, so far, seemed just a blur; I played with more finesse and confidence, but Coach Melling seemed to use me exactly as my freshman year; when we needed points, I was called to action.

Or, if we were getting our asses kicked and Bullet heard enough of my friends in the stands yelling for him to play me, would seemingly do so out of guilt.

I really did not care, and my team mates all were stellar with respect to my attitude and role on this year's squad. They seemed to find it in their hearts to forgive my apathy, and one thing is very sure with athletes, especially on a higher level; they do know talent, and respectfully acknowledge so, no matter the competition with each other. Our players, especially the other guards: Mark, Blakely, T.J., Mitch and Jimmy, all "knew" how good a player I was, and this was some sort of redemption for me. I mean I loved this game and busted my ass to be the greatest player I could imagine, and they all knew so.

The East Tennessee Valley Hornets were obviously worse than last year's team; losing Joe and Kelly was more than we could resolve, especially with a coach that was clueless with the college game and its players.

I did have a bit of liberation, ironically, when we again played Lee University at their gym, again getting our asses kicked, worse than even last year there. I hit all but one of my five shots taken, and gathered a few assists while playing fairly well defensively; all of this in front of Sharon's school's fans, who by now were well aware of our romance.

Still, it did not truly matter to me, and even though she was very proud of her boyfriend and was sincerely demonstratively so on the court after the game, understood my spiritual pall, as she was all too conscious of my pain of not having my sister there to witness her brother's moment!

By the grace of God we did not have another damn Christmas tournament this year. The "All Tennessee Classic" rarely invited any school back for consecutive appearances other than the tournament winner, and sometimes a particular team that had miraculously performed, such as we did; but, we were bypassed much to Coach's chagrin, and to all of our relief.

I sort of suspected that our team's "ritual voodoo prayer," concocted by me, and performed after the Lee game without Coach's knowledge but with full consent and support of all of us players, contributed to our extended Christmas vacation. Most likely however, and more accurately, the reason for our lack of a holiday tournament was Melling's misguided and hopeful belief in the invitation that was not to be, and thusly never pursuing other options, of which there were several!

Bullet lost; we won.

Again, thank the Lord!

Every single one of us was an extremely happy camper, and all had wished my sister well through their sincere invocations to me.

As said, the holidays were a sad reminder of actual life, and every one of my adored and immediate circle was affected greatly.

\*        \*        \*

Jess was heartbroken, understandably so. He played an entire football season without his beloved girlfriend witnessing a single play, and while this did not affect his play overtly so, it most definitely impacted his demeanor in the locker room and off the field.

My best friend was a very popular student/athlete, even as a sophomore, but could not mask his heartbreak with his naturally gregarious demeanor. On occasion there would be the Jess Butkus we all knew and loved, but just as my personality had taken a major hit, so had his!

We tried to see each other every day, as I was his lifeline to Loretta, and we both knew well that when there were others to share one's pain, it helped, most assuredly so.

Still, he lamented his girlfriend's dire battle and I could see the pounds ever so slightly burning off of his magnificent body, and the stress lines etching their way upon his very handsome face.

In our circle, Jess' pain was unique to only him, as he was losing his potential life mate, and apparently the girl of his dreams. He worshipped my sister, in a very healthy manner; that is of having such a profound respect for one of the opposite sex, which when found was truly something to cherish!

He adored my sister, and she him. Their relationship was one of a slowly and most surely developing friendship and love for one another, stealthily gaining ever the slightest momentum towards a lifelong journey together. Jess full well knew that Loretta was his soul mate, and was fearful of losing something he could never hope to regain.

My friend confided to me that he quietly cried himself to sleep every single night; this most awesome specimen of a young man hurting so much was sometimes more than I could envision, as I did exactly the very same thing.

Jess watched Loretta fade away, with her health declining towards its inevitable conclusion. He would drive to my house, sometimes by himself, just to share an evening with her and my parents.

Loretta was so kind to him, taking their conversations many times in unexpected directions; talking about football, opera, his own family, and life after college. This helped her boyfriend quite a lot, as my sister always seemingly knew how to tap into one's spiritual serenity. She also assured Jess, many times, that they would reunite again; that he just needed his faith to mend and guide his broken heart.

I hurt so badly for them, and prayed for the very same things they did. These beautiful young people deserved their lasting union, and hopefully with God's grace, this would be so.

Their devotion would continue to grow, even until Loretta's leaving this earth. It may have been the most magnificent love affair I would ever be privileged to witness, and at the same time the most crushing.

I thanked God for bringing Jess Butkus into my life; to be a best friend and to share my pain, to laugh with me, and most of all to let me know that my sister had truly found romance of the very highest order with this amazing person.

We both would be devastated, and we both would need each other to somehow find our way back into the realm of sanity and some measure of peace here on earth!

*    *    *

As said, my parents suffered the very most unimaginable of pain; that of saying goodbye to your child.

Later in life I would know the most profound happiness and indescribable love of holding your child, close to your chest, and whispering in her little ear that everything was going to be alright; but of course at this time I had no clue as to the resonance of such an endearment.

Mom and dad were also physically and mentally changing before my very eyes, with both seemingly visibly growing older by the day. They were heartbroken as well, but in a way unbeknownst to me, Jess, Sharon and others. Only Loretta seemed to understand their grief, and was continuously reassuring them of her "beginning a new life"; too hard to witness, and even harder to realize.

Mom was very cryptically, ever so slightly going crazy, and I could see this in the little things that were her daily routines. She would forget who she was talking with on occasion, even momentarily, but alarming so just the same. She also would get very angry with me and dad, surprising us with her outbursts, yet we forgave her nearly always excepting those few times we retaliated without thinking due to our own feelings of utter despair and roller-coaster emotions.

Mom was also spending more time in church, trying some way to connect with a God with whom she was truly angry and at times unforgiving.

Slowly she started to find peace, but watching my mother transform into someone I did not recognize at times, was very disconcerting.

She and Loretta would talk every single day, with mom holding onto her only salvation, that of a miracle occurring, which I guess was always a possibility.

I certainly grabbed onto this lifeline a well, but could not convince myself of its reliability.

Mom, actually had stronger belief, and let my sister know of her convictions in this regard, with Loretta so wisely agreeing, to save her beloved mother whatever ounce of pain possible, whenever she could.

These two women so influenced and enriched my life that I could never hope to repay either one, yet they both knew that I was somehow "chosen" to hopefully empower other women in this world; maybe daughters, maybe girlfriends, and quite possibly the ones chosen for those most sacred of relationships with the opposite sexes.

At any rate, Loretta and mom seemed to unite spiritually, giving each other strength and perseverance, with my mother letting her know of how very proud and amazed she could be of such a young girl.

I still do not understand how my mother survived her daughter's death, and for years we would laugh and cry remembering how very special this extraordinary young lady was; how wonderful it was to just be a part of her brief life.

Mom would say to me as long as she lived: "I had the privilege and honor of knowing Loretta her entire life!"

*     *     *

Dad was changing as well, but more so physically than mentally. He actually got very sick a couple of times, and I can only attribute this to anxiety of the highest order.

I feared for dad, as I knew in my heart that as physically strong as he was, he did not possess my mother's internal immune abilities to fight those silent and yet most deadly of all human enemies; those "stress arrows" and subsequent wounds that inevitably took many of us out.

Dad would, as well as mom, spend some time every single evening with his daughter, caressing her and re-living many of those nearly forgotten moments of her childhood; and, maybe more importantly much of his own life experience, as he did seem to find solace in Loretta's countenance and thought, which would somehow relax my father, as dad did carry an extreme amount of guilt from an extremely rough childhood, parental and spousal mistakes, and of course the horrors of the World War in which he and so many others had valiantly fought.

Loretta also very presciently realized that her father would have a much tougher time surviving her death than her mother. My sister was fully aware of mom's strength, and of dad's liabilities.

Women have for time immemorial proven to bear witness to, and then find some miraculous way to carry on with the worse that life offered; with their men falling along the wayside.

God's selection process for the survival of the human species? I truly thought so then, and know so now!

This amazing sex has taken the worse imaginable beatings enacted upon, morally, spiritually and physically, and yet found the strength to continue.

I knew in my heart that the just maybe the singular most important lesson for me in all of this grief and turmoil was the realization of this, and the subsequent learning and absorption of said qualities!

Dad and I talked when I was home to see Loretta, but for some reason would not get on the phone with me while I was away at school during this time period.

At first I was slightly offended, but gradually realized that his health was failing and he simply could not bear any more pain, especially from a son who reminded him of himself, and he was quite possibly embarrassed by his own lack of resolve.

Of course, I never thought of my father as anything but tough, but it was his thoughts that counted here, not mine!

Loretta would tell me, when no one was within earshot: "Jesse, it's dad that you have to care for, not mom, you know. I am so worried that he will not survive me leaving, and will need you to save him. Please be there for him, he will need you so badly, and Mom's help will not matter as much as yours; this I honestly know, it will be up to his only son."

I knew she was deadly accurate on this account, and felt even more pressure bearing its suppressing weight upon my soul.

Loretta was so wise! She would for the rest of her days give love and support and unbelievable faith to both of her parents, whom she well knew were crushed with the reality and guilt of losing their child;

and, she would always add in her prayers one last modicum of hope for our father's survival.

*     *     *

Sharon's grief for my sister was an amalgamation of feelings projected in several directions, all at the same time, confusing, disappointing and changing her personality and demeanor into that of a young woman for whom she did not care whatsoever!

I forgave her for her lapses into bitchiness, as I knew well that losing her father in divorce was very effectively crushing her spirit, as she both idolized and hated this man; conflicting emotions literally ripping her personality apart!

She saw Loretta only once after the holidays, and that was when we both had a weekend free together, which was becoming even rarer than before.

That late winter weather added further insult to injury as the winds howled outside my sister's bedroom, accentuating the utter despair of a dying young woman, and another young girl's layers of grief.

I left them alone for several hours which was good for Sharon and Loretta, and yet at the same time unbelievably painful for me as every moment I was within literal grasp of my beloved sister, and could not physically touch her, hold her, or just look at her, frustrated me like nothing I've experienced. Still, I knew these two girls needed their own special time together.

Apparently Loretta had said some very enlightening things to Sher, as on our way back to our respective campuses, my girlfriend seemed visibly relieved, even though she dared not say so, for fear of appearing self-indulgent.

Again, my sister had proven her most amazing of healing powers;

though her body was wasting away, her mind seemed to grow, and this was borne out in everyone she touched in her last days.

Sharon knew she would survive her parents divorce, and sensed that her own mom and dad would eventually come to some sort of reasonable conclusion to, and affirmation of the life they had shared, most importantly knowing that their marriage had produced two incredible daughters.

I would experience in my adult life these very same conflicts regarding the ending of a storybook romance and marriage, realizing too that my wife and I had accomplished something extraordinary, and that was the miracle of two beautiful and healthy young girls.

Once again, my soul mate and sister was preparing me, through Sharon, for my future survival.

*       *       *

My last days with Loretta will never, ever be forgotten; not even the smallest of details, as I purposely and diligently cataloged seemingly every single thing we did, everything we discussed, and every prayer spoken together.

My sister was just magnificent, and there's simply no better way to describe the wonder and utter amazement I experienced with this stunning person who was my closest friend in the entire world!

I can clearly recall three distinct phases of the final weeks of my sister's life. The first being a still self-sufficient Loretta, with her being able to get to the bathroom on her own and feeding herself in the kitchen, with her intellect as sharp as ever, and demeanor that of the girl we all knew and loved.

We must have reviewed our entire lives together in those precious days, laughing, crying, and recalling the all too vivid emotions spent with each of our lives' events, together and apart.

We took advantage of a couple of late winter days that God had so graced with an aberrantly warm phase, to walk outside, and actually relax on a couple of lounge chairs, soaking up the sun's most lovely rays, and napping while holding hands.

This will always be one of my most precious and fondest of all memories, and mom would equally recall this particular snapshot, as she had lovingly witnessed us from her vantage point in the house.

This phase also saw Jess visit as often as he could; getting away from school was not as easy for him being not directly related to our family, even though we all considered him to be so.

Watching these two was good for me, but I clearly sensed that Loretta was ever so slightly pushing this great friend of hers and mine away; and, so benignly that he did not realize anything. Again, this was my sister's way to help preserve and at the same time nurture her most beloved of all boyfriends.

Jess would be spared the last days, not because of his wishes, but Loretta's, and truthfully, this was better for both.

I slept in my sister's bedroom every night I was there, sometimes strumming my guitar quietly until she fell asleep, and again giving our parent's maybe that greatest gift of all; that of sibling's love for each other.

I would kiss her forehead and eyes while she slept, saying prayers for her safe passage; these invocations were maybe my most artistic creations ever, but they took their particular toll on me as I sometimes could not finish, choking on my tears, and shaking uncontrollably, letting God complete whatever I could not.

We promised each other the next world, and I took it upon myself to find a way to truly believe in our future together.

Loretta was still my normal sister at this point, and I so tightly held onto this vision and experience.

The second phase of her moving towards God was extremely tough to take, but somehow He gave me the strength and wisdom to not only cope, but maybe excel when I was really needed by Loretta.

This was when I was given an official leave of absence from school, and I certainly took advantage of East Valleys' good graces!

I had already sort of moved back into our house a few weeks earlier, but now I would stay every single night, regardless of the time spent.

I ran baths for her daily, carrying and placing my most beloved soul mate into said warm waters, soothing her aching body.

The scars on her chest were all too familiar reminders of this entire ordeal, yet they only enhanced her profound loveliness.

To many it would seem bizarre for a brother to see and act with his sister in a manner such as this, but to us, and as equally important to mom and dad, it was the only way, it was our way, period!

I would wash her hair for her, and gently help her clean her own body with those favorite cloths she had kept from childhood.

One day, she took both of my hands and slowly placed them where her breast had been removed, giving me that wonderful look of hers, winking and telling me she loved me more than anything; and, only until my first daughter was born, many years later, did anything even remotely come close to that epiphany, for I knew then and there, that Loretta had been reborn, and thanked God profusely for delivering her!

These days were precious and few and I cannot imagine not having shared them with her. I was so fortunate to be in a place in my life where this was possible, as many times for others it is not, and how awful that must be.

Still, here was that proverbial double-edged sword again carving me into pieces, as I would have her, and then lose her.

My sister finally slipped into the coma we were all prepared for, yet still found it hard to believe and accept. She seemed very much at peace, and I would, as mom and dad, whisper into her ears our most sacred of vows.

One afternoon, another sunny one at that, I felt an overwhelming feeling to be at her side.

I heard Loretta slightly gasp, grabbing a few precious and agitated yet unconscious breaths.

I knew what this meant, and called out for my mom, as dad was at work, forgetting that mom was also away on an errand.

Loretta took an intense swallow of air, appearing to resurrect herself, but again, I was ready.

I whispered in her ear those words of mine for her that will never go away, and let my sister die in my arms, holding her tightly to my chest, and giving her to God.

I had lost the singular most beloved person in my life, and for the longest time could not remove myself from her bed, with my head on her stomach, holding on, not wanting to let her go.

Finally I did so, kissing her eyes for the very last time!

*     *     *

Loretta's funeral was stunning, with several hundred in attendance; so many that were there to acknowledge this magnificent young girl's life, and to give thanks to my family for providing her to the world!

Jess looked liked a millions bucks, as did his family, who finally met my parents for the very first time, albeit under such somber circumstances yet important to our cause with each other as best friends.

My friend was regal in his bearing, yet at the very same time a worn and beaten young man; an honorable one, though to be sure, who cherished and literally worshipped my sister, but most importantly respected her.

TJ, Barbie and Sharon all drove up together, which was so thoughtful of my team mate, as he knew Sher could not have made it on her own in her current state!

It was wonderful to see my girlfriend again, but we both knew things had started to change, yet it really did not keep us from sharing a few memorable kisses, and somehow connecting on an otherworldly manner with regards to the friendship we had developed, and the love we had shared. We both intuited that our relationship would somehow survive, but apparently not in our collective and immediate futures and this truly seemed fine for us. I guess we were indeed growing up; I only hoped that on some level we would again be able to regain our passion and laughter.

For now though, my heartbreak was one girl and, only one. Loretta's death seemed to erase much of what was wrong with my life, giving me a much greater perspective in general, but also some of the good stuff was affected, Sharon being the most obvious.

It's funny but I was not at all concerned anymore with my place on the East Valley varsity basketball team. I had only missed one of our games that season, and I had miraculously still managed to play decently, even if it was on Coach's never changing sporadic timetable; and ironically, the very last game saw me contribute maybe one of my finest efforts ever. Good way to go out, I would later think!

My team mates sent flowers, Coach Melling did so as well, and Coach Harding wrote me a wonderful letter, which I still keep to this day.

Ostentatious as it was, the grandest floral arrangement came from my friend and New York Mafia Family Godfather Giovanni Caruso, with an "endowment" to be set up by my mother and father in Loretta's honor, where and whenever it deemed fit.

Mom would do so later in life, conceiving and developing our county's very first rape-crisis center.

Many, many friends and family all came to pay their respects, and I truly was touched by all those Loretta had so obviously affected. I thought to myself how she would be just grinning at this ridiculous, yet endearing turnout.

We all prayed, and I delivered a brief, yet apparently moving story of one of our childhood nights together, staying up, and figuring a way to take on the world.

Well, my sister and I did just that; only sometimes the greatest of all of us die much too early for the rest of us to actually understand the endgame that was projected and eventually would have been enacted upon.

Still, Loretta and I conquered quite a lot, and of this I was most proud. There really was no need to say anything more, as it was obvious to all the love I shared with my sister.

We laid our wonderful Loretta to rest, and I went back to college that very afternoon, thankfully with Jess at my side.

We did not shed a tear the entire trip; I suspect we were all cried out by then. Instead, we laughed and laughed, and resurrected our own brief life together, promising to continue on in the very best of friendships this earth had ever witnessed, quite obviously influenced by the girl with whom we had shared our love.

\*　　　\*　　　\*

Three weeks later my father dropped dead in his tracks, walking from our kitchen into the den.

His daughter's death had literally broken his heart!

# Chapter Twenty Three

"The lady is the sea,
She shimmers gracefully,
The lady is the sea,
Always there in his life...."

The Lady is the Sea

# XXIII

Just before my sophomore year ended I had made up my mind to transfer to the University of Northern Virginia at Fairfax, a small Division I school less than an hour from my home, for my junior and senior years. The head basketball coach was very interested in me playing for him, as my high school coach and he were close friends that communicated often, and the progress I had made in the last two years was more than enough for him to offer me at the very least a partial scholarship, with the caveat of a full ride if I could earn it practicing with the team this year, while not officially playing; the inter-collegiate rules required that I "red-shirt" (or sit out) one year because my transfer was not of the hardship category.

Now it would take me three years to graduate, but I really wanted to be near mom and home; we had taken too many hits and truly needed each other.

The upside of all of this was that I would have another year to improve my skills, and many locally would get a chance to see me play college basketball, and most importantly of all, my mother!

Mostly though, I was still overwhelmed by my sister's death, and somehow just being near the house we grew up in made me feel closer to her. I knew logically that this was ridiculous, but my emotions greatly influenced this conclusion.

Jess and I had talked for countless hours regarding my decision, and again, my best friend was heartbroken but understood well my feelings.

Jesus, does life ever fucking run smoothly, or possibly a little comfortably? I was once again seriously having my doubts.

I also missed Sharon greatly, to be sure, but we had cautiously and consciously drifted our separate ways this past summer and for the time being this was necessary for both of us to heal!

Added to that, and even though my chances of playing should have been excellent, or at the very least pretty good at East Valley with Mark, Blakely and T.J. all lost to graduation, I truly did not trust Coach Melling's intents nor his acumen; I still envisioned myself forever glued to the proverbial pines, wasting away my college years as a player, much of it due to simply being in the wrong system.

Missing my team mates, friends and professors would be tough, but the real heartbreak, though, for me would be not seeing my very best friend Jess on a daily basis; the countless hours we had spent together during these past two years of college were beyond memorable, they were life changing, and how does one shed something so internal, so meaningful?

He was still in shock, as all of us, but we had to move on, and I promised him, as only the very best of friends could, that we would not lose contact, ever!

That summer we did get the chance to spend a glorious week

together at the beach, just hanging out, swimming, tanning, drinking just enough to stay out of trouble, and reminiscing about the girl we had both so adored.

*     *     *

My first day in class at my new school was significant in one very obvious respect; I had not paid one ounce of attention to anything my teachers had said, instead drifting into my thoughts, in every single class, of having made the wrong decision.

My instincts were on high alert, and that evening after talking with my mom for a good two hours, called Jess to share my thoughts.

"I would be one happy son of a bitch if you came back here Jesse," my friend stated, "but I know it's confusing and is this something you truly want?"

"I'm not sure brother," I replied, "transferring is a major pain in the ass; Jesus, just getting in here was a hassle!"

"Anything I can do?" he asked.

"Maybe; let me first call Big A.L. and see if he can pull any strings," I answered.

A.L. Lamb was the dean of admissions, and just so happened to sponsor our unique and crazy ass fraternity. Many years later I would dedicate one of my books to Big A.L., which had greatly pleased him, telling me so in one of the infrequent, yet most meaningful letters we traded; and later according to his sister who had told me again, soon after he had passed away from finally being just too old and much too tired to carry on with life.

"Shit Jesse, if anyone can make it happen, it's Big A.L." he added.

We all revered the man.

"I'll call you tomorrow," I said; "I need to talk with mom some more, but she is very much in favor of my finishing down there with you, which totally surprised me. She said that later I would understand even more so, but basketball was simply not worth the pain and anguish, especially when best friends were involved!"

"She said," I continued, trying to recall her exact words, 'your happiness is my life, Jesse; never doubt that for a second.'"

"Your mom is the best," Jess stated, "just the best!"

"Yes she is my friend," I concluded.

Jess and I said our goodbyes, still very tough to do so even after all that had happened, but I guess this is one aspect of what friendship and love truly means.

The next day I went to all of my classes, with much the same inattention as the day before, and had made up my mind to transfer back to East Valley, however much effort that it might take.

That afternoon I talked with my new coach at U Nova, and he was more than understanding; several years ago he had also ironically lost a sister to cancer, and truly understood the chaos and emotional scarring that I was experiencing.

He added that whatever path I decided upon, it would be the right one; something of which I took to heart and thought of often.

I called A.L. Lamb, and from the tone of my voice he knew something was troubling me greatly.

"Jesse, it's so good to hear from you, but what's wrong dear boy?"

"Big A.L., I think I made a mistake in transferring here. I thought that I really wanted to play ball near home, but I miss all of you, and it doesn't seem right that I am here! Would it be possible to get back into East Valley this fall? I don't even care about playing for Coach Melling anymore!"

A.L. was well aware, as most of the East Valley student body and administration, of my on-going dilemma with the head basketball coach; too many had seen me play pretty well in the last two years, and

I did have my small but effective core group of fans that would be very vocal during our home games!

Big A.L. would say the words that I would recall decades later, while giving a speech at one of the homecoming alumni weekend events:

"Son, you just get your things and come on home; I will take care of everything!"

And, take care of everything Big A.L. did: the avalanche of re-admission paperwork, my class schedule, my new housing, which would last through graduation and be my very favorite abode while there, and every single ounce of university protocol and mind-numbing procedure that needed attention.

This wonderful man had stepped up and taken care of one of his boys; something I'd never forget.

People sometimes were just magnificent, delivering affection and resolution with no other interest save for the one in need!

I returned to East Tennessee Valley College, my home away from home, the very next day.

*     *     *

Interestingly enough, the very first day back I ran smack into Coach Melling just outside his office, which was in the East Valley basketball arena complex, while on my way to another of Coach Ellen Harding's advanced science of movement classes.

"Jesse, it's great to see you; I had heard you transferred, are you coming back?"

"Yes, coach, I thought I wanted to be near home, but this is also my home," I replied, probably not without a little edge.

"I am very sorry about your sister, Jesse; same for Mrs. Melling."

I knew this to be true, as I really liked Coach's wife, and remembered our conversation nearly two years previous when she had made that glorious breakfast for our entire team, commenting on how proud she was of my now infamous fight with Reece Davis defending my sister's honor.

"Please give her my best sir, and tell her thanks!"

Melling continued, "I look forward to you playing this year Jesse, I think we will be pretty good with the new freshman and two transfer players we got."

I had no idea of what Coach was talking about; after last year's season had ended I literally had deleted from my thoughts East Valley basketball operations in general, and Bullet's actions specifically. Plus, I now only had a couple of close friends on the team that were there with me when we were incoming freshmen, and it seemed like a different ball club altogether.

"Coach, I am not playing this year," I emphatically stated, "it's no fun for me," adding very matter of factly.

Melling had the most quizzical look on his face and replied, "I thought you transferred to that Division I school to play ball."

"I did, Coach; it's here that I do not want to play!"

I politely excused myself, needing to get to class, and have never to this day forgotten how good that brief exchange made me feel; to say what had been building inside of me for two entire years to the Coach who had never respected my basketball skills, without being rude in the slightest. I felt that I had grown even more so.

After class with Coach Harding, she motioned for me to stay for a few minutes and again take another walk with her.

I had no idea other than maybe she wanted to simply welcome me back, and again extend her condolences.

"I heard you and Coach Melling in the hall this morning," she began; "wow, sitting on the bench for us this year doesn't appeal to you, Jesse?" she added smiling very sweetly.

Coach Harding, as I had often said, was so ahead of her time in many, many ways, and I believe truly influenced hundreds of college women, and some men including me, over the years in manners that were wholly unique and extremely important. She was all too aware of the two year clash I had experienced with the East Valley's men's head basketball coach.

"Well, it's great to have you back," she continued; "I can only imagine how you feel after losing your sister, and again I am truly sorry for that, but do believe you belong here for many reasons dear Jesse, especially in continuing the adventures with your friend Jess Butkus," winking and adding a bit cryptically, knowing that seemingly ALL of the East Valley campus population was not only aware of, but very used to our now somewhat infamous exploits!

"I am happy to be back here, Coach," I replied; "I am going to miss playing this year though, in fact I don't know how I will occupy my afternoons."

She, as well as the entire East Valley coaching fraternity, was very cognizant of the hours I spent in the gym, before and after our practices, perfecting my skills and obviously improving at a rate that was beyond the norm.

"Well, that is exactly why I wanted to speak with you Jesse; I have a proposition for you, something I think might interest you," she offered.

I just looked at her, inviting her to continue, as I had no clue as to what she had in mind.

"A.L. Lamb informed me of your impending return yesterday, letting me know of your intentions not to play this year! And, then earlier over-hearing you and Coach Melling brought me to this offer that I had entertained in my mind for the last day or so; I'd like you to take over my duties as the head Junior Varsity women's basketball coach, and let me add that this would help me to concentrate on the varsity squad!"

Budget cuts and other reasons, one of which I suspected was "the good ol' boy network" of thinking that women's sports in general, and basketball in particular, were just not as important as the men's side of things, demanded that Coach Harding oversee both the varsity and jayvee teams, which she had done so for many years.

She added, "I do not expect you to give me an answer right now, just think about it for a few days and let me know; either accepting or declining will be fine with me Jesse, please believe that!"

I looked at this remarkable woman, and I guess my very obvious grin was my answer, as she returned my smile and said "congratulations Mr. Mouchebeau, you are now the head coach of the East Valley Hornets women's junior varsity basketball team."

Coach then hugged me, something much unexpected but welcomed, and added, "Are you free for a meeting this afternoon, maybe 3 o'clock?"

"Yes maam, I'll be in your office then; and thanks Coach, this means quite a lot to me!"

Once again I was overwhelmed by yet another woman's absolute intellect and insight, and even more so touched by her departing words: "no Jesse, this means much more to me, and my girls!"

\*         \*         \*

This year's basketball season came and went. I had a terrific time coaching the girls and they apparently were just as enamored by the attention and respect I gave them, playing extremely hard and delivering a just barely yet totally acceptable winning season. It was everything that I had hoped for, and all of us were greatly rewarded by this experience!

Coach Harding had very graciously stayed out of the way, only counseling me when I requested so, which was maybe thrice.

She had also given me high praise with regards to my composure on the bench when things were going poorly; she still knew that I was prone to confront certain situations of conflict, but obviously I had matured.

My "girls" honored me with a beautifully framed team photo, all signed by them and Coach Harding, thanking me for enriching their lives, and also making a very endearing reference to my sister Loretta; of course my eyes welled up with tears as I was extremely proud of the effort my team made in the course of our time together.

Maybe the best part of all of this was the fact that I had impressed my players, other coaches, students and faculty with my skills as a head coach, and was made very aware of this through their various letters, notes and verbal acknowledgements, again, most notably Coach Harding's.

Melling was not surprisingly absent from this praise as his team suffered through their worst losing season yet, and I actually thought that he was on the way to getting fired from East Tennessee Valley, as he was progressively getting less and less results from each succeeding team that he coached.

Funny thing is, I missed playing ball, but not as much as I had thought that I might. My friends still on the team asked if I would play my senior year, and again I said unequivocally "no thanks."

I did keep my skills sharpened, though, by playing in the intramural "A league," which was loaded with former (and some of them good enough to play in college) high school ballers, averaging 30 points a game and leading our team to the championship. The one major difference, aside from the obvious aspect of talent, from playing varsity ball was that I had an enormous amount of fun!

Coach Melling was even seen at a couple of our games; duly noted to me from Jess; my best friend had also come to all of my jayvee girls' home games, and was truly impressed by my abilities to lead these girls into battle, and exhibited his booming and very fine tenor voice in cheering them on when needed!

How cool was my best friend? The coolest!

Jess was there for me, for many reasons, but most importantly to remind me of the fact that I had a bigger game plan in life than college basketball; this profound concept was not lost upon me in the least.

The remaining couple of months of my junior year at East Valley went by quite quickly. After the basketball season had ended it seemed as if all I did was go to class, study, play fraternity league softball and party more than a little. I guess I needed the respite.

My female liaisons were infrequent, yet extremely meaningful in that I was only looking for companionship, and I luckily happened upon two East Valley co-eds searching for just the very same results.

You know sometimes we just need the proverbial escape; maybe both of these lovely young women had suffered through similar tragedy as I (we never got that far in dialogue), and were also looking for release from said pain! At any rate, we gave each other comfort and pleasure, truly wanted by us and not questioned whatsoever.

Mom seemed to be finally settling in and adjusting to all of the previous years' tragedy and suffering, as I could see glimpses of her old self, just occasionally mind you, but there nonetheless, and this made me feel just a bit better.

Jess had come home with me on spring break, and he, mom and I had some beautiful moments together, crying a little but more importantly laughing a lot!

Sharon and I exchanged a couple of letters in the course of the year, but since her parents divorce she had measurably changed, maybe not much for the worse, but I knew full well that she needed to come to some sort of resolution with her life, if only for her own personal well-being, and ultimately for anyone involved with her.

Did I miss her? Yes, heartbreakingly so sometimes, but I had seen enough of life to survive even romance, and that my friends is often the toughest thing to do!

All in all it seemed like the year flew by, and I truly knew this is what God does many times when you have too much pain; he "fast-forwards" you into a new phase, keeping your memories intact, but not giving you quite enough time and energy to hurt yourself!

Thank you dear Lord for my first year post Loretta Mouchebeau; it was special in that I actually survived without the most precious girl I had ever known.

It was also special because I actually had hope for the future!

# Chapter Twenty Four

"We need not be afraid to face Him,
Those who disbelieve cannot get near,
Your trust He senses as you honor Him,
He walks with you..."

The Old Man

# XXIV

Summer was always my favorite season, and this last one before my senior year of college was no exception. As far back as I could recall I was very aware of seemingly losing a small piece of my soul at each and every summer's end; yet another spiritual chattel that my sister and I had in common with each other.

Even though my marriage proposal to Mary Jean Lowell, who had been my high school dream girl and Loretta's absolute favorite, had been turned down with genuine sadness earlier that spring, I still had managed to put together a very remarkable and memorable three months.

Yes, I had gone to see maybe the most beautiful girl I had ever known, and certainly so when we were sophomores at White Oak High, for what I knew now was the wrong reason. Feeling a supreme moment of weakness and despair with the first anniversary of my sister's death approaching, and I guess Sharon's sometimes extremely noticeable absence in my life adding to my melancholy, my inner self seemed to coerce me into doing something purely emotional, with rationale being a faint glimmer.

I survived that brief yet powerful encounter of course, but it sure was a bittersweet one to say the least. It did refresh, though, my nostalgic pension for a time when we all were younger and full of that high school passion and zeal for life; it was also a beautiful reminder of when Loretta and I were in our wonderful early teens, and I knew I would continue to treasure each and every moment of my sister's life that I happened upon, for whatever the reason and whenever the chance!

This summer vacation was extremely important in many regards, not just for me, but equally for Jess and my mother; we obviously had made real progress in healing ourselves individually, but also each other, with our heartfelt interaction and shared thoughts.

Jess had come up to stay for two weeks, and noticeably we all were happier, as one more year removed from our collective tragedy had slightly softened our anger and despair, and broadened our hopes.

God does heal, but sometimes our scars are so internally imbedded that we must seek our own unique and very personal approaches for recovery. As proven over and over with so many occurrences and for us especially with Loretta, death had found numerous and different ways to crush us all. We in turn needed as many inventive and significant means with which to cope and then carry on.

Mom had started LMC/RCC, the Loretta Mouchebeau Center for Rape Crisis and Counseling with Don Giovanni Caruso's most generous endowment. She had a chuckle over the summer with Jess and me reliving her experience of finally getting around to opening the envelope included with Don Giovanni's flower arrangement sent for Loretta's funeral.

It was maybe six weeks after my sister had died when mom started going through the multitudes of letters and cards sent in honor of Loretta, as losing my father literally less than a month after my sister's death threw all of us, needless to say, into an unbelievable tailspin.

One of the things that struck my mother was how beautifully hand engraved the writing was on one particular envelope, with an obviously original drawing of a stunning angel in the lower left hand corner, also noticing that the gold ink was somehow "alive," taking on various hues with different angles of observation.

"Well boys," she told us, "I opened it very carefully as I wanted to preserve this gorgeous work of art, and about fainted. Inside was a most touching letter from Mr. Caruso and a check for one hundred thousand dollars with a smaller note attached saying that this would be matched when needed!"

"That was it," she continued, "no suggestions on how to use this most generous gift; no caveats whatsoever!"

Jess and I had just gasped, and this made mom giggle some more, which was so heartwarming to see and participate in, as mom was recovering ever so carefully yet undeniably ever so powerfully.

"Jesus mom," I asked, "this was how Lamb's Rock got funded originally?"

Lamb's Rock was mom's most appropriate and spiritually inventive catch phrase for the LMC/RCC.

I had no idea, nor Jess, of Don Giovanni's most amazing gift, as he had wanted this just between my mother and him, at least until things got under way.

What was equally wonderful was the fact that the Don just knew mom would do something courageous with the money; something meaningful, extremely important and very necessary!

As a result of this, my mother retired from the public school system, where she had been a guidance counselor for several years, the summer after Loretta and dad had died, and that fall had miraculously found some very economical commercial space to rent and begin what she now referred to as her remaining life's dedication.

The center had started with just two women; mom doing the main administrative work, counseling and fundraising, and Norma, a former teacher and one of her best friends, as another counselor and also liaison with the various media outlets, generating public awareness and community support.

"That's how it all began," she concluded.

Mom paused, we were speechless, and she smiled.

"Oh, there's one more thing," she added, "not only did Mr. Caruso send us another check for the same amount, but he promised ten thousand dollars a year ear-marked for continued support, you know a sort of 'perpetual living endowment.'"

Upon hearing this my thoughts drifted back to when I was a camp counselor at the New York Military Academy, just two summers previous, but seemingly so much longer ago; watching over Don Caruso's son Joey, then a very intelligent yet frail young boy, and helping him grow into a tougher, happier and much healthier kid, all duly noted by his father's most sincere expressions of thanks at that camp's conclusion.

"You still here, Jesse?" my friend and mother literally asked at the very same time, as obviously I had taken a momentary leave of absence.

They both were well aware of my exploits that most memorable summer, especially with Don Caruso and his bodyguards all kissing my cheeks and hugging me when little Joey and I had said our tearful goodbyes.

"Just thinking of how all this started." I bemusedly replied.

We all had sat at the table, lost in our collective thoughts on where our lives were headed, hopefully integrated with our continued love and respect for each other.

Mom truly looked upon Jess as her second son, and this most profound show of affection had helped my best friend to somewhat recover from losing his soul mate, another aspect we all emotionally, spiritually and physically shared.

We had gone to visit the LMC/RCC facility that very day, as wanted by all three of us; I remembered Jess and I literally being overwhelmed by the recent painting of Loretta that mom had commissioned from one of her friends, who knowing Loretta of course had donated this beautiful work of art, sitting in its most proper place, as you first entered Lamb's Rock.

My sister was simply gorgeous, just as I visually remembered, and Jess and I both began to cry, holding hands just like two little kids, with mom caressing us from behind.

A beautiful moment indeed, and heightened even more so with the framed letter my father had written to my sister several months before she had died, expressing his undeniable love and devotion to her, placed just to the side of Loretta's portrait.

Just below this most touching letter from my father, and equally ensconced, was Mr. Caruso's original check, his brief note to mom, and his most exquisite envelope; both of these chattels serving as a reminder to all of us that knew Loretta, and quite possibly more importantly for the girls coming to the center in need, that there are many men in the world who are compassionate, loving and honorable with regards to their sexual counterparts, and will defend most passionately their safety and well being!

All in all we had needed that day's catharsis, as finally life was moving ahead, with real meaning and purpose, and most importantly with renewed energy and sincere anticipation.

Jess had left that next day for his final collegiate football season's August camp, with mom promising him that she'd attend one of his games. By now he hated this month of hell, before the official fall semester classes began, and made it clear to me that if somehow I could come to school any earlier than necessary, that would please him to no end, as any break in this militaristic routine could give him a truly needed respite from the other players and coaches.

He was looking ahead to maybe even improving upon his 2$^{nd}$ team all-conference status as a junior, and his senior year he would do so, getting 1$^{st}$ team honors and even a couple of honorable mention all-American nods!

I was also contemplating my upcoming senior year, as a good deal of time this past summer was spent reminiscing much of my college experience to date; many of the ballgames I played were still so vivid in my mind, and I have to tell you that the thought did cross my mind to play my senior year, and possibly continuing for another year as a graduate student, as the intense passion and regard for my most beloved of all sports was still clearly there.

Funny though, Coach Melling still miraculously had his job, and all it took was a close remembrance of literally any of our interaction the two years I played to convince me otherwise.

I was also that summer very aware of an undeniable transition within me taking place with regards to my newfound infatuation and outlet of creative writing, and it was no coincidence that the intensity of these last two years, needing some sort of cathartic release, found so.

Going into college as a freshman I had felt such a strong desire to study physical therapy and psychology (with intentions of later pursuing some sort of sports related career), and had done just that, luckily having Coach Ellen Harding for several of my declared major's classes, and learning quite a lot about the human body's capacity for endurance and healing. Of course I was even more so profoundly educated by my sister's personal experiences in said arena, and realized that college was just that; classroom interpretation of real life, which, while important, would never take the place of existence in general.

Now though, as an upcoming senior, my desires and talents were shifting, and I somehow intuitively felt that professionally I would someday write, not even caring that my higher education's focus was neither English nor Literature, or any of these related genres. I knew that I had it in me to accomplish what I wanted, and felt somehow truly serene and most secure in these thoughts.

I was very glad that I had chosen to transfer back and matriculate at East Tennessee Valley College; so was mom and Jess, and I was positive Loretta felt exactly the same, wherever she was. I just knew this in my heart.

A phase of my young life was ending, to be sure, and I was honestly saddened by this reality.

I had recalled near the end of that summer mom's friend Norma's smiling words to me four years previous and just before I had left for college as a freshman.

"Jesse, you will have the time of your life, and treasure every moment you possibly can," she had said, looking over at me on the passenger side, while driving me to wherever we were headed.

"Life will just never be the same," she continued, "it will be wonderful in so many regards, as you will see, but not as amazing as these four wonderful years of fulfillment unencumbered by the various burdens later thrust upon all of us."

Reflecting many years after college on her exact words had proven her right, of course. Most of us would agree, I think, that these school years were special indeed, as life most assuredly found novel ways to pound the ever loving shit out of each of us, sometimes even on a daily basis.

Yes, this last season before my senior year was truly appreciated.

I had not talked with Sharon one single time that summer; having instead, chosen to write just two letters, the first in June, and the second in July, benignly asking how she was faring, and filling her in on the details of Jess', mom's and my plans and status.

I was mildly disappointed with no response to my first communication, but let it go, as I had no way of knowing what was going on with her personally, never minding her family and just possibly the fact that she was romantically involved.

I did, though, hear from her after my second letter detailing the LMC/RCC, with mom's accounting of its inception to Jess and me; and, adding the good news that this facility was gaining solid momentum in its most noble purpose.

Sharon had responded very sweetly, and I definitely believed that thinking of Loretta's entire battle had given her another shot of inspiration and even courage with her own self. These two young women had shared quite a lot in their brief friendship, and that simply does not vanish with passionate and cognitive people.

I also had momentarily, yet most intensely, felt some of the previous love and affection I once had for this beautiful young woman, with my thoughts drifting to a few of our most treasured times.

These too, would not disappear, for I very definitely had my sister's influenced quality of "looking back for those smiles," when we needed hope and strength.

Still, I had been hopeful for a phone call from Sher, and was again chagrinned by not hearing from her, even if casually so.

I knew that we were through as lovers that spring Loretta had died. I mean this was more than a year ago, many events had since transpired, and I had accepted this as necessary experience. Yes, we had also been very close friends, but the emotional gauntlet she and I had run was truthfully too much to overcome, especially at our tender and youthful age.

After saying a very tearful yet joyful goodbye to my mother, most appropriately at Lamb's Rock, I headed to college for this final time, and upon Jess' request, was going to arrive a little more than one week before classes were to begin, living again in that most wondrous house Big A.L. had found for me when I had transferred back to East Valley nearly one year ago.

Since this would be the last week of football camp before school began, the players would get a little more free time in the evenings to not only deprogram themselves out of an extremely intense and Spartan training regimen, but to re-acclimate back into a more "normal" existence with the incoming general student population.

As non-football athletes, we collectively knew how to accomplish said behavior, but football players were undeniably a different breed, and the practice of this one-week adjustment period had been instituted by, of all people, Coach Ellen Harding several years previous; and, had cut down on first semester altercations involving football players by 90%, which was just astounding.

As said, she was way ahead of her time!

Jess was very excited that I was coming, and we had made plans to go to a few movies, share some meals, and just hang out, but most importantly I would be nearby, and he would know so.

Who knew, maybe I would even get some serious "alone time" in the gym, as I once did, having still kept the facility's keys that our trainer Phil had given me when I was a freshman basketball player, so long ago.

*      \*      \**

I smiled to myself, again reminiscing the entire drive:

*Of first meeting Jess in the gym that day, and seeing his handsome black face knowing he was beyond special, knowing he was for my entire life;*

*Of all of my team mates, particularly Burton and Joe, my roommates when we threw the now infamous homecoming party, and most definitely T.J. Cooper, who's insight and life skills I would always remember, and not forgetting that it was he and his wife Barbie that had introduced Sharon to me and helped nurture our romance;*

*Of my playing time that was exceptional and still clear in my mind, with several games being relived, especially the Southern West University contest, all Lee University games, as that was Sharon's school, and our fabled and not soon to be forgotten Christmas tournament;*

*Of Coach Ellen Harding's hiring me to be the women's junior varsity head basketball coach, and me again now smiling inside remembering when my girls had called me "Coach Jesse," as "Coach Mouchebeau" was just too easy for slaughter;*

*Of Big A.L., one of the singular most compassionate men I would ever have the privilege of knowing and loving, and who's unfailing dedication to his charges would be remembered particularly by those of us directly affected, and in general by this fine University;*

*But most importantly, the hundreds of heart to heart and soul to soul phone calls my sister and I had shared throughout my first two years of school; promising each other our undying love, support and affection for all of eternity.*

This is what I would miss most of all, now and forever!

*     *     *

It was such a lovely late afternoon as I pulled into East Valley, driving through the campus slowly savoring the moment, knowing this was the final chapter.

Our house was on the other side of the school grounds, just off the western end of campus, in an older neighborhood, populated mostly by families long since established, with sporadic college students homes filtered about here and there.

I drove onto our tree lined street, turned the corner and crept into our shaded driveway.

My heart stopped.

Sitting on the front porch facing me was Sharon McGee, replete in one of her renowned sundresses wearing dark glasses and that smile that had taken my heart nearly three years ago.

She was stunning!

I could barely get out of my car as my legs seemed to just quit on me, quietly closing the door and ever so cautiously moving towards her.

I had no idea what was going on.

She took off her sunglasses and I could see that she had been crying, very likely for quite some time.

I noticed a suitcase at her feet, and upon seeing this she spoke.

"Jesse, I had never stopped loving you; just myself."

I let her continue.

"I would be so happy if I could keep these clothes in your closet, so they would be there whenever I came to stay with you?"

Just maybe the kiss we next shared was the very best this world had ever experienced!

# Epilogue

Dear Loretta,

It has been nearly twenty years since we've held and kissed each other, and I miss you so much. I really never thought I would survive the unbelievable heartbreak I felt when you died that afternoon in my arms, much less last this long; but here I am, finally writing to you after all this time!

I know we have talked countless hours over these two decades, as there were so many times I truly needed your guidance and wisdom, much like when we were babies, then little kids, then teenagers and on. You have been with me every day and will always be my final thoughts on anything important in my life.

I realize that you already know this, but I wanted to express myself in written words for mom and others to read and know.

So much has happened since you've been gone, and there's simply not enough time to record all of these amazing events.

Jess and I are still best friends, but rarely see each other as his opera career has kept him in Europe nearly this entire period. Sometimes we will go a full year without talking, but then a phone call will quickly link us back together as the brothers we've grown to be, not missing a beat in our relationship, and always talking of you.

He has done quite well over there but it did put too much pressure on his family here and eventually his marriage to a very beautiful girl, also an opera singer, ended in divorce. They did produce two gorgeous children, a boy and a girl, and apparently he and his ex-wife get along pretty well and the kids have been fine.

Mom has been nothing short of amazing, and the Loretta Mouchebeau Center for Rape Crisis and Counseling clinic she started just a few months after you left has served countless young girls and women in their respective recoveries from the various traumas life has dealt them. She now has a full-time staff of six women and men, and every summer hires at least six high school and college students for their part time jobs.

I volunteer there when I have the time, which is not as often as I would like, but mom understands and always thanks me for whatever time I can give, and especially the donations I have helped to raise over the years, as a result of mentioning her clinic on the back covers of my books and in interviews.

I recently have begun to have some decent success as a creative writer; not big-time, but well known enough to make a good living.

Mom is extremely proud of me, and I never

forget to acknowledge not only her, but both dad's and your influence on my abilities as an artist. This never fails to make her smile.

She misses you too, babe, and I sense that she has her own very special and private moments with you and dad.

My two daughters, whom you well know, and they you, are so funny and smart, even as little kids, and they remind me of us at that age. God does this make me smile, but still I sometimes lose my composure and quietly break down and cry if I am not careful. They both sense things, as we did, and are as intuitive as you were, which is obviously a direct tribute to you their aunt, and of course their own mother.

I miss Sharon and us as a family, but we always seem to keep our girls' best interests at heart never failing in this regard; something we both are extremely proud of. She is a wonderful mom and you would be proud of her. She mentions you often.

Our daughters, we both know, are the very

reason we were put on this earth, and even though I was too young for marriage, could not have found a better mate with which to carry on this most amazing legacy of girls.

Lastly my most beloved sister, my soul mate and very best friend, I am finally ready to begin the book that I now truly know needs to be written.

It will be a tribute in general to women's intuitive powers, strength and intelligence, and also their abilities to just survive; but most importantly it will tell the story of a brother and sister's most profound and unique love for each other, and their exquisite spiritual connection.

It will be entitled "The Girls of Yesterday."

I still so love you Loretta, and I will see you again someday!

Jesse